A PROMISE OF WATER

SHARON SCARBOROUGH

ENCHANTED INDIE PRESS

A PROMISE OF WATER

by

Sharon Scarborough

PUBLISHER'S NOTE

**Printed and Published in the United States of America by
Enchanted Indie Press**

Digital Edition (v2.4.3)
ISBN-13: 978-1-938749-41-4
ISBN-10: 1-938749-41-3

Print Edition (v2.4.3)
ISBN-13: 978-1-938749-40-7
ISBN-10:1-938749-40-5

ENCHANTED INDIE PRESS

A SPECIAL NOTE ABOUT TEXAS RANGER BADGES
AND THE COVER

Larger than the Lone Star State itself, Texas history reflects a combination of fact, fantasy, and legend, especially with regard to the story of the Texas Rangers and the wide variety of badges they wore from their beginning in 1823 until 1935, when the first official badge arrived on the scene, and continuing to the present day with a new badge used from 1938 thru 1957, and changed again in 1962.

Cover design for *A Promise of Water* symbolically reflects the four most important elements of the story: drought, murder, a *promise* of water that hasn't yet arrived, and, of course, our hero, retired Texas Ranger Oswald Nightingale. No other symbol can so effectively characterize Nightingale's role in the story, so it seemed to be a simple matter of finding a suitable image of a badge. The variety of possibilities that appeared within milliseconds of initiating a search, however, made the task of choosing one anything but simple.

The Texas Ranger Hall of fame and Museum website offers a fascinating article titled, "A Short Course on Fantasy, Replica, and Toy Texas Ranger Badges," directed specifically at folks who would like to own an authentic badge from the legendary law enforcement agency. But the fact is that there are very few genuine Texas Ranger badges, and unfortunately, a brisk and fraudulent market exists in which scam artists offer badges with fake certificates of authenticity.

The badge image chosen for the cover is clearly labeled as an "Old West Obsolete Texas Rangers Company B" replica, with detailed information about how the badges are manufactured. And while no one can claim that the seller is offering it as genuine, the word "replica" would indicate that it is a duplicate of a real badge. According to the Museum article, however, this is one variation on what is known as an "1890's flag badge," and the wreaths are from a design found after 1961. This badge is no more authentic than the ones made from five or ten peso coins (as early authentic badges often were) and sold online with claims of being the real thing, in spite of the clearly visible evidence on the rear of the badge that it was made from a coin minted in 1947 or '48. The caution, "Buyer beware!" apparently is too often ignored.

For the purposes of cover design, the image need not reflect a genuine badge to carry the message that *A Promise of Water* is about a Texas Ranger. He's not a real Texas Ranger, of course, and it seems appropriately respectful of those who are for our hero to wear a fictional version representative of this unique law enforcement agency.

DEDICATION

To Shannon, Kelly, Mickie, and Jessica, who have made my life worth living.

AUTHOR'S NOTES

About the Subject

The worldwide water shortage has been a concern of mine for years. My family has heard this repeatedly, but clean drinking water is truly something about which we should all be concerned. Consider putting it on your radar.

About the Book

This is a work of fiction, and while Austin and Lubbock exist, the other places mentioned are just that—fiction. Alas, the people, too, are fiction, but they are the products of dreams from men and women I have known, people who say, "I always wanted to be a cowboy."

1

Oswald Nightingale walked from one painting to another, looping his Resistol hat around his hand as he walked. Sitting didn't work. He was too tall for the small eighteenth-century settee, and it was lumpy—probably still filled with horsehair from some beat-up elderly horse a hundred years ago. So this was the governor's outer office, where peons waited next to the seat of power. Looked old and smelled musty with a faint hint of furniture oil.

He'd never been summoned to the big house. Should be impressed. Instead, he had these doubts. If this was the way she treated everyone, it was no wonder nothing got done in government. Granted, he showed up ten minutes early. Still no reason to make a guest wait.

The room had doors to the east, the west, and the north, each one with frosted carved panes in the top half. The wall to the south had windows covered with heavy drapes. An antique bar stood between Nightingale and the eastern door.

Roy McGowan shoved open the door behind the bar, so that the glass rattled. A half-apologetic smile swam across Roy's face as he stuck his hand out to shake. "Glad you could come, Oz. We'll have some beers and discuss old times later."

Nightingale liked Roy in a way that he couldn't explain. The point man had a hell of a job because his charge was to always give the governor the truth, even when the boss didn't want to hear it. Nightingale had grown up with McGowan. In junior high, Roy had quickly shown his talent for politics by running for class treasurer and winning. Now Roy worked for a semi-conservative woman in a very conservative state and had helped her win.

Patricia Daniels, with her maternal air and dimples, had taken much of the state by surprise.

Nightingale and McGowan had been in touch through the years. McGowan had worked hard to get to be the right-hand man to the governor. His rise in status came as no surprise to anyone.

McGowan wore a pink shirt and gray tie with a gray suit. His reddened face protested the heat with dribbles of sweat. McGowan must have come in from outside, or he had just had a cross-purpose encounter with someone. Nightingale searched the man's face for clues about what lay ahead, but McGowan avoided his eyes.

As a Ranger-Investigator, Nightingale had been the go-to man for several previous governors, but one case involved a murdered friend and left him wondering about the direction of his life. Then a different case led to accusations, fingers pointed at him for, of all things, theft. He was pulled into his former boss's office, and in a moment of outrage, he quit.

He'd decided to be a detective and a writer. That was a few months ago. He'd received a letter from his boss, which he had ignored. Now there was a new lady governor and, a couple of days ago, a call from McGowan: "The governor wants to talk to you. How soon can you be here?"

At the time, Nightingale had hesitated, all the while feeling the urge to get out of Broken Rock. "You know I've got my own business now?"

He heard the smile in the voice of his childhood friend. "I keep up, Oz. You're not that busy."

The truth was that he liked powerful people calling on him, and he found writing to be a challenge. Three pages of narrative over a few weeks' time did not bode well for his literary career.

McGowan delivered the final plea. "The state needs you."

So Nightingale packed a duffle bag and drove, mulling over what could be so important. He'd heard nothing in the news. What was this female governor like? What had Roy McGowan told her about him? How much did Roy know about his job situation? And most important, what did the governor want from him?

The governor walked in behind McGowan. As she stuck out her hand in greeting, she had on the political smile that he'd seen on TV. "Mr. Nightingale, I'll call you Oswald if that's all right. Thank you for making this trip. Does your back hurt after that drive?"

Her left hand covered his hand as they shook. Nightingale felt the pull of power, but more than that, she had an aura. She exuded intelligence and influence like he had seen in many politicians. Had to be the eyes, a deep brown that switched on the warmth—or ice—as necessary. She'd be hell in a poker game.

"I've learned to get out and walk every couple of hours," he said.

She turned away before he finished answering, obviously not interested. She wasn't used to power yet. With such a capacity, she could be dangerous. He guessed she didn't believe much of anything unless a poll backed it up.

McGowan herded them to the room next door, made sure the doors were locked, and ordered iced tea for the governor and coffee for Nightingale. Governor Daniels chose a big leather chair, and motioned to Nightingale to sit in one across from her. She was a good-sized woman at about five feet eight. Well-padded but not overweight, she sat comfortably in the big chair.

"I don't know whether to throw these out or get more," she said, patting the buttery leather arm of her chair.

Nightingale studied the room. It was about six hundred square feet of wide-planked hardwood with oak and pecan tables, chairs, and cabinets divided into areas for living, eating, working. A gargantuan desk sat in front of two windows draped in heavy green fabric. The head of a buck adorned one wall; several old maps of the state covered another. A Remington sculpture sat in the middle of a small table in front of them.

The governor sat on the edge of her chair and leaned toward Nightingale. "The state needs your help, Oswald." She put up one hand to stop a protest before he made it. "I don't know you personally, but I know your reputation. I need you as a Special Ranger up in East Texas."

"Do you know about my troubles in my job?"

"Yes," she said. "This is more important than some man making accusations. I go by your history. Just hear me out."

Nightingale shifted in his seat. Never hurt to listen.

"We're in the worst drought since 1956," the governor said, "and it's hurting the state worse than the one in '56 because we've got people moving in every day."

Drought? This woman had no idea about dry weather till she'd been to his home. Anger crept into his gut. "I wondered when anyone up here would help us out in Broken Rock. Lubbock and Amarillo are suffering, too." Usually more thoughtful, he stopped the rush of words.

The governor wasn't listening anyway. "I haven't been in office long, and people who should know"—here she raised an eyebrow at McGowan—"people who advise me say you can't run a state like we have for the last few years with no thought about water policy." She got to her feet and carried the glass of tea to a massive conference table. She turned to face him. "I grew up about as poor as you can in this state, and I know what the people want, but I'm worried that we are on the verge of great growth with not enough water to keep up with it. The legislature supported my water plan, but we've got folks buying up water rights before we can implement the plan." She walked closer to the window, lost in her message. "Legislators love power, and if they see a chink in the action, they'll turn on me quicker than a dog in heat." Tiny lines crisscrossed the skin of her jawline. At sixty-two, she was fourteen years older than Nightingale, but still a fine-looking woman.

Nightingale glanced at a glass shelf of books to one side of the window. Along with the books, another Remington cowboy kept watch. The room still showed a person in charge. Her voice brought him back.

"So, I have this plan where we can make a difference. We've got to have the whole state, including your area, to agree to help each other, and what we've got is one woman in Beulah standing in the way of a legacy of progress. We've all got to sacrifice. Don't you agree?"

Nightingale nodded, thinking that drought and legacy made it clear what the governor wanted. After years of the state doing nothing about the water problem, Patricia Daniels had decided to do something.

"We can declare this a matter of eminent domain, but I don't want to do that because the state will look like a bully. I know how touchy that subject is to you." The governor looked at McGowan.

Nightingale sat up straighter. His parents had lost a major portion of their farm to eminent domain when the government took their land for a railroad. His stomach tightened. He looked at McGowan. This was a set-up.

"One little old woman stands between you and greatness—is that it?"

McGowan stood up, glaring, and stepped toward Nightingale.

The governor stopped pacing and squinted at Nightingale. She flushed, and a flash of animosity glinted in her dark eyes. Then she smiled and patted the air for Roy to sit, making clear that she could choose to be angry or she could let it slide. "The press will see it that way, but that's what we need to avoid. It can't be seen as her against me, or the state."

Nightingale bit back a retort. He usually regretted moments of grand honesty. Now was the time to listen and see if bullshit from the promiser-in-chief could ever mean anything.

"Roy, why don't you tell him the rest."

This was smart on the governor's part. Roy gave out the orders to save the chief's hide if anything ever got in court. Nightingale glanced around for any sign of a camera or tape, but saw nothing.

"We want you to meet a man named Posey up in East Texas. I'll call and set up the meeting. He's to get the land procured from Mrs. Dearborn, the lady who's stopping this whole thing," McGowan said.

"Why this man?"

"He's a lawyer," the governor said. "I know his family, and he's a good man. Got his degree in real estate law. He hasn't been in state in a while. He's not used to the rough edges of some folks. He needs help persuading the seller to sell."

"There's an environmental group—some elves or forest creatures—who've said they're gonna help the woman," McGowan said. "You can keep 'em from getting out of hand."

"Be sure and take your gun." The governor sat back down in the big, soft chair and leaned in.

Nightingale had read she once said it was hard for a woman to get anywhere on brains alone.

The governor put a strand of hair behind one ear. She had her elbows on her knees, her voice low. "You know this affects the whole state. People are angry. The state is seething. You can help make life easier for the folks in Broken Rock—they can have water, I give you my word—if you help us grease the way on this last bit of problems."

They stared at each other for a minute. He'd just been told—not directly, but with innuendo—how things would be. Meanwhile, everyone in Broken Rock, Obsidian, and other small towns in the way would suffer for a while longer, but he could be their savior. He hadn't expected this. Silence seemed best. He tried to think if he had any choices.

He clasped his hands, leaned forward into the governor's space. "Your word."

She nodded.

He hiked himself out of the over-soft chair. "Seems to me the best thing for the state is to get this done quick. Let's get in touch with Posey."

2

Nightingale left Austin early the next morning and mulled over the governor's comments as he made the six-hour drive to East Texas. The people of Texas loved oil. More correctly, they loved the money from owning oil wells; however, need for water, the thirst for water was primal and basic. Men might go to war for oil, but they would kill for water. That was the reason the governor wanted Nightingale watching over the man named Posey. So Nightingale sat at a table in the Laughing Cow Bar, doing what she wanted. McGowan had set up the meeting, then told him what to expect: "He'll have a briefcase. You'll know him."

Nightingale leaned back in his chair at a table in the bar. He watched Posey, wondering if the man knew how high the stakes were.

Sure enough, Posey stood for a minute with the door at his back, surveying the room. Dressed in starched khaki pants and a white shirt, he had the look that Nightingale had worried about. The tell was the pinkie finger that twitched on the handle of his briefcase.

Several men watched the stranger, their eyes hooded or

hidden under the shadow of a cap. The man didn't belong in this dark, small place. A trucker turned from the bar, smiled, and whispered to his companion. Nightingale admired Jack Posey's grit but wondered about his common sense.

Posey hesitated slightly, then beelined to Nightingale's table. Sweat ran down the sides of his face and dripped on his shirt. He slid his sunglasses to the top of his head and looked at Nightingale before glancing around the room. "I'm Jack Posey," he said. His voice, a high-pitched tenor, seemed to carry through the walls.

When he reached for a chair, his jacket bulged in the back with the shape of a holster. Nightingale's worry quotient went up.

The briefcase hit the floor and toppled over on the uneven wood. Posey leaned closer, whispered, "Is this place typical? What kind of ambiance did McGowan think was here?"

Nightingale stood, pulling over an extra chair, hoping to quiet the man. At six three, Nightingale stood about five inches taller than Posey. He'd known him for five seconds, and already he didn't like him.

"You're Ranger Nightingale?"

"Nightingale is my name."

Posey frowned. The chair squeaked as he sat down. "You've been appointed as a Special Ranger. The governor told me that."

Nightingale sat down and took a pull on the Dos Equis. "She has a way with words, doesn't she?"

Posey raised his eyebrows. "What are you drinking? I'd like one of those."

"Yes sir." Nightingale stood, grateful to walk to the bar and order. While he waited for the beers, he watched Posey in the mirror over the bar.

Posey pulled out a handkerchief and wiped off the table before putting his briefcase on the surface.

Nightingale pulled in a long breath. The governor said Posey's parents were friends. But there had to be more to it.

He passed on the offer of glasses, noting a lipstick smear on one rim. He walked back to the table and stood with the bottles in his hand, waiting for Posey to close the briefcase and put it back on the floor.

He sat down. "So, what's your plan? My understanding is you'll do all the important work." Nightingale didn't know what Posey'd been told. For his part, he hoped to be an unobtrusive observer.

Posey glanced one way and then the other, grasped the beer bottle, and stared at it. "Not so loud. I don't want people noticing us."

Nightingale took a long breath and tried to muster patience. "Mr. Posey, you've been seeing too many movies."

"I don't think so." Posey's voice lowered a notch. "You come out to my car. I need to show you something, and we can discuss what needs to be done."

This was just the kind of blowhard to cause a lot of trouble simply for lack of common sense. The bar had gained a few customers. Nightingale took one last drink and stood. Better get him out in the open.

Posey jerked the briefcase off the floor. Outside, in the noon sunshine, he pointed a pale hand toward a Hummer. "The black car over there is mine."

Nightingale couldn't help his squint of distaste. Vehicles that big and shiny brought immediate attention in this land of winding, dusty roads. He yanked his hat brim down. He had a job to do. He'd get water for Broken Rock out of this deal or die trying. Should have put off that stop-smoking pledge.

Inside the Hummer, Posey puffed up, sat taller. A gold band with diamonds sparkled on a chubby finger when he reached up to pat the dashboard. Gadgets lit up the dash like the instrument panel on an airplane. Nightingale looked out the window to hide the smile that snuck up on him. Boys and their toys. Reckon McGowan knew what this man was driving?

"We don't need to go far." Posey started the car and sighed in the blast of cool air and garage band that accosted them. He swerved around a small truck, left the radio going full volume, and pulled onto the highway without looking.

Nightingale tried to not stomp the floorboard and fumbled around his waist to be sure the seat belt was fastened. With the other hand, he grabbed the dash.

"We're going to a farm up here. Some woman won't let us have the land we need. The legislature put this into law, but she's refused reasonable offers. I drove up here earlier to test the navigation system." He patted the dash, smiling.

Nightingale took in a few landmarks, mainly noticing the tall pine trees. "Why is this so important? Can't you put it off a little while?"

"We've got the whole package ready to go forward. People in West Texas are suffering, so they signed everything. We're surveying, and construction will start soon out there. We've been talking to this woman for months and got nowhere. The governor wants this to be one big happy family deal," Posey said. "She may not be realistic." He pulled the car to a wide, grassy shoulder of the road, and they got out.

Posey took a few steps through the weeds before facing Nightingale. His next words had only the slightest evidence of the missing 'r' from his days at Harvard. "There's going to be a reservoir built here. It requires about half of Mrs. Dearborn's land —a couple thousand acres."

"Why? People up here have water."

"Cities to the west are going dry. Not just Dallas, but Denton and smaller towns. It takes twenty years to get a reservoir built and working. Some people will have to make a little sacrifice. She owns several thousand acres. The plan is to start in the Panhandle on the west side and here for the east. Course, people out there are willing to sell their first-born child for relief. Here, not so much."

Several things ran through Nightingale's mind. If you lived in Texas, you cherished every grain of dirt you had the good fortune to own. Folks pulled out firearms if you talked about taking their land. The drought he lived with didn't seem as evident here, so he guessed empathy for anyone else in the state with low water would be lacking.

"What're you offering her?"

"Market price."

Nightingale glanced around at the damaged skeletons of brown trees mingled in the woods along the road attesting to the dry few years. The lakes he'd seen on his drive into town had broad shorelines, sometimes hundreds of feet, leaving dry land in their stead. But some perverse instinct in him reared its head, reminding him of Broken Rock and the people who would count their blessings if they could see a shrunken shoreline.

A mixture of pine, oak, and scrub trees grew in profusion about twenty feet from the edge of the pavement. Cut grass and stubble ran to the tree line. Several yards up, barely in sight, two figures on horseback exited the line of woods, crossed the black-top road, and walked toward them.

Nightingale nodded toward the horses. "Anybody you know?"

Posey squinted and adjusted the hat that seemed to bother him. "I don't know anybody out here. The house we passed is Mrs. Dearborn's. That's probably her."

"This lady you're fighting—is she married?"

Posey kept his eyes on the advancing figures. "Widow. Husband died in Iraq. Soldier, I guess. I don't know details. Just know it makes it hard for our side 'cause she's got this hero in the background."

As the riders came closer, Nightingale saw that one of them was a woman, but he couldn't tell her age. The other rider was male, his face concealed under the brim of a battered hat. The woman sat tall, knew her ride, and stopped just far enough away from him and Posey that she raised her voice when she spoke.

"Can I help you gentlemen, or are you just admiring the landscape?"

"I'm Jack Posey, ma'am. Are you Mrs. Dearborn?"

"And if I am, what would your business be?"

"Governor Daniels sent me," Posey said. "I'd like to talk with you about buying some of your land."

"Stealing it, you mean." Her voice remained low, trembling with power. She might be able to deliver a curse or cast a spell with such a voice.

The governor's man hesitated slightly as he glanced over at Nightingale. "No, ma'am. A fair price. The people of Texas need your land for water, and we're willing to pay for it. We need to talk."

"Mr. Dosey, I—"

"That's Posey. Posey is the name."

"Sir, I suggest you and your hired helper leave my land. I will not sell what has been in my family for generations to a governor who is wanting to cover my land with water so her rich friends can have pet projects and water their lawns in Houston and Dallas."

Nightingale dropped his head and, in an undertone, said, "We need to leave. We'll choose a better time."

Posey's face reddened, almost glowed, with anger, but he turned with Nightingale and went back to the vehicle.

The two horses stood with their riders. A car sped down the

road and the horses didn't budge, despite their mane and tails flying from the wind as the car went by.

They looked like statues.

All sorts of irony in those animals at the side of a paved road, but Nightingale didn't examine that. Instead, he wondered what he'd do if he was in Mrs. Dearborn's place. His home territory was drying up, literally and figuratively, but he had promised the governor that he would convince this woman to give up part of her home for the good of the state.

If he lived in Mrs. Dearborn's shoes, would he fight or do the "right" thing for his fellow citizens? Would fellow citizens acknowledge, be grateful, give two hoots about what she'd given up? He doubted it. He saw no way around the dilemma, but he didn't know the right answer. The one thing he did know: the woman sitting atop that horse was not giving in without a fight, and the governor had given him orders to see that she lost that fight.

Muttering a curse, Posey threw the big vehicle into gear and squealed tires, driving so close to the horses that Nightingale wondered about the man's stability. After he made a U-turn in the middle of the road, a sullenness came over him, reminding Nightingale of an ill-tempered child.

Posey continued to mutter.

"You need to calm down," Nightingale said. "This isn't the end of the world. You've got the upper hand. Doctor told me about blood pressure. You'll pop your vessels."

"It's easy for you to make fun of this whole thing. If I don't get her to sign and sell, we'll be years in litigation. The state will suffer. People will suffer and the governor's reputation will suffer."

"You more concerned with the people of the state or the governor's reputation?"

"Such remarks don't help things." Posey glanced sideways, a

brief, hateful look. "I don't know why the governor wanted you and your smart-assed attitude to work on this."

"Couldn't agree with you more. But we're stuck with each other."

The governor's man didn't argue, so when the Hummer screeched to a halt at the bar, Nightingale got out, gave him a head start, and followed on the same road, thinking he'd wait for Posey to cool off.

Posey parked at a Bed and Breakfast.

Nightingale circled the block and soon found a Holiday Inn Express. From there, he called Josephine Holly.

"You any closer to knowing what they want?" she asked.

He pictured her standing in the kitchen, making bread or cakes for the next day's meals. He'd known her for almost a year and considered her his best friend. He loved her, but he didn't know if that was enough. And he knew she didn't care. He wanted to marry. She didn't. She just wanted a dependable man friend. They were what he called intimate, and people in their town of Broken Rock knew it.

"The folks in charge want a woman up here to sell her land for a reservoir. I'm supposed to keep a watch on the man in charge of puttin' this deal in writing. They figure we all need water, so we'll be dancin' a jig to make the people here aware of the good things their reservoirs could do for our state."

"I can't see you dancing for anybody. Nobody over here is gonna be happy about a lake over in the east. They need to consider the western part of the state for a while." Josephine sounded testy, which was not her usual demeanor.

"Anything wrong?"

"You mean more than me trying to run a Bed and Breakfast and asking the guests not to shower? No Oz, there's nothing wrong. Every damn plant is brown. I've got people leaving pee in the commode to save water. There's a cow carcass rotting in my back field, and my roses are dead. I sound really bad because things are bad, but you know that. I need to hang up. Call me tomorrow night. I promise to be in better spirits."

The connection ended with a soft click.

Nightingale took a shower, mulling over Josephine's frustration, knowing that the rest of the state had a bare notion of the desperation of the people around Lubbock and Amarillo, but most people couldn't taste the food that wasn't on their plate.

After his shower, he went downstairs and drove into town for supper. Knees banging the underside of the wooden restaurant table, he began to read the newspaper he'd bought.

An article about Mrs. Dearborn and her fight against the state's power of eminent domain filled the top of the fold. A small picture of a young Constance Alexander Dearborn was inset in the last part of the story that continued onto page three. Next to that, in a shaded two-column brief, ELF, the Environmental Law Foundation, was mentioned. According to the writer, the organization might help the Dearborn woman.

Out of the corner of his eyes, Nightingale saw white orthopedic shoes.

"She's the closest thing we've got to a celebrity," the waitress said when he looked up. "Lot of folks didn't much like her before this, and now they don't know what to think."

Nightingale ordered, and when the chicken fried steak arrived, looking delicious next to the mashed potatoes and gravy, he realized he hadn't eaten since breakfast. The green beans, chosen for health's sake, lay limp next to a piece of fatback.

"What do you think of all this?" he asked, poking his fork at the newspaper.

His waitress folded her arms. "I've got kinfolks out west. They need water. I don't see how us having another big lake will help them. May help Dallas, but I'm not inclined to want to help a big city. We won't ever know the truth of it for several years. By then, I'll be dead, and it won't matter."

She laughed and told him dessert was chocolate pie with mile-high meringue.

He finished reading the story, which included a review of the state plan for water conservation and a mention of the oil pipeline that had already taken a swath of land from several farmers. While the writer didn't say it directly, the implication was that Mrs. Dearborn might put up resistance, but she would lose her fight against the state just as others had lost.

Back in his room, Nightingale spread out several articles he had printed off the Internet before coming to meet Jack Posey.

He was into the first paragraph when the bedside telephone rang. No one knew where he was, so he wondered what the call could be about.

No one immediately answered his hello. But then a gruff voice, someone speaking through a rag maybe, said, "Go back where you came from. Don't be here nosing into our business. We'd just as soon kill you as look at you."

Nightingale glanced toward the window and, despite the drawn curtains, stepped closer to the wall.

The voice stopped.

Nightingale put the receiver down and called the front desk to confirm that, while the call was logged, the hotel had no way of knowing the place of origin.

He wrote down everything he could remember about the call, then he pulled the pistol out of his back holster and laid it on the table within easy reach.

3

By midnight, Nightingale had read all the printed articles and decided to try to sleep. Maybe insight would come in the night.

At 6:00 a.m., the alarm beeped, and at 6:10, his cell phone rang.

"Is this Nightingale?" The voice sounded stressed, a familiar baritone.

"Nightingale? This is McGowan. Damn it man, I just tried to call Posey's room and got no answer. Where are you, and why did he call me last night saying he was gonna fire you?"

"Roy?"

"Yes, this is Roy McGowan." Crisp, enunciated words.

Reality washed over Nightingale, and he came immediately awake.

McGowan was all business. Evidently, this was not an odd 6:00 a.m. call for him. "We need you to find Posey and see what's happened. We'll worry about the rest later."

Roy sounded like his teeth were gritting sand.

"At the Bed and Breakfast?" Nightingale said.

A female voice fired with anger cut back at him, short and

succinct in his ear. "Mr. Nightingale, get over there. He's at some place called the Sycamore Bed and Breakfast. I want him on the phone in half an hour. No publicity. Keep it low-key."

The connection broke.

Nightingale smiled and shook his head, glad the governor had clarified his role.

He dressed, walked down to the front desk, and asked directions to the Sycamore B and B. He wondered about Posey. Why didn't he answer the phone? Probably left it in that Hummer. Nightingale shook his head. Greenhorn.

The young desk clerk gave instructions while pointing out the continental breakfast that came as a package with his room.

Nightingale tipped his hat in thanks, said he might take in the breakfast later, and went to his truck.

Very little traffic flowed in the early morning. He wished for his dog as he drove, hating how often thoughts of the big shepherd came to him, and knowing he would never admit such a weakness to anyone. He drove slowly, looking at the old-fashioned houses with big front porches. Reminded him of his cousin's house in Obsidian. Finally, a familiar picket fence signaled that he'd driven by this house when he followed Posey.

At the Sycamore B and B, no one stirred.

A sheriff's car hugged one curb. An officer Nightingale guessed to be twenty-five years old stepped out of the car as Nightingale parked.

The officer walked over to him. "Are you Mr. Nightingale?" The young man's cheeks shone with a nervous blush.

Nightingale was eye to eye with the man. "Yes, sir. I am."

"I'm Amon Toohey. The governor's office called us and said someone wasn't answering the phone here. They wanted me to meet you and explain to Mrs. Jackson that you are official and need access."

It seemed to Nightingale that Toohey's nerves needed the

soothing strokes of protocol more than his own did. "By the way," Nightingale stuck out a hand to shake, "my first name is Oswald."

He almost heard the relief as Toohey shook his hand. "I hope you can let me know what this is about."

"Curiosity killed, so I guess I'd better protect you a while," Nightingale said.

"I take orders, so I'll settle. My boss, the sheriff, will be here soon."

"Let's go on in," Nightingale said.

Toohey pulled the brim of his hat as he nodded and walked up the steps.

Baskets of petunias hung around the porch, adding to the ornamentation and old-fashioned feel of the place.

Nightingale had shined his boots the night before. He looked at his feet, glad for the extra effort, wondering why he felt so off-balance in the early morning light, like the scene was surreal. He readjusted his hat, trying to corral the summer humidity before it trickled down his temples.

On the sign in the yard, small print declared, "Emma Jackson, proprietor."

Nightingale nodded toward the light coming through the windows. "I'm leaving this up to you," he said. "Did you talk to McGowan?"

Toohey straightened his spine, just the slightest bit of pride in his posture. "Right. I met Mr. McGowan during the campaign. His call is good enough for me."

Nightingale raised his knuckles to knock, and the door swung open to the sound of arguing voices. The aroma of fresh coffee and cinnamon rolls filled the air, along with an unstated tension.

Toohey raised his eyebrows. "Sounds a little hot."

A dark-haired man and blond woman clasped luggage and faced a woman at a writing desk.

"We just want to leave." The man set his suitcase down and tried to smile, but the movement looked more like a tic than a genuine smile.

The woman at the desk glanced at Toohey and Nightingale but continued her conversation with the man standing at her desk. "I understand that, but you stayed all night. You have a bill."

"That animal kept us up all night," the man said. "I think a reasonable person would ignore any charges, but we're leaving whether you do or don't."

Toohey held the front door open for them. The blond lady looked straight ahead. Nightingale guessed she was about half the age of her companion. The man glanced at him and the officer, then defiantly stalked to his car with his friend, or wife, or girlfriend in tow, muttering about the lack of civilization.

The woman at the desk had the deep crevice of a frown between her eyebrows. "Amon, why are you here this early?" She peered around Toohey. "And you would be?"

Nightingale stepped forward and extended his hand. "I'm Oswald Nightingale, ma'am. Officer Toohey knows me."

Toohey stepped closer and lowered his voice as he leaned to the woman. "The governor's office wants this Ranger to check on Mr. Posey. Mr. McGowan called me. They been trying to call Posey but get no answer. Sheriff Patterson is on his way."

"The governor's office?" She looked Nightingale up and down, not hiding her skepticism that a light-brown man with the almond-shaped eyes of a foreigner had any authority.

Nightingale shifted his jacket slightly so the edge of his badge showed.

The lady raised her eyebrows and stuck out one hand, limp, as if she offered a favor. "I'm Emma Jackson, the owner of this establishment. I'll go with you."

Nightingale shook her lifeless fingers.

She pulled a key from under her desk and went to the stairs. The two men followed.

At the door to the room, Nightingale said a polite, "Excuse me, ma'am," stepped in front of her, and knocked. "Mr. Posey, are you awake? We have a call for you."

When no answer came, Nightingale extended his hand for the key.

"Ma'am, please step back," he said.

For the first time, she seemed cowed.

Nightingale turned the key and pushed the door.

In the middle of the double bed, Jack Posey lay partially naked, his butt and back shiny in the light coming through the window, a tangled sheet over his legs and feet. A small device lay on the bed next to him.

From across the room, Nightingale couldn't tell what it was, but it looked like it was connected to Posey. Nightingale stuck out a hand to keep Mrs. Jackson and Toohey back.

"Jack," Nightingale said. "Jack, are you okay?"

He heard the short, panicked breath of Mrs. Jackson.

She squeaked as her hysteria built. "He's dead, isn't he?" Then she screamed.

4

Moving quickly to the bed, Nightingale said over his shoulder, "Toohey, get her out of here and call for back-up."

The young officer put his arm around Emma Jackson, pushing and pulling, while craning his neck to watch what was going on with Posey.

Nightingale touched Posey's shoulders, which were warm. "Officer, get a doctor."

There was no blood. Nightingale pulled at the sheet, shifting the device so it looked less like a bomb and more like an insulin pump. A small tube ran under the front of Posey's body.

The apparatus blinked and swished.

Posey didn't raise his head. He groaned and muttered into his pillow. "Orange juice. Nightingale, orange juice."

Mrs. Jackson had turned her head to Toohey, who was awkwardly patting her back. Both ignored Nightingale's orders.

"One of you get orange juice, quick. This man is diabetic."

Emma Jackson jerked to attention. Her squeamish whimpers ceased. "I'll get it."

Toohey seemed to come out of his trance. "I'll call the medics," he said

"Jack, can you talk?" Nightingale hunkered down to Posey's ear.

"Sick. Undo . . ." He pulled one hand to his belly and yanked. The light on the small box went out.

Nightingale pulled the sheet up to cover Posey's rear. He had no experience with sick people. He'd been well most of his life, and he didn't like this helplessness. He turned to the deputy. "Toohey, have you called the doctor?"

"No. I don't need a doctor," Posey said.

When Emma Jackson returned, she had a glass of juice and a pitcher on a silver platter. The tray trembled as she put it on the edge of the bed.

Nightingale helped Posey move so he could turn his head and drink. Nightingale and the others stood back and watched as the color came to Posey's face.

"Not too much," Posey said. "Damn, Nightingale, cover me up."

"You are covered. Your pump is disconnected," Nightingale said. He stood up, glad to hear Posey complaining. "We'll call a doctor."

Posey's head still drooped, but he looked at Mrs. Jackson. "Thank you, ma'am and officer. The Ranger here can help me. I know my condition, and I don't need a physician."

Toohey and Mrs. Jackson backed out of the room, and the door clicked shut.

"Thanks," Posey said. He put his feet on the floor and began to reconnect the pump. "I need food."

"What happened?" Nightingale asked.

Posey tried to pull the sheet around like a toga. He still didn't look steady. "I got drunk last night. The pump went crazy."

"You got drunk, and you're diabetic." Nightingale didn't try to hide his disbelief at such stupidity.

"Yeah. I live with it. Hand me my pants." He looked up at Nightingale, defiance in his eyes. "Never mind. I need to get my equilibrium. I'll set here a few more minutes."

A loud banging on the door stopped the conversation. "Mr. Posey, are you all right? I'm Sheriff Patterson."

The sheriff pushed the door open. Toohey stood in the hall, but the sheriff and another deputy walked into the room. They paused when they saw Nightingale, shifting their gaze from him to the man sitting on the bed.

The sheriff spoke first. "I guess you're the Ranger. I talked with McGowan. This is Ed Howard, my deputy."

The deputy almost grimaced. His eyes turned stony, lacking anything human, except possibly hate. "Yeah, we met in Amarillo."

Nightingale grinned. "As I recall, it was Lubbock, and you didn't think I should be a Ranger."

Howard reddened and took a deep breath. One side of his mouth curled in a sneer.

Nightingale knew several people like Howard. For them, Nightingale's complexion was too much like an Egyptian, just a shade too dark, or the shape of his eyes made him look like an Arabian. Or, God forbid, he might have Negro blood.

They had met by accident when Howard showed up at the Ranger office inquiring about a job. Nightingale didn't know why he was in the office that day, but Howard had made some comment to the director when Nightingale walked by. Nightingale figured Howard blamed him for the fact that he didn't get the job.

The sheriff frowned at his deputy. "That's not the way he feels now, is it Howard?"

Nightingale stuck out his hand to shake, thinking that to Howard the South had not lost—they simply took a break.

Howard ignored the outstretched hand.

Posey seemed oblivious to the tension between the two men. He told the sheriff he had a bad insulin pump and he'd be fine as soon as he could dress and get breakfast. "I'm here doing the governor's business. I'll let you know details as soon as I can," he said.

"We need to be in the loop, so to speak," Patterson said. "I know the governor is trying to buy the Dearborn property. It'd probably go smoother if she'd let us know how we could help."

Despite his recent bout with diabetes, Posey seemed to view his illness as an aggravating detail. He acted like he felt superior to this country sheriff. "Right. I'll tell her that. Nightingale will see you out."

Patterson's face blazed. "Don't bother. We can make the few steps to the door without an escort."

Nightingale watched, wondering what the payback would be.

After the two officers left, Posey sank back on the bed. "I need food," he said. "We need to talk."

"Do you remember anything about last night?" Nightingale asked.

Posey sat on the edge of the bed and pulled the sheet over his lap. A half sheepish grin came to his lips. "Not much." He yanked the covers higher over the pale roll of stomach that fell over the sheet.

A faint knock came at the door.

"Come in," Posey said.

The door swung open and a college-aged young man stepped aside for Emma Jackson to walk in with a large silver tray. She gave the man a queenly nod, and the door swung shut, leaving him in the hall. Still holding the tray, she turned to her audience. "I didn't know what was best, so there's coffee, toast, and more juice." She slid the tray on a bedside table, then frowned at Posey. "Maybe you should go to the hospital. I'm not equipped for the sick."

Posey looked at Nightingale, his scowl reflecting his unhappiness with the situation.

Posey slid closer to the edge of the bed. "No, ma'am." He moved like he might stand, and the sheet fell just enough to expose pubic hair. "I'll be fine in no time."

Nightingale stepped in front of Posey.

All color left Emma Jackson's face. She stared at Nightingale's face, then pivoted quickly and left without another word.

Posey buried his face in his pillow to contain his laughter.

Nightingale shook his head. "McGowan said you called him."

Posey sat up, became serious. "Yeah, funny thing about me and alcohol. I become the orator. I've had this stuff so long I just punch in new numbers when I need sweet control. In this case, I was still pissed at you, so I didn't pay attention." He stopped to drink more orange juice. He shook his head as if the motion would bring clarity. "First off, I want to know what the governor said your job was."

"My orders were to keep you safe. I didn't see that as a problem."

"I'm sure they didn't mention the threats they've had over this water deal."

"Threats? No. Wait a minute. You weren't sabotaged last night, were you?"

"Of course not. Blood sugar issues make me paranoid, but that's not the problem. I've got a briefcase full of incidents involving militants wanting water and taking it—to hell with the consequences. There's a *National Geographic* about the worldwide water shortage." Posey stood and yanked the sheet tighter. "We're up here to try to take water away from people who own it and give it to big cities." He wobbled a few steps and grabbed the bedstead. "Doesn't take a damned genius to see that we're the enemy."

The toga slipped off his shoulder.

Posey dropped heavily on the edge of the bed, as if his energy had left him. "That stubborn woman on that stupid horse may have problems we don't know about. I got a phone call from someone threatening to beat the crap out of me. 'Keep the government away from our water,' they said."

"Was there a name, a phone ID?"

Posey's sour look showed his irritation with the question. "No. I don't like this." He looked at the window, worry lines creasing his forehead.

"Most people only talk big—especially over the phone," Nightingale said.

"So what do you plan to do to protect me?"

"First thing is I'll move in here. Have you had any threats besides the phone call?"

"Governors get threats. I thought what they were saying was aimed at her." He waved one hand as if to vanquish the worry, then picked up the toast, "I read too much last night. This blood-sugar thing always makes me depressed. Soon as I get a contract from that woman, I'll be fine."

"I'll go talk to Mrs. Jackson. I'll get a room here while you get dressed," Nightingale said.

Posey nodded, let the sheet drop, and started toward the bathroom.

5

Nightingale found Mrs. Jackson in the dining room. "How is he?" she asked.

"He'll be fine. I'd like a room here."

"I have two vacancies now. One is in the house out back and one is upstairs, not far from Mr. Posey."

"Upstairs is fine. What do you need?"

The woman took his credit card and personal information just as the sheriff walked in from the dining room. The sheriff had a wrapped cinnamon roll and container of coffee.

"So, what exactly are you and Posey doing here?" Sheriff Patterson said.

"I'm just tagging along because the governor asked me to," Nightingale said. "Only Posey knows the details." He looked around. "Howard gone back to the house?"

"I sent him back. He's a good employee, but you need to tone down the smart-assed attitude. We're still in charge."

Emma Jackson interrupted. "I've got a business to run, Tommy. If you'll excuse us." She handed a key to Nightingale. "I'll show you the room. If you want to leave, that's fine, but if you spend the night, I expect you to pay. Those folks earlier stayed the night and didn't want to pay for it. Had a good supper, too—roast beef." Mrs. Jackson seemed to catch herself in the midst of her diatribe. She swallowed, blushed, and seemed to realize how she sounded to a guest.

She looked up at Nightingale with a plastic smile. "We'd love to have you stay more than one day." Her huge brown eyes had a downward slant, giving her a constant look of sadness.

Nightingale followed her.

Upstairs, she opened the door to a room down the hall from Posey. A queen-sized bed with a carved headboard and a yellow satin duvet filled the space. Lace trimmed the pillows. A Queen Anne chair and desk sat by the room's only window.

Mrs. Jackson raised her eyebrows, studied the room, and looked apologetic. "I guess I forgot that there's so many curlicues and swirls in the furniture. This room doesn't look like you at all, but it's comfortable." She walked to the window and pulled the curtains apart to show off huge trees shading a peaceful fenced yard.

Nightingale thought of Josephine.

"This room is fine." He patted the bed. "Bed is firm—just like I like. How many rooms do you have?"

"Three up here and two small houses out back. I usually cook breakfast, but not today." She threw one hand nervously into the air. "We'll have a light supper." She waved the hand, repeating a memorized script, but going through the motions of offering hospitality. "Call downstairs if you need anything." She indicated the phone on the desk and closed the door.

Nightingale turned to face his new surroundings. Something wasn't right. He sat in the Queen Anne chair, but it wasn't comfortable. He went to the desk, set his briefcase beside it, and returned to the window. The telephone sat like a bullying elephant in his space.

Then it came to him. Someone was in the room, and it wasn't

his dead dog, whom he talked to occasionally when he needed to work on a problem. "Okay, dog, do you get the same feeling that I'm getting?"

He quick-stepped to the bathroom and jerked back the shower curtain. From there, he bent down to look under the bed. That left only the closet. He pulled his weapon from under his jacket. "So what do you—?" With that, he jerked open the closet door.

A youngster—probably fourteen years old—stood rock still, with his arms at his side, his eyes closed.

Nightingale said nothing.

One of the boy's eyes popped open.

Nightingale reached in and pulled him into the room. The instant Nightingale touched him, he began to slap and kick like a mad raccoon. Finally, Nightingale held him with his arms behind him, wondering where he got so much power.

"Hey, you can't molest a child," the boy said. "There are laws."

"Only if they find a body." Nightingale was surprised at the resistance the skinny kid offered. "We can go downstairs right now, if you want to."

The threat worked. The boy quit squirming and kicking, but Nightingale continued to hold him at the shoulders while he tried to guess the boy's age.

"Just let me go. I wasn't doing nothing."

"Then why were you hiding?"

"I help around here."

Nightingale wondered about the truth of that statement. "That still doesn't answer why you were up here in my closet."

"Okay, okay. I fell asleep." The boy's muscles loosened and Nightingale turned him so they were face to face. "About midnight, I heard a knock on the door at the end of the hall and I looked out."

"From this room?"

"No." The boy rolled his eyes. "I was in the hall closet. There's a little space where I've hid before. Anyway, this woman knocked on the door and went in the room, and I went back to sleep."

"A woman? You're sure?"

Again, the eye roll. "This morning I heard Mrs. Jackson come to clean this room, and after she left I came in." He shrugged as if that explained everything.

"Did you see the woman leave the room at the end of the hall?"

"No. I'm hungry. You got anything in that briefcase that I could eat?"

Nightingale felt sorry for the kid. How much of what he said was truth and how much was fiction might take a while to sort out. Posey hadn't mentioned a woman.

"Where do you live? I can take you home and get something to eat on the way."

The kid started to sit at the desk stood up quickly. The Queen Anne chair couldn't hold him either.

"Let's get something straight." Nightingale stood, chastising his inward bully for intimidating a child. "You're underage. I don't know your name. And I don't know if anything you've told me is true. You're coming with me."

The boy looked like he might cry but drew in a long breath and stood by the door. "Okay. I guess I'd better give this back to you." He held out his right hand, and in his palm was Nightingale's initialed pen. The kid had picked his pocket.

6

The phone on the desk rang just as Nightingale's hand touched the doorknob. "Stay right there, kid."

He stepped toward the phone and heard the door open behind him.

The boy was down the hall and had hit the stairs.

Nightingale cursed and followed. At the top of the stairs, mid-step, he realized how bad this could look. He slowed his pace, trying for nonchalance by the time he reached the bottom stairs.

Mrs. Jackson stood in the dining room with a note pad under one arm and a cup of coffee in her hand. "I saw Cayden run out. He shouldn't have been upstairs. Was he bothering you?"

Nightingale did a quick mental critique of whether he wanted to start a search for a child who might be telling tall tales. "He said he did some chores for you sometimes. I thought he might show me around town. If he comes back, you could tell him I'll pay him as a guide."

She placed the coffee cup on the table and then the notepad. "He's a funny kid. You may want someone else as a guide. Would you like some coffee?"

Nightingale smiled and declined. Then he went back to his room, retrieved his keys, the phone, and his hat and walked to his truck, ignoring the dining room.

Outside, the air was cooler than he was used to in August but still in the 70s. The B and B was in a residential area, and as he drove, he absorbed the neighborhood. Two other houses down the street sported small, tasteful Bed and Breakfast signs. A typical small town in Texas, he guessed. Sidewalks cracked from age. Streets with a few potholes. Look far enough and you'd find a city struggling to keep up city services. He wondered if the main industry was the sale of antiques.

He continued on to the outskirts of town to the hotel of his previous night's stay and told the man at the front desk he needed to check out.

The man was gracious. "You had a call this morning, but the caller wouldn't leave a name or number."

"Female or male?"

"A man."

Nightingale mulled over the information. "I had a call in my room last night, but I didn't think anyone knew I was in town yet. How would that happen?"

"Someone knew where you were staying, but our staff wouldn't have put a call through to your room unless the caller clearly identified you. Did you tell anyone you were here?"

The man seemed sincere, so Nightingale didn't ask further questions. Whoever was hiding behind a telephone would show up if they really wanted to, and he'd deal with them then; otherwise, the threat should be ignored.

Nightingale took a different route going back to the B and B. He needed to think. Since the drought, he'd read about the Water Board of Texas. The new board had three paid members, all appointed by the governor. In the past, everyone worked out of the goodness of their heart, but the drought had brought the need for change. Now people wanted to be paid to work on water problems. In the past five years, the state's dismal response to the drought had been a topic of much discussion, but there seemed to be little will from politicians to cooperate and get anything done. Instead, they had meetings.

Course, how could he blame the state for Mother Nature and human reaction? Soon as you had a few drops of rain, everyone except farmers thought everything was back in good order. In his opinion, cities kept the citizens in the dark about the shrinking aquifer. State officials were no better. They debated the philosophy of who owned the water. In his calmer moments, he knew that people would solve the conflict locally and then the state would probably do what was expedient. But editorials he'd read lately hinted that people with lots of money were buying land over the aquifers in an attempt to control the future.

Each purchase he read about was of land in one or two water districts. Speculation was that the owner of the most land would control water in that district. That owner would ship the aquifer water to the highest bidder in any state, and Texas be damned. The idea made his skin crawl.

His phone rang, and he maneuvered the truck to the side of the road. Roy McGowan didn't bother with cordial exchanges. "What have you found out?"

Nightingale pulled the phone away from his ear. Roy's pushiness grated on him.

"I haven't found out anything new, Roy. The Dearborn woman is not selling."

"The governor knows she's a problem. Posey may not be able to handle her. You talk to her. Hell, I don't care what you tell her, but see if you can find out why she's determined to be a burr under the saddle."

"I'll ask her. You told me to protect Posey, and he's worried. He's had threats."

"He can join the club. I was afraid he'd wimp out."

"I have, too."

"Really? What kind of threats?"

"Telephone. Gonna kill me. I'm guessing his was the same."

"Hell, we all get those. I've had my share. We need you on this, Oz."

"I'll do what I can, Roy."

His father came to mind. The elder Nightingale liked to point out the downfalls of too much pride, which he had sometimes seen in his son. He'd teased Nightingale about showing off his star, and Nightingale admitted he was proud of his job. He loved being a Ranger. Early in his career, some shady land sales had caused him to pull out of one of the state's "requests for assistance." He had made it clear to the powers that be that he didn't need work so badly he would help them make some dollars for retirement.

Now he couldn't be so pure. He needed this water agreement as bad as anyone in the state—including the politicians. He smiled to himself. Karma—you had to love it.

He put the truck in gear and headed toward Mrs. Jackson's pride and joy.

When he walked into the Sycamore, Mrs. Jackson was standing at her desk, the telephone clasped to her ear. Her pink cheeks and pursed mouth told him she was not happy.

Nightingale tried not to overhear, but that was impossible.

"I can't do anything." Mrs. Jackson's words came out stiff, almost formal. She turned her back to Nightingale. "Has anyone called Tommy?"

After a short silence, she put the phone down. Nightingale had started up the stairs, trying to listen but be unobtrusive. Mrs.

Jackson touched her desk, as if she needed the support. "That was someone who knows my sister, Constance Dearborn."

Nightingale had practiced his solemn, no-surprise look for years. It came in handy, especially now, finding out that the two women were sisters; he'd had no idea earlier. "Is anything wrong?"

"There was an explosion just now."

Nightingale turned and walked down the stairs. "Where? Was anyone hurt?"

"No. Apparently, it was at my sister's ranch." Mrs. Jackson stood still, staring at the telephone.

"Your sister?"

Mrs. Jackson turned to him, her face red and her eyes like steel. "Yes, though we haven't spoken in years."

Nightingale tucked that information aside. "Has anyone called the sheriff?"

Mrs. Jackson paused, staring into space. Surely she realized how odd her reaction would seem to a stranger. She ran a hand through her short hair and seemed to make an effort at speaking. Her fingertips still touched the desk. "Yes. Tommy, Sheriff Patterson, will go. He's our kin. She needs someone to take charge."

"I'll go see what I can find out. Do you want to go?"

"No." Another strange expression crossed her face as she looked toward a horizon he didn't see. "I have to stay here to watch over things."

She straightened herself again, like she was willing her entire body to be strong. "I'm sure my sister does not want me to come."

Nightingale walked to his truck wondering at the conversation. In the last few years, he'd lost the desire to tiptoe around protocols. Some people wanted good manners more than honesty. He usually found that true in political situations, but sometimes people were so stubborn with their feelings that they shut out family and friends and died totally alone, but with their stubbornness intact.

"Damned fool notion," he said.

Again, he missed his dog. He needed a dog to replace the dead one. At least people would understand him talking to a real dog. This way he just looked like he'd lost his mind. Dogs never deserted their people; they loved them with or without money or a good mind.

The sheriff's car passed him, siren screaming, as he drove toward the Dearborn place. He returned along the roads he and Posey had driven the day before. He couldn't make heads or tails out of Mrs. Jackson's reaction. That cool distance was unlike anything he'd ever seen between sisters. Brothers, yes, but women usually didn't hold grudges. Or did they? He tried to keep the sheriff's lights in view but finally gave up.

From the newspapers and Internet accounts, he remembered that Mrs. Dearborn owned several thousand acres. Posey had pointed out one of the markers to her property line.

The forest was made up of pines, oaks, sycamores, and other trees he didn't know; he wondered how deep it went. He had not grown up around trees, so he soaked in the welcome coolness. The woods showed signs of the drought, the brown trees evident in spots through the branches of survivors. Then he recognized the drive where he and Posey had stopped before the woman and the other rider confronted them.

He slowed the truck and stayed on the blacktop road. After two miles, a dirt path went to the right. He pulled onto the path, drove a little piece, and stopped at a deep gully, where he got out.

Further up the way, a patrol car occupied a portion of the shoulder of the road. He squinted toward the vehicle and saw the young officer that he met at the Sycamore Bed and Breakfast step out of the car. The obvious eagerness of the man reminded Nightingale of a younger version of himself.

Officer Toohey strode through the weeds, grinning and mumbling. "I guess I'm not surprised you're here." He paused before motioning Nightingale to follow. "Mrs. Jackson told the Sheriff she'd heard you were one of the best Rangers alive."

7

Nightingale said nothing. Where did Mrs. Jackson hear such a thing? He tried to not enjoy the flattery, instead aiming for a sliver of the younger officer's eagerness for himself.

A plume of smoke rose above the trees farther into the woods. "Mrs. Jackson told me there was an explosion. Is that true?"

"The sheriff and Ed are up there checking. We heard that some environmental group was planning on causing problems." Toohey squinted toward the smoke.

"Have outside groups shown up before?" Nightingale asked.

"Not that we know of. Mrs. Dearborn said she was getting help from some 'concerned groups.' You know how some of those nutcase environmental people are."

They headed into the trees, shaded from the sun. The cooler air carried the smell of pine. Wild grape vines hung from some of the trees. Greenbriar and hawthorns nicked their pantlegs.

Nightingale took long strides, swiping branches when they whacked at his head. Now, actually walking through the trees rather than driving by them as he had been a few minutes ago, the damage from the drought was more obvious. Most of the pines and evergreens had brown needles or were dead, testifying to the effects of the drought.

Nightingale had not thought he was claustrophobic, but the woods seemed to close in. He remembered Casey, a crime photographer from the Tennessee hills, who had come to Broken Rock when her uncle was killed. "People from the hills are more insular, more suspicious," she had said. "They believe the land protects them. The hills and the woods are their friends."

He wondered if these folks were like that. For all the variety of people he'd met, he'd never left West Texas, except for brief stints in Austin. He regretted that his life had been so one-dimensional.

Mosquitoes nipped his face; gnats swarmed. He swatted at the insects, trying to keep the gnats out of his eyes. He stopped a minute, getting his bearings, still swatting.

"You ever had dealings with these environmentalists?" Toohey asked back over his shoulder.

"No. How about you all? You think this was caused by them?"

Toohey walked backed to Nightingale, lifted his hat, and wiped sweat with a handkerchief. "Don't know. They sent some stories to the paper. Pete James, the editor, told the sheriff about it. Come to think of it, I guess there was only one story. Pete put it on the opinion page."

Toohey started walking again.

Nightingale got in step beside him. "So this isn't the first time they've caused trouble over here?"

Toohey grunted and smacked a hackberry limb out of the way. "I don't know. Seems like it was in the papers last spring. Nobody pays that much attention till it gets in their back yard, and now the state has put us between a rock and a hard place. People are not happy."

They'd been walking up a hill. At the crest, the scene opened up into a large clearing. The hollowed-out land looked like a parking lot for trucks and trailers. One of the trailers had broken in two, as though a small blast had gone off in the middle, splintering the trailer bed and leaving a hole in the dirt. Debris was scattered around the trailer, but from a distance, it was hard to see exactly what had been destroyed.

The sheriff and Deputy Howard stood to one side of the trailer. Further back, up the opposite hill, two figures stood next to two horses. Looked like the Dearborn woman and her companion of the day before. They stood in the shade of the trees, staring toward the sheriff.

Nightingale and Toohey started down the hill, the incline now much steeper than it had been on the walk through the trees. Nightingale's boots slid on the short grass and the even slicker pine needles as he picked his way down. On the other side, a damaged path of broken branches and beaten, small trees twisted into another forest. Apparently, the tractors and trailers had shoved aside anything in their way to get onto the land.

At the bottom of the hill, the sheriff walked over to meet them. "I guess Posey was too puny to come?"

"Yes, sir."

Tommy Patterson glanced at the woman on the hillside before he directed his question to Nightingale. "Reckon you can get any of those tech people out here like you see on TV to check on this bomb and such?"

"I'll ask. Probably not. Nothing in real life works like that." Nightingale saw the goodwill drain from the sheriff's face and regretted his quick honesty. "What happened?"

"Hell, it's pretty obvious. Something exploded." The sheriff threw both arms in the air, not mincing his own frustration.

"Mind if I look?"

"Yeah, fine. I guess you know what to touch and what to leave alone."

Nightingale picked his way around the destroyed trailer. At the edge of the mayhem, under leaves and dirt, a shine of metal caught his eye. "Toohey, Sheriff, don't move."

The quick intake of their breath made him think they would stay back.

"What do you see?" the sheriff asked.

"What I know about explosives you could put in a hat band," Nightingale said. "I see some bars of putty, or clay, or plastic that have metal caps. Could be C-4." Nightingale recited as he stood still, trying to remember.

In some class, the instructor had said C-4 didn't explode without a firing mechanism. It was a stable explosive. Even firing a bullet into it would not set it off. That same instructor had three fingers missing.

"I don't see a firing mechanism," he said.

He bent toward the light brown bars, looking for wires or a trip mechanism. He wondered if the sheriff or Howard heard his heart pounding against his chest. He tried to stop the trembling in his hand. Slowly, slowly, he touched the first bar. The metal cap fell off. His breath of relief moved the blades of grass around him. He picked the bar up and smelled. Clay. He did the same with the other one.

Behind him, he heard footsteps. "No wires? Was there a timer?"

Nightingale jerked around at the sheriff's voice. "Not that I see. Just makes me wonder."

"Me, too," Patterson said.

Nightingale heard the sound of horses and muffled voices. He turned and saw the two figures at the top of the hill had mounted and were riding out of sight.

"Guess Mrs. Dearborn decided to leave when we didn't get blown up," the sheriff said. "Since your boys can't help us, I'll call the state fellows to come out here and see what really happened."

The pleasure in his voice made Nightingale sure the man enjoyed this show of power.

"We've got to talk to Mrs. Dearborn," Nightingale said.

Patterson turned a sideways glance. "I'll tell you what." Here he paused and squinted toward the debris on the ground. "Howard and me will talk to her. If it's anything you need to know, I'll tell you."

A half-grunt and chortle came from Ed Howard's direction.

8

M urder. Constance Dearborn had wallowed the word around in her mind many times since she first met Jack Posey. She could have shot him and the man with him and never regretted it. Anger and hatred billowed in her heart. But murder would only lose the battle, lose the farm, probably her life.

From the slope overlooking the valley, she watched the sheriff, his deputies, and that meddling Ranger poke around in the scattered pieces of machinery and trees where the explosion had happened. Good diversion from someone, but blowing things up usually didn't help matters.

"Let's go back to the house," she said. She and Faulkner walked the horses to a level spot before mounting.

Faulkner mounted his ride easily despite his prosthetic leg.

After topping the hill, she heard another commotion, but didn't turn back. They could find her if they wanted to—they always had.

She used the ride home to consider her options and try to quiet the rage inside. Faulkner, never a man of many words, said nothing.

Her father would have encouraged all-out war at the threat

that someone would take this land. The gall. The cheek, the very idea, made her boil with anger. Shoot them all—that's what they deserved. What made this year so civilized that anyone could trample on her rights? Not to mention the land. She wanted revenge for those tractors and trailers on her land. She closed her eyes, let the horse choose his pace. Anger accomplished nothing, so she tightened her lips, sat taller in the saddle, and looked straight ahead.

She dared not try to explain her feelings to Hank Faulkner. He seemed good-natured, despite the war's damage to his leg. He'd been through enough. He'd been a godsend to help her with the heavy chores that she couldn't handle. Every once in a while, she wondered what he'd been through and what he expected of his life ahead, but she didn't probe. She had no energy to help him, even though he had helped her.

For the last several months, all she had thought about was this government threat. This war was hers. Maybe those people from the Environmental Liberation Front could help. But, surely, they had not thought planting explosives would help.

At the stable, she handed her horse's reins to Faulkner and walked to the house. She'd repainted the shutters and trim a dark green after she inherited the house. The choice was for her mother, not her father, and she still liked it.

The easy turn of the key made her twist the key again. She was sure she had locked it. A tremor of unease ran across her shoulders. She marked the tension up to anger.

Then she saw him. She stopped breathing.

He stepped from around the side of the house. "Ma'am, I don't want you to be scared. I'm from the Environmental Liberation Front. We want to help you."

Constance dropped her hands from the doorknob and took a step backward. She scanned him for a gun. Did she have time to get one? Where was Hank?

"I have a friend talking with Mr. Faulkner," the man said. "My name is Jason Keel."

A noise came from behind her.

Jason Keel's eyes grew large and frightened.

A grunt like an animal that had been hit hard made her turn. Someone was shoved hard and fell beside her.

"Mrs. Dearborn, there's a man here who said he needs to talk to you." Hank Faulkner stepped into view. He bent to place a gun against the temple of the man on the ground.

Jason Keel paled.

His friend was crying, shaking in terror. Had to be in his early twenties. Stringy blonde hair fell around his face when he looked up at his partner.

"I didn't sign up to die for this, Jason."

"If you'll just listen," Jason said. He held his hand up in Faulkner's direction, shaking his head.

Faulkner stood and stepped back. "Kids can be dangerous, too," he said. "We found that out in Iraq."

Constance didn't speak for a minute. She listened to the quick, scared breaths, the choked whimpers. She made a choice from her gut, hoping no one, including herself, would be shot.

She stepped closer to Faulkner, keeping her voice low. "It's all right Hank." Her instincts told her to not cross him.

Keel and his friend became quiet, obviously grateful for any help against the man facing them.

"Hank, Mr. Keel was telling me that they want to help us. They don't have guns."

"They could lie."

"We're not lying." Keel shook his head, his voice quivered.

Constance stepped between Faulkner and Keel and began to whisper. "We'll listen. Then send them away. How about you put the gun down?"

Faulkner waited for a moment, staring at her. Finally, he put the safety on and gave her the Walther. She couldn't tell what he was thinking, or if his mind was in the present or in the past.

She let the gun dangle from her right hand. She hadn't held a hand gun in several years. It was heavier than she remembered. She barely turned her head. "Y'all had better leave now."

Jason Keel helped the young man up from the ground, where he'd been kneeling. They walked around the side of the house, never looking back. Faulkner waited a few minutes before following them.

When he reappeared a few moments later, he stuck his hand out for the gun. "Don't worry," he said. "They're gone. They had a car at the bottom of the driveway."

She handed the gun to him, not knowing if that was the right thing to do but not sure what else she could do. He stuffed it in the back of his waist. The quiet became uncomfortable. "I was scared," she said.

His mouth twisted into a half-grin. "Of them or me?"

There it was, out in the open.

She returned his stare. "Both." She couldn't read his face and, deep in her gut, she was surprised to find this was the truth.

His jaw tensed, and he turned away from her. "That about says it then." He picked his hat off the ground and hit it against his knee. "I'm gonna finish brushing the horses."

"We need to talk." She raised her voice toward his back.

He stopped, then turned slowly. "No, ma'am, you need to talk. I don't need anything. I may want some things, but I don't *need* much of anything except my leg back."

His voice came at her steady. Dark eyes that had been wild a few minutes before now looked over her shoulder, away from her gaze. He took a deep breath. "I'm sorry. I didn't know who they were or what they might do."

"You were right to protect me." She dared a step closer. "Let's just calm down. I'll fix coffee."

They went into the house, and she measured water while he walked to the living room, looking out the window facing the road. Likely, he wanted to be sure the men had stayed gone.

When he came back into the kitchen, he laid the gun on the counter.

Without turning from the coffee maker, she said, "What did that young man do?"

"You mean to make me suspicious?"

She nodded.

"He stepped out from around the barn and called me Mr. Faulkner. Nobody calls me mister if they're a friend. Then he put his hand in his jacket." Faulkner shrugged like a schoolboy. "That move made me think . . . and I pulled my weapon and walked him to the house."

"I didn't know you carried a gun."

"This is Texas; it's legal. Besides"—He looked out the big window toward the woods—"I got used to it in the service. Never know when you'll need one."

She pulled out coffee filters, then put them back. She measured the water and forgot how much she'd put in the pot. Her mind spun around many things besides coffee. She'd learned a lot in the last hour: people could get to her house, and probably inside, when she didn't want them to, and Faulkner, her husband's army friend, had more tension bottled inside than she'd ever guessed.

Her husband had written to her about Faulkner. No details, just something about cooking a big meal to repay the man who'd saved his life. Because they were over forty years old, her husband wrote of them as "two old farts trying to keep these youngsters alive." As it turned out, Christopher was killed and Hank lost part of one leg in a roadside bombing. Faulkner had grown up in the same county as both of them, and when he came to see

Constance to talk about Christopher, it seemed natural for her to offer him work.

They talked a little about the war, more about growing up in the same area. She knew he was nervous, didn't sleep well. He flinched at sudden noises, but generally she thought he simply put the war into a category that he didn't want to discuss. She figured he would talk about it if he wanted to, but today the PTSD he had mentioned in passing—"Everybody has a touch of it if they've been in combat"—had become very real.

And those two strangers from ELF were another problem. Coming to her like thieves didn't impress her, but if they could help, she'd listen. Showed how desperate she was to even consider them.

The coffee maker beeped, bringing her back to reality. She took down two cups.

Faulkner remained standing, looking out the window. "Do you reckon those fellas will call you?"

"You think they were really from an environmental group?"

"Don't know. I've got some tree-hugger friends. I'll see if they've heard of these two. Do we know the second one's name?"

"No. The one with me said he was Jason Keel. I don't know if we should believe them." She put the coffee cups on the table and pulled out a chair. "Hank, I need to talk to you."

He grinned, and she wondered if he found her nervousness amusing. He was a man more handsome than her husband had been, a man who had saved her husband's life, only to have him lose it a few weeks later.

The slightest ice of fear entered her belly. She had no idea how much to say. She knew Faulkner was fond of her, possibly too fond, but she didn't want that.

He sat down and blew into the hot coffee.

"Are you taking anything for this, this . . ."

His mouth tightened as he reached for the sugar and jabbed a spoon into the bowl. His hand started trembling.

"Look at me," she said. "I'm your friend. I want the best for you."

The spoon clattered as it fell from his hand, spilling sugar across the space. "Right. Let's be honest Mrs. Dearborn, today I scared the hell out of you. Sometimes I can't control my anger. I figure I'm due a few tantrums after what I've seen. I'll leave if you think I'm dangerous."

"That's not what I said." His taunting, childish remark pissed her off. She didn't care what he did or thought. Her anger matched his. "If you're so damned much in control, then listen. I'm not the enemy. I'm uneasy when I see men with guns lose their temper. It shouldn't be that hard to tell me if you're on medication."

Astonishment passed over his face. He began to laugh. "You've got a worse temper than me."

He reached over and covered her hand with one of his.

She flinched.

The laughter stopped. She couldn't look at him. She stared at their hands and gave the slightest tug away from him. Her mind clamped down: too soon, too soon.

He jerked his hand back. "Sorry, didn't mean to get too close." He slugged down part of the coffee and stood. "I'm going home now. It's early, but my sister had some chores for me. If you need me tomorrow, call me. Good evening, Mrs. Dearborn."

She waited to hear his truck leave before pulling the bourbon out of the cabinet and adding a generous amount to her coffee. Bourbon had cured a lot of ills for her father—might work for her, too.

9

Nightingale walked back to his truck, batting away the gnats and mosquitoes and his own curiosity. Leave it, he told himself. Stick to the charge from the governor. Any outsider blowing things up was Sheriff Patterson's problem, so let it go. He had a duty to the governor, the state, and his hometown of Broken Rock.

But it was an old habit, this poking and prying at things. He had to tell Posey what had happened, and with that came the questions: Who had planted explosives? Why plant fake explosives among the real? Why blow up Dearborn's property? Prying had served him well as a Ranger, but he'd retired—needed to tamp it down. Let the sheriff take care of it like he wanted to do.

It was early afternoon, so after a milkshake at the Dairy Queen, he headed for the Sycamore Bed and Breakfast and Posey's room.

Posey answered the door in his bathrobe. A pale man anyway, his diabetic bout had left him with large, dark circles under his eyes. The dark-rimmed glasses made him look even more like a nerd. His skin hung loose on his frame, as if he'd lost weight but no one told his outer casing. Even his reddish-brown hair seemed thinner.

"You feeling better?" Nightingale asked.

"Much. Thanks. Where've you been?"

After offering coffee, which Nightingale declined, Posey began to pace like a caged animal. Nightingale sat down and gave a quick rundown on the explosion at the Dearborn ranch while he watched the back and forth.

"Lord knows we don't need some lunatic tree-huggers complicating things," Posey said. "You don't think it was a bomb?"

"What I found was fake, but something blew up a wagon full of tools. The sheriff doesn't want me asking questions, but he asked for me to call in the Ranger lab people to help. I didn't think they'd help, and they won't. Maybe when you talk to Mrs. Dearborn, you can find out who she suspects," Nightingale said.

Posey made a slight grimace. "You are an ex-Ranger and a busybody. That's not how this works. As far as I can figure, you're here to help me, nothing else."

Nightingale felt his mouth tighten. "So, what do you want?" he said.

Posey didn't answer directly. "From what I've heard, her father was a piece of work. He told each girl what she would inherit but didn't stick to that in his will. Now, the sisters don't talk to each other. I was told Mrs. Dearborn needs money to help with farm expenses. Let's visit her and offer to help."

"I'll drive my truck," Nightingale said.

A locked gate greeted them at the Dearborn ranch. Nightingale pushed the button for the intercom. Background music played but no one spoke.

"My name is Oswald Nightingale. I'm here with Mr. Posey to see Mrs. Dearborn."

Without a reply, the gate buzzed open.

Nightingale drove up and parked in front of the house. He looked at Posey. "Do you know how to use your weapon?"

"Sure. I took one of those required six-hour classes." Posey reached toward the bulge.

Nightingale didn't feel a burst of confidence. "I don't think you'll need it. Keep it covered." He scanned the porch and yard for places that might provide cover.

At Posey's skeptical look, he said, "I'm a very tan man in front of a house in East Texas. I've lasted as a Ranger 'cause I'm no fool. When she comes out with a gun I want my badge and my gun to be the first things she sees."

Recognition lit Posey's face. "Yeah, I read about how some of these folks are about a hundred years behind. Might be dangerous for you."

Nightingale shook his head in dismay. "Right. Nobody seems to notice my white half."

Posey stood a few feet back on the steps.

Nightingale knocked and raised his voice. "Mrs. Dearborn, I'm Oswald Nightingale. I'm here with Mr. Posey."

The door flew open and a twenty-two rifle, held by a skinny woman, greeted them.

Both men stepped backward.

She looked to be on the young side of forty, full of piss and vinegar. By herself, probably. Otherwise she wouldn't be putting all this bluster into opening a door. "Why're you here without calling first?" She waved the barrel of the gun at Nightingale.

He didn't back up again. One hand held his badge, and the other pushed his jacket back so he could reach his weapon if needed and so she could see it. Who the hell thought women were the weaker sex?

"Ma'am, you don't always answer your phone. This water situation is mighty important, and Mr. Posey's daddy said anyone who was a daughter of Judge Alexander would listen to reason.

That's all we ask, just listen." Nightingale rushed his words, trying to get to the point.

She looked around Nightingale to Posey.

"How'd you know my father was a judge?"

Posey's frightened eyes bulged behind his glasses. He stared at the gun barrel. "My daddy served in the Vietnam era, but your daddy was a judge, and he wrote a letter that kept my father out of combat."

"Who is your father?"

Posey's voice squeaked. "Jim Bob Posey from Dwyer."

"Why would he write a letter for someone in South Texas?"

"I don't know. Dad said he knew your mother from Tech."

Nightingale felt his admiration growing for the lawyer, if this was true. If not, there'd be hell to pay.

"What about my baby brother?"

Posey kept his hands a respectful distance in the air. "No idea, ma'am. I didn't know you had a brother."

Mrs. Dearborn's mouth twitched with the beginnings of a smile. The gun barrel drooped toward the floor of the porch. "All right, say your piece. You're not coming in my house."

"I have some information here." Posey lowered his hands a little. "It's a paper with some ideas for you to read. The legislature passed a law to put a statewide water plan into action. There'll be reservoirs across the state, some dams, new studies on desalination, a lot going on. We need a reservoir for Dallas and the other cities southwest of here. People are like frogs put in warm water and then the heat is turned on. They're cooking, and they don't know it."

The lady smiled, almost laughed. "Too bad for them. Other people were here. Said they came from the governor, too. They showed me plans. Have you seen how dry these lakes are around here? Why don't you fill them? Taking my land to build another lake to pump water to Dallas or God knows where, when you can't keep these filled, makes no sense."

"I'm prepared to offer you better than the market price for part of your land. You'll still have a huge ranch and the money to buy more. The state needs this."

"I see that you can be polite at gun point. That's a pity. Should have tried it sooner."

Nightingale thought about the governor's threat. "Ma'am," he said. "We need to talk. If you don't sell, you'll be run over by bulldozers."

She raised the rifle, turning it on him. "Guess I'll go down shooting."

Posey said, "You think about all that money, ma'am." His words were followed by the sound of his boots hitting the porch steps and then the gravel as he headed to the truck.

"We'll be going now," Nightingale said. He touched his hat brim and walked backward down the stairs before turning toward the truck.

They had reached the road before either of them spoke. Posey drew long breaths.

Dusk was settling around them, giving the sky the pinks and blues of sunset.

Nightingale turned sideways toward his passenger. "Do we need to stop? You've been wiggling since we left that woman's house."

"That dump of a bar where we met—is it near here?" Posey asked.

"Yeah, but after last night I—"

"You don't have to watch over me. Or do you?" Posey's tone relayed his suspicion. "You want to tell me the real reason you're here?"

Nightingale felt Posey's stare and kept his own eyes forward.

"You've got to be expensive," Posey said. "We definitely need a drink." Posey let out a gallows laugh. "I wonder what McGowan is not telling me."

As Nightingale parked the truck, Posey muttered to himself about drinks and a caretaker.

"You're an adult; drink if you want to," Nightingale said. "I'm not your babysitter. Tell me what to do if you pass out."

A smile spread across Posey's face. "I propose a truce, Mr. Nightingale. I'll have one beer, and we can talk. Believe it or not, too much alcohol is not usual with me, not because I don't like it, but because I don't like the morning after."

In the evening shadows, the bar looked more inviting than it had in the daylight. Low lighting illuminated a few couples scattered at the tables and two men at the bar. The smell of French fries reminded Nightingale that he hadn't eaten in a few hours.

When he asked for a menu, the barkeeper handed him a greasy 4 x 6 note card with appetizer choices. Everything was fried.

"We close the kitchen at ten, so if you want food, better make up your mind."

Nightingale ordered fries and two beers, and they settled at a small table in the back.

Nightingale let two swallows of cold brew settle in his stomach before speaking. "You called this meeting. You start."

"The way I figure it, the governor is returning a favor to her friend, my mother, by hiring me."

When Nightingale raised his eyebrows, Posey grinned. "It's politics. I put the early deals together in the west of the state. This was supposed to be a done deal, so everyone could feel good. The Dearborn lady is a problem. But you—you're the odd part to this, and the only thing I can think is they may be worried about my getting out alive."

Nightingale glanced at his beer. "Why would they worry about you getting out alive?"

Posey shook his head. "Apparently, people up here don't want this to happen. But the governor's plan should help them reconsider." He patted a zippered case resting against his foot.

"Was this supposed to be easy?"

"Mrs. Dearborn is in deep water—no pun intended—as far as needing money for the farm, so yes."

"Won't she get a large amount because of her husband dying in combat?"

"There's some question of what he was doing, but how do you know so much about her situation?"

"The governor's staff gave me a stack of reading material. What do you mean 'question of what he was doing'?"

Posey shrugged. "Something about drugs, probably nothing serious, but the delay is not helping. According to what I was told, she was almost ready to sign, then cooler weather set in and we had a few local elections. Politicians aren't famous for getting along. The scramble that followed got us to this point."

"You didn't show that you had a plan a couple hours ago."

"Right." Posey took another drink and laughed. "That gun scared me."

Nightingale grinned and warmed to the younger man as they talked. Posey didn't mind admitting his foibles.

"So why are you here?" Posey asked.

"Like you said, they were afraid somebody might hurt you. Maybe they knew that Mrs. D had a gun."

"You think she'll let us come back?" Posey asked.

"Yeah. She's got old-style values. She'll let us come back. I think she likes you, but she'll make us wait. She set us up. We'll need to be polite, not barge in."

In the smoke and low light, Posey laughed. "I've seen some mean sellers and buyers—never somebody come at me with a rifle. I'm calling McGowan when we get back and telling him we've got to stretch that deadline."

"She had a good point about the lakes drying up. What's your answer?" Nightingale asked.

"A reservoir is built and aimed at the water needs of the cities. Lakes are already there and can't be redirected to take care of those needs."

"So Lake Meredith, out in my area, has dried up. What then?"

"I don't know." Posey's mouth twitched with frustration. "For God's sake, I'm not here as a water expert. But if you had good political grit you'd use this to get some more water to your area." Posey looked sideways at Nightingale. "You son-of-a-gun."

Nightingale downed the last of his beer, admitting nothing. "You ready to go?"

They didn't speak again until they were back at the B and B.

Inside the living room of the establishment, the youngster who had been in Nightingale's room sat on a couch opposite Mrs. Jackson's desk, reading a thick paperback.

"I'm going to my room," Posey said.

"Same here." Nightingale walked with Posey, ignoring the boy.

He didn't look back. Be damned if he'd encourage the little criminal. In his room, Nightingale hung up his jacket and opened his laptop. The wireless connection looked doubtful for the present. Maybe later.

The knock on the door was so firm, he thought it might be Posey. Instead, the boy stood at the door with his book in one hand. "Mrs. Jackson said you needed a guide to show you around town."

"I mentioned that, but I don't cotton to thieves. I believe in rules." Nightingale crossed his arms.

"Figures."

"In business, you keep your sarcasm to yourself," Nightingale said.

The boy jerked his head to swing the hair out of his eyes. "Are you paying, or am I supposed to work for free?"

"I'll pay you twenty dollars. Shouldn't take more than a couple hours."

"I'll be here at 8:00 a.m. tomorrow."

"How're you getting home tonight?"

The boy had gradually backed away from the door. "I'll walk." He was halfway down the hall, waving his hand, before Nightingale could protest.

"Do it your way," Nightingale said.

The kid acted worse than some abused dog. Nightingale had seen kids like that, but each one had a different story. And with every one, he felt he'd missed a chance to help—all the way back to the first one. He felt inadequate when it came to children, especially teenagers.

When the boy was out of sight, Nightingale went downstairs in search of Mrs. Jackson. She was in the kitchen, not cooking, but writing.

She looked over the rim of her glasses at him. "I'm planning the breakfast menu for the week. Are you allergic to anything, Mr. Nightingale?"

"No, ma'am. I was wondering what you can tell me about that kid named Cayden? I've asked him to show me around town."

She put down her pen and stared at her hands. "Not a good idea. He's too young to know our history. He's had some bad influences in his life." She stared at Nightingale like he missed her point. "His last name is Shepherd. He has a tendency to tell tall tales."

"I might enjoy that."

Nightingale didn't say more. Cayden had flat-out lied to him, but he pushed that aside. He wanted to know more about this self-sufficient child. He'd shot a teenager years before. He had decided then that boys needed help more than criticism. He jerked his attention to the chore at hand, went to Posey's room, and told him about the plan for the next morning.

"You are certifiably crazy," Posey said. "We don't have time to 'tour' or see the sights. We've got work to do." Posey stood at the closet, hanging one shirt and then one pair of pants—pants together by color, same with shirts.

"Of course we've got work." Nightingale leaned against the wall near the window. "But we've got to know the people and what's going on here. This is a political message as much as anything else. That kid can talk to us about what everybody thinks. Then we can see how to approach this."

Posey raised his eyebrows in mock wonder. "When did you become politically astute? That kid doesn't know politics."

"No, he'll tell us what he sees, and you'll decide the politics."

Posey looked at his watch.

"You expecting company?"

Posey gave him a sarcastic lift of the left eyebrow. "In this hole in the road? You've got to be kidding. I thought I'd call McGowan and tell him your plan. He might have pointers."

"Good idea. See you in the morning."

"No, I'm sleeping late. Don't bother me with a walk led by a child."

In his room, Nightingale tried the Internet. He had no luck with messages, but read a few articles about Texas water. He was getting ready for bed when his cell phone rang.

"This is Garrick. Thought I'd see how you're doing."

That was a lie. Garrick was probably bored.

"What's going on back there?" Nightingale asked.

Garrick, a retired Ranger and general curmudgeon, had shown up in Nightingale's last case and had begun to show up at

Nightingale's house or Mrs. Holly's place on an irregular basis. They'd been friends for years. Nightingale suspected that Garrick had a soft spot for Josephine Holly's pies, but he helped her with chores, too. Rumor was that Garrick was his biological father, but Garrick had never admitted that, and Nightingale liked his past as it was, so he hadn't pressed the idea. Most of the time he figured the rumor had been started by people who hated both him and Garrick.

"I thought you needed to know that Josephine is poorly."

"What'd you mean? I talked to her yesterday and she sounded about like normal. Maybe a little madder than usual about the drought, but . . ." He stopped for a minute, trying to recall the conversation. He had credited her dismal conversation to her worries about the lack of rain. "I've never known the woman to feel bad."

"She's not telling anyone."

"What? How serious is she?"

Garrick coughed and Nightingale heard the jingle of ice in a glass. How much of this was alcohol induced? "Listen, I'm telling you she looks gray—not her usual self. She's not got her pep like usual."

"Do I need to come back?"

"You'll have to decide. That's all. Do you need me to help up there?"

"No, I don't need help." Nightingale told him goodbye and wondered about the reason for the call. Garrick knew how deeply Nightingale cared for Josephine Holly, so a call was the way to get to him. Nightingale paced for a few minutes. He cursed his lack of passion. For years, he had worked at not caring for much of anybody. He'd seen some men cry, usually over family deaths. He didn't cry. He practiced stoicism like it was a religion.

His two cousins, both near his age, were his only family in Texas. He saw them on holidays, but work had been his balm and existence. He had a soft spot for Garrick but had never pursued questions about parentage, feeling disloyal to his mother and father, who had made sacrifices for him and whom he still loved deeply.

Then he'd met Josephine. Her determined stance on friendship—not marriage—had intrigued him. In his late forties, the emptiness of his life was becoming obvious. He'd always avoided hurt, and he finally realized that made him avoid the chance to love. He realized that he loved her and she didn't return his love. She hadn't misled him. He couldn't persuade her otherwise, so he agreed to her terms: he kept a distance. And that was what they had.

Garrick had done a fine job of inserting worry.

It was after nine o'clock. He called anyway. On the third ring, she answered, sounding groggy.

"Josephine, I thought I'd check in and see how you're doing."

"I'm sleepy, Oz. That rascal Garrick didn't call you, did he? How are things up there?"

"It's early for you to be in bed. I was thinking about making a quick trip home, if you need anything." Lord, that was clumsy. Why not just say, "I'm worried about you"? Because he didn't know what to say—wondered if he ever would.

"I'm fine, Oz. I've got a headache. I'll call tomorrow." With that, she hung up.

He looked at the phone, almost dialed again, then realized he had to stop. He was acting like some lovesick teenager.

He cursed Garrick for planting the seeds of worry, and himself for letting the seeds take root. He couldn't get to sleep. The Internet worked clear and quick in the late-night hours. He found plenty to read. Huge companies were buying thousands of acres of land to make their own water districts. No one shipped water out of Texas aquifers yet. Rain had graced a few counties. Speculation about man's vision and

God's plan for the state was rampant in editorials and chat rooms.

Nightingale couldn't imagine selling water to another state when Texas was in such dire need. But some men had a different moral compass. His mind jumped from water worries to thoughts about Josephine Holly. Sound sleep never came.

10

The next morning, he called Posey's cell phone and got a recording. He left a message, thinking that this was the same pattern as the day before, but Posey had said he was sleeping late.

Cayden knocked on his door at 8:00 a.m. He had on a wrinkled tee-shirt and jeans. His shoulder-length hair was wet and parted to one side, slicked off his face.

"Glad to see you're on time. Have you had breakfast?" He didn't give the boy time to answer, just guided him to the truck. "I need some coffee and toast. While we eat, you can tell me where we're going."

"I ate earlier," the boy said.

"Fine. You can watch me eat and tell me what you've planned."

"Might as well start at the haunted hotel," Cayden said. "They have breakfast there."

Cayden directed Nightingale as he drove to the cobblestoned Main Street and turned right to the Blue Willow Hotel. In the parking lot, the aroma of ham, eggs, and sausage greeted them.

Despite the good smells, the restaurant was not crowded.

Cayden picked up a brochure from the front desk as they walked in.

"So why is it haunted?" Nightingale asked.

"The ghost of some woman roams around the second floor, but only certain times of the year. She caught her boyfriend with another woman and drowned herself. If we didn't have this drought, you could see the water from the front porch."

"You believe the story?"

"Yeah." Cayden looked too somber for a fourteen year old. "People can be real stupid, especially women."

Nightingale wondered what event brought that observation.

From their breakfast table, he saw trees and the river banks—no water. He persuaded Cayden to order a pancake, and between bites, the boy said his plan was to go from breakfast to the Beulah Mercantile. Posey was probably right and this would accomplish little, but Nightingale had already promised, and keeping promises had to be done.

After the Mercantile, where they bought a bag of candy out of a barrel, they went to Allison's Antiques. Furniture from the 1920s and earlier rested in every corner. A lady who Nightingale assumed was the owner asked if she could help them, but when Nightingale said, "Just looking," she told them to let her know if they had questions and disappeared into the back of the building.

In the Railroad Museum, an elderly man poured forth about the importance of the railroad to the area and the legend of Jay Gould, who cursed a neighboring city and helped blow up the dam that had produced wide, deep waters for riverboats. After the dam was gone, river traffic ceased.

"The lesson is, 'Don't piss off the people with money.'" The old man stood tall and grinned at his own wit. His pressed shirt and creased jeans reminded Nightingale of Garrick.

"What about politicians?" Nightingale asked.

"You're referring to that water business, I guess."

Nightingale nodded.

"The thing is that our new governor campaigned hard in these parts about a water plan for the state. Said we'd keep the lakes for recreation. Nothing was said about taking somebody's land to build a reservoir." The man cocked his head and squinted one eye at Nightingale. "I'm betting you work for her or some of her people. She's trying to give that appearance of equality."

Nightingale almost grinned. Usually, people were not so direct in their comments about his color. The white heritage in him usually didn't have a chance to surface—people always seemed suspicious of him and assumed he was as prejudiced as they were. "I do work for her."

The man nodded, continued his look. "She shouldn't of sent you. We've got a bad taste in our mouths. Even your people here in town don't like her anymore. She'll take the land of the poor, too. I'm not a fan of the Alexanders or Dearborns, but the government is not doing Constance right. And the thing is, if they'll do it to one, they'll do it to all. Tell her Pete Coleman said that."

"I'll tell her, Mr. Coleman, but this isn't settled yet. Mrs. Dearborn may decide she wants the money."

The man laughed. "And pigs may fly."

Nightingale and Cayden walked gingerly out of the museum, elbows close so they didn't touch tiny reproductions of trains from the past or knock off fragile-looking lanterns perched on every inch of counter-space. Outside on the wide-planked porch, Nightingale stared toward the street for a minute. This was shaping up to be the governor against many, not just a particular woman. He looked at his watch.

"Let's go back to the B and B and get Posey roused. I'll pay you for the day if he's got something else he needs to do."

"I want you to get your money's worth," Cayden said.

"I understand, but I decide on the hours and the wage."

Nightingale said. They walked across the street to the truck. "I think our agreement was twenty dollars a day. Right?"

"Yes, sir."

At the B and B, Cayden went upstairs with Nightingale and stood back as he knocked on the door and called Posey's name. The "Do Not Disturb" sign still hung on the door handle, and Nightingale had noticed the Hummer still parked out front.

Nightingale had mixed feelings about what to do next. Posey was an adult. He might be angry, but he also might need help.

After no response in the room, he walked slowly down the stairs.

Emma Jackson pursed her lips in annoyance when Nightingale asked for the key. "I don't like this," she said.

She went to the room with them and handed the key to Nightingale. The minute he opened the door, he knew everything was wrong.

Posey was face down on the bed again, a sheet covering the lower part of his body. No sweat glistened on his back. Cold air filled the room.

Behind him, he heard Mrs. Jackson's gasp of surprise.

"Stay out," he said. He shut the door and walked to the bed and touched fingertips to Posey's neck. Nothing. The door squeaked as it opened. "You two don't come any further. Call an ambulance and the sheriff." When Mrs. Jackson didn't move, he walked to the door and repeated, louder. "Now, call now."

He closed the door again and surveyed the room without disturbing anything. Everything looked neat, reflecting the character of Posey. His briefcase sat on the floor. His laptop, closed, occupied the desk. Heavy curtains covered the windows. A bottle of Jack Daniels sat on the desk, still over half-full, and beside that a bottle of red wine that looked like a few glasses had been consumed. A tissue and a paper cup were the only things in the trash can. Nightingale swung open the closet only to see pants and shirts hung neatly and sorted, dark to light, just like Posey had hung them the day before. The boots he'd worn sat on the floor. Three pairs of shoes sat beside them. More shoes than a woman, or maybe he planned to stay longer than advertised.

The room was cold. Someone had left the thermostat on fifty degrees. The body was cold. The sheet fell over the shape of the insulin pump the same as the day before, and when he lifted the sheet, it was disconnected. Nightingale walked to the desk. He glanced back. "Cayden, are you in the hall?"

The boy opened the door. "Yes, sir. Is he dead?" Fear and curiosity mixed in his voice. He took one step inside.

"Don't come in."

The boy's eyes grew even bigger. "Was he murdered?"

Why did he think that? "No."

The shrill screams of police and ambulance sirens combined outside.

Nightingale made a beeline for the door and pushed the boy into the hall, as he pulled the door shut. They stood in front of the door, waiting.

Sheriff Patterson topped the steps with a furrowed brow and a snarl. Behind him, Deputy Howard looked happier than anytime Nightingale had seen him.

"Nightingale, you seem to always show up at the wrong place and time. I hope you haven't been in this room and contaminated anything," Patterson said.

"Your concern for Mr. Posey is moving. I didn't touch anything except his neck to check for a pulse. I didn't find one."

Men with EMS equipment topped the stairs, and Patterson shoved his way to the door. "We'll talk later," he said to Nightingale. "This way, boys. We don't know for sure he's dead. He's diabetic. Had a spell night before last, too."

Nightingale motioned to Cayden and the two of them went

down the stairs to his truck. "I'm driving you home. Give me directions."

"I can walk."

"I don't know your reasoning, but I don't have the patience for it right now. If you don't tell me, I'll ask Mrs. Jackson."

The threat worked, and after driving ten blocks north, Nightingale stopped where the boy directed. "If you need a guide anymore, let me know."

"I've got some figuring to do," Nightingale said. "You did a good job." He pulled out his wallet and gave the boy a twenty, then watched as he walked into a house that looked like it was built in the '50s. Briefly, he regretted that he couldn't know Cayden better. But now he needed to call McGowan. He wanted more information about Posey. Somehow, he felt responsible, even though it looked like he'd died of his own excesses.

He turned the truck around and pulled to the curb to call McGowan. In the rear-view mirror, he saw a young woman standing on the front porch of the house he'd just left with her arm around Cayden's shoulder. In the waning light, he couldn't see much, but he guessed this was Cayden's mother. He wanted to meet her, and something inside told him he would.

Nightingale couldn't decide why he thought Posey's death was strange. It really should have seemed normal after the incident of the previous evening. But that was it—it wasn't normal. His gut didn't feel right.

"McGowan, I've got bad news. Posey is dead."

"I couldn't have heard you right. Sounded like you said Posey is dead."

"I did."

"Wait a minute."

Nightingale heard a door slam. Then McGowan grunted, and Nightingale continued.

"I found him less than an hour ago. Sheriff didn't want me there, so I'm telling you and trying to stay out of it."

"How'd he die?"

"Don't know. More of that diabetes trouble, I guess, like night before last. I'm gonna find out what I can, but cops here are tight-lipped. It doesn't feel right. I need to know what they find, but I doubt they'll tell me."

"God, I hate to tell the governor this. I'll be calling the sheriff. There were threats, you know. Find out what you can."

"Posey thought the threats were for the governor."

"We've all had threats. Nobody thinks about it," McGowan said.

"The sheriff doesn't want me nosing in."

"We'll see. Have to be careful of whose toes are stepped on."

Nightingale drove back to the B and B, examining his suspicions. It was his nature to wonder about death. He hated that Posey was dead, and he felt responsible. If he could know whether evidence of foul play was found, he knew he'd rest easier. The man had been worried; he'd been threatened. Maybe McGowan could get something out of the sheriff, even though his words sounded half-hearted. Everything was political.

But the issue was not really the sheriff or McGowan. The issue was that he himself had retired in a moment of anger and now he regretted it. He needed to resolve his discontent, but had no time to think about it with the current problems. One thing was clear. For the second time in his life, he had done something without thinking about the consequences, and again it had come back to bite him.

11

He walked to the porch of the B and B, needing fresh air. Lights of the ambulance were disappearing down the street. One car from the sheriff's office still hugged the curb.

Back upstairs, he went directly to Posey's room. It was locked but he hadn't seen the officer belonging to the car, so he knocked. Amon Toohey opened the door.

"Mind if I come in?" Nightingale asked.

Toohey blocked the entrance. "Sorry, I can't do that. Sheriff said we have to treat this like a crime scene until we know different."

"I see. Was there a doctor here?"

"The medical examiner is a doctor. I've got work to do." He stepped back into the room and shut the door, relegating Nightingale to the hall.

Nightingale mulled over Toohey's lack of friendliness, so opposite from his earlier meetings. His phone rang.

McGowan's voice bristled with tension. "The governor wants to talk to you."

No problem. He wanted to talk to the governor, too. With the phone to his ear, he walked down the hall to his room.

"Mr. Nightingale, what happened?"

He admired the way she got right to the point. "I don't know for sure. He wanted to sleep late this morning, and when I got back here, he didn't answer the phone. I went in the room. Looked like he died during the night."

"Just died? No wounds?"

"That's what it looks like."

"You sound less than sure."

"Seemed awful young to me."

"Yes, young." Her voice took on a distance, like she was looking out a window, or thinking of something else. "I want to know, for sure, what caused Jack's death. His mother is one of my best friends. I'll have to call her. An ambulance will come for him today. There will be no autopsy in that county. I want you to stay there. See that there are no mistakes." She hung up.

Why did people get suspicious when a person died in their bed? Why did he think Posey's death was odd? In less than two minutes, the governor had given him another job. She hadn't mentioned water.

He straightened his hat. First things first.

Had to see the sheriff. He'd passed the office on his drive through town after meeting Posey. The office was in a small building near the railroad tracks, and the size made Nightingale think that crime in the community had to be on a small scale. He'd found that the size of jails, like football stadiums, was in direct proportion to the emphasis the community placed on law and order.

He parked across the street. The door had a jingle bell like a retail store. The receptionist wore a gun. Or maybe she wasn't the receptionist. She glanced toward him as she set down the coffee pot at a make-do set-up in a back corner of the room. Oswald took off his hat and waited for her to acknowledge him.

She sipped and grimaced, then eyed him over the rim of her cup. "Can I help you?"

"I'm here to see the sheriff. My name is Nightingale. He knows me."

The uniform blouse snugged her middle, a button threatening to pop. The slacks, unfortunately, were just as tight. She didn't look like she enjoyed her job. "I'll tell him you're here." She set the coffee cup on a desk and walked down a hall.

Construction dust clung to her desk and in the air. Down the hall, a piece of sheetrock lay on a sawhorse. Doors to cells stood open.

When the woman returned, she had worry lines between her brows. "Sheriff said to come on in. Down the hall to the left. Try to ignore the construction."

Nightingale thanked her and went to find Patterson.

The sheriff didn't ask him to sit down. "The governor called. So I'm not supposed to conduct an autopsy. I didn't argue. Guess she's got a doc who's better than ours." The sheriff shook his head, a disgusted sulk on his face. "I wish you people would stay in Austin and out of my hair. I ain't had a minute's peace since I laid eyes on you."

"What'd I do?"

The question seemed to catch the sheriff off-guard. He pulled his hand down over his face. "Let me ask you something, Mr. Ranger. How would you like it if somebody from another city came and nosed in on your investigation?"

"So, it *is* an investigation. What'd you find?"

The sheriff rolled his eyes. "You know as well as I do that not getting insulin could kill a diabetic." His voice rose as he stood and walked closer to Nightingale. "I'm a cop, damn it. I'm not supposed to know much. One thing I know is not everybody in these parts is of the political persuasion of you and that governor."

"Yeah, I'm wondering how many votes she got up here." Nightingale immediately regretted the remark because McGowan had said she'd won easily. "I'll try to stay out of your investigation from here on."

"Right." The sheriff's tone clearly showed his disbelief.

Nightingale walked to his truck, still analyzing what he knew. No autopsy by a local medical examiner meant there would be a political price to pay. He wondered how much McGowan had told the governor. Did she think about political fallout or was that McGowan's arena? And what did he—an outsider—care, except that politics made everything harder.

Back at the B and B, the deputy's car was gone. The wooden front door had been left open with only the screen door standing like a welcome reminder of times when people trusted their neighbors and didn't lock their doors.

As he entered the front room, a woman to his left spoke. "Mr. Nightingale, we need to talk."

He stepped back, felt the screen door with his hand, waiting for his eyes to adjust to the shadows. The woman wore a straw hat with a large brim. He could barely see her face. No obvious weapons. No purse.

"Do I know you?" he asked.

"No. You know my grandson." She stood stiff and strong, like a cadet, then folded her hands in front of her waist. She didn't smile. Her voice mesmerized, low with the vibrato of smoking, or maybe a love of whiskey. "Cayden is the reason I'm here. My name is Audie Louise Shepherd."

In the moment that followed, Nightingale thought through his hours with the boy. Nothing had happened to cause a grandmother's discontent, but this lady was not happy. "He's a good guide. Is there a problem?"

Emma Jackson came into the room at that moment. The two women stared at each other. Audie Shepherd reminded him of a

Shawnee soldier who had served as a guide when he first became a Ranger. The man said little; his eyes conveyed everything, and he killed with no remorse. Emma Jackson's usually sad eyes reflected hatred for the other woman. Nightingale was glad the women hadn't brought weapons.

Mrs. Jackson moved first. "How dare you come here!"

With the aplomb of royalty, Audie Shepherd said, "Come, Mr. Nightingale, we'll go outside to talk."

He opened the door for her, and she walked down the steps of the porch.

"Mrs. Jackson and I don't get along. She shouldn't leave her door open if she doesn't want company." At the sidewalk, she turned to the right.

They walked in silence to the end of the block.

She was about five eight, but when she stopped to speak to him, she looked up. The sun glinting in her eyes seemed to frustrate her, so she turned to look at the street. "Cayden is young and impressionable. His mother and I raise him. While I know he needs a good male image, I would rather it be under different circumstances. I'm sure you're an outstanding officer."

"Did I do something to bring this about?"

"No. He came home happy. This is one of those things. . . . Mr. Nightingale, did your mother ever tell you to do something because she knew what was best? No other reason?"

She glanced up at him from under the brim of the hat, and he saw the beauty she used to be.

"Yes, ma'am." He could see her determination in the way she held her head.

"In this case *I* know what is best. He enjoyed himself. But this water issue will be sticky before it ends, and he doesn't need to be involved."

She sounded like she had a crystal ball, but Nightingale didn't want to cause trouble for the boy. "He'll wonder why I didn't call for more work."

"I'll tell him I spoke with you and the other man's death stopped your project." She spread her hands out as a martyr. "He'll suspect me. Probably be angry with me, but he's a teenager. He's angry a lot."

Nightingale had known women like this. He liked the kid, who would be a criminal or cowed after a life with her. Too bad. He touched the brim of his hat. "I like Cayden. He's a hard worker, but I won't call him again."

They said goodbye, and Nightingale went back to the B and B. Down the street, he saw a dark blue truck.

The truck parked, and a familiar figure opened the door.

In a few long strides, Nightingale stood by the truck. "Sutton Garrick, what the hell are you doing here?"

The older man continued his slide out of the truck. "I was bored." He craned his neck, glanced around at the trees, then nodded in the direction of Audie Shepherd. "There's some nice scenery around here. Never see trees like this in West Texas."

"I don't need you meddling here. I've got a job that's not Rangering." Nightingale tried to maintain a cool demeanor without pissing the old man off. Lord knows, he had a hard time doing that most days.

"I know the score." Garrick held up his hands in protest. "I'm gonna spend a few days looking around. Got friends here. Never had a vacation. You won't even know I'm here."

"Where're you staying?"

"At the Holiday Inn Express at the edge of town. Young man said somebody died at one of the B and Bs last night. You know anything about that?"

Small towns—you had to love 'em. Everybody in town had more details than he did, all of them partially wrong. Garrick didn't have the patience for real estate games with Constance Dearborn; hopefully, he would go back home as soon as he saw how tame Nightingale's new job really was. It was futile to try to keep the old guy out. Nightingale took a long breath and offered to buy coffee. "I'll tell you what I know, but it's not much. Not worth staying for."

Nightingale climbed into the truck with Garrick, and they drove to the Blue Bird Café, where Nightingale slid into a familiar booth. "How's Josephine doing?"

"She's better. Got a lot of women coming in and checking on her." Garrick looked around the restaurant as if spies might pop out at any moment. "What's the governor got you doing up here?"

Nightingale gave a pasteurized version of McGowan's call and the happenings before Posey's death.

"So you were supposed to take care of him and he died? Guess no one understands 'natural causes,'" Garrick said. His tone had a touch of sarcasm.

Nightingale bristled in spite of himself. "I couldn't do anything to prevent him dying in bed."

Garrick leaned forward in the booth, keeping his voice low. "But if the governor thinks this is fishy, she's gonna look to you if something shows up."

Nightingale didn't like it, but the old man was right. "I don't have anything except this feeling. The night before, when Posey got sick, there was a boy who said he saw a woman go into the room. Posey denied that."

"So this was the second time you found Posey?" The old Ranger was quick into questions.

You never got over being a lawman, Nightingale thought.

"No one had been there. No signs of violence," Nightingale said. "Window toward the back of the room looked like it was painted shut. No struggle. Nothing out of place. Door locked from the inside. I didn't get to the bathroom."

"Did the sheriff ask for an autopsy?"

"Didn't have time. Governor's office called and said they wanted the body brought back to Austin."

"That coroner doesn't have jurisdiction," Garrick said.

"Looks like the governor doesn't care."

"So you're stuck till you hear from the coroner. Too many cooks to suit me." Garrick picked up his hat and stood. "I'm going back to my room. What are you doing tomorrow?"

Nightingale hadn't planned, but a few things were obvious. "Need to see the sheriff and Mrs. Dearborn. May drop by on the kid."

Garrick left him at the Sycamore. Garrick was a wild card. He'd been out of the Rangers several years and had never been good with by-the-book rules. Even though Nightingale needed help, he was glad the old guy had no more questions, and he couldn't shake off the concern that made his gut uneasy and his neck itch.

Sutton Garrick could be a help. He could also be a hindrance.

12

Constance Dearborn reached for the whiskey, then pulled her hand back. Nope, she didn't need to start bawling. She poured the coffee she'd made for herself and Hank down the sink. Methodically, she measured water into the pot and added coffee, with an extra scoop to get the caffeine boost. She wouldn't sleep much and didn't care. This was all Christopher's fault. If he hadn't tried to be a hero and gotten his fool self killed, he could be here bearing the weight of this farm. She knew him. He went over there to play army, kill some rag heads, and come home. But nothing had been like he expected.

His letters told the story. Like when he left, he'd written, "I'm old and need to be working on machinery. That's where they'll put me. I'll be there a few months and then home to your loving arms. It's no big deal."

But it was a big deal. Constance poured coffee and swiped the countertop with a damp rag. "Damn you, Chris. What made you think war was short term?" She'd had this argument with her dead husband before, and it accomplished nothing. She didn't know if the heartache would ever end, so she pushed it aside to focus on the current worry.

How long could she hold out against the state? There was no money to hire lawyers for a lengthy offense. She'd been lucky that they'd not already sent people to her porch. She balled up her fist and pounded the counter. She looked around like someone might see her coming unglued. Anger had become such a part of her life, she hardly recognized it. "Well, that did no good."

Now she'd have a bruised hand and more questions from Hank Faulkner, and that was a whole other problem. She turned to the cabinet and pulled down the whiskey, then poured a hefty measure into her cup. The caffeine should counteract the whiskey.

Today confirmed her fears. Hank Faulkner wanted to be more than an employee. She cared for him, but she didn't love him. Sometimes she thought he would be easier to live with than Christopher, but he had problems with anger; or was she just being sensitive? He was a friend, but she needed time to settle. Time to get over Christopher's death. Time to put away her own anger.

She picked up Posey's card from the counter. In the morning, she'd call him. Daddy used to say she was the best bluff in poker he'd ever seen. She'd see what Posey was really holding, besides a lot of hot air.

Sunshine shot through the blinds the next morning. A headache pounded behind her eyes. She deserved it. Stayed up too late and drank too much. What else? She hoped she didn't get out and drive. She had one goal today: call Posey and find out what the state's bottom line was as far as time and money.

She walked to the kitchen, poured out the coffee from the night before and remembered Faulkner's last words from the day before, "Call me if you need me." He'd been angry, but now it didn't seem any worse than her own meltdown.

She turned on the radio, wondering if the local news would say anything about the men from ELF or the explosion. She didn't have the patience to listen. As soon as the caffeine calmed her headache, she called Posey. No answer. She didn't leave a message—that would give him the advantage. She cleaned the kitchen, got out her laptop, and scanned the news, reading about the drought in the west. There had been some rain in the state, things were better, but they were still bad. Farmers had it worse than anybody. Cities still thought everything was fine because no one really told people in cities that the tap might run dry in the next few years. That kind of talk didn't get votes.

She called again. When Posey still didn't answer, she called Nightingale's number.

"Mr. Nightingale, I was trying to reach Posey, but I get no answer." In the silence, she pulled the phone from her ear and looked at it. "Mr. Nightingale, are you there?"

"Posey's dead."

A chill came over her. She needed to speak and finally found words. "What happened?"

"We don't know. Just happened last night. Would you mind if I come over? There's been some changes."

Constance did a quick run-through of her options. She pulled the phone away from her ear and shook her head hard to try to get back on track. She didn't know why Posey's death had filled her with such darkness. She took a deep breath.

Nightingale was second best, but she might have a better chance to negotiate with him. Maybe she could get a better offer. The man sounded upset. "Yes, please come. I'm sorry about Mr. Posey."

She hung up the phone. She'd just invited the enemy into her camp and was hoping she'd have an advantage because of a death. She called Hank Faulkner.

"Hank, if you can come over this morning, I'd appreciate it. Nightingale is coming here, and I want to be sure I'm asking the right questions."

"I've got some chores around here first." He didn't sound eager, probably still pissed from the day before.

She waited and heard him draw a slow breath.

"I'll be there in a little bit."

He might want an apology, but she wasn't ready for that. He was still the man she'd hired to help, but she had no one else. She had to face the bald truth.

She had no one. Her sister hated her. She had surface friends —those who were curious because she stayed to herself and buried her head in work. She'd had one close friend for a little while after she and Christopher married. But Mary had had babies and moved away. There was no one else, and she guessed it was because she was a surface friend herself. She didn't trust easily. She wanted no one knowing her thoughts or secrets. She'd been a loner for so long that she knew nothing else. What she had for support was Hank Faulkner. What a mess.

The fleeting thought of a poker game came to her. She felt herself pale, her hands ached with sudden cold, and she grasped the coffee cup. She'd die before she let any man anywhere read her.

Nightingale took his time getting dressed, trying to map out a plan. He had to quit thinking about Posey. His death was unfortunate, but until he heard from the autopsy, he had to let it go.

As he drove to the Dearborn farm, he focused on water. Maybe common sense would triumph, and in an epiphany, Constance Dearborn would know that fighting the state was a losing battle.

McGowan's call made his chore harder. He acted like the governor now depended on Nightingale to get this sale closed.

Nightingale felt out of his comfort zone. And the governor had said nothing about him taking on Posey's job. He hoped Mrs. Dearborn would be willing to help her fellow man—for the right price. In the back of his mind, Nightingale accommodated his role in persuading her to sell with getting her a higher price than the first offer. The governor had to be willing to negotiate, too. The payoff for the coup would be a dam or reservoir, or something in the way of relief, for West Texas.

Nightingale still felt enclosed, almost claustrophobic, as he drove through the envelope of trees bowed overhead. In some places, the road narrowed and the tree tops reached across, their limbs touching. He couldn't get used to it. He never would feel protected here. He'd only feel that someone might be hiding in the trees. He shook his head, trying to rid himself of morose thoughts.

At the Dearborn house, he cursed when he saw Garrick's dark blue truck. The truck almost had the personality of its owner, occupying a space like it belonged.

Nightingale walked up onto the porch and knocked, reminding himself that he'd hidden nothing from the older Ranger the night before.

Constance Dearborn opened the door and stepped back for him to come in. "Your friend, Mr. Garrick, arrived a few minutes ago. He's been telling me about the drought in your area."

Garrick stood as Nightingale walked in. "I told Mrs. Dearborn that I'm retired. Came up here on a wild hair."

Mrs. Dearborn looked pleasantly amused. "You all work together?"

"Used to. Not now," Nightingale said. He couldn't be a total grouch. Mrs. Dearborn was already charmed.

Garrick continued to stand.

Nightingale would have to say his piece with the old man listening.

They all exchanged uneasy looks, slow to address the point of the visit.

"Why don't you come in the kitchen?" Mrs. Dearborn said. "I'll make coffee."

They followed her through the archway into a bright dining room. Nightingale saw the strategy. He was at a disadvantage in the woman's home, where she offered food and drink and hospitality.

She put cups out for coffee while the men remained standing. "What happened to Mr. Posey?" she asked.

"Died in his sleep," Nightingale said.

They bowed their heads. Garrick shuffled his chair and broke the silence.

"Seems odd," Mrs. Dearborn said.

Nightingale nodded. "The governor talked to me this morning. I'm here to talk to you about a better offer than you've had previously."

The back door opened, and Mrs. Dearborn jerked around. She smiled and looked relieved. "This is Hank Faulkner," she said. "He's here at my request. Hank works for me. He knew my husband." She looked at Nightingale. "It seems quite unfeeling to be discussing this so soon, but I guess the governor is in a hurry."

Nightingale shared the sentiment but only cleared his throat. "My understanding was that market value was not enough for half of your acreage. Would you sell the entire farm if we doubled the price?"

Surprise swept across her face. "Did I just hear you correctly?" She cocked her head a bit, as if she had a hearing problem.

Nightingale thought she might have paled a bit. He knew he sounded clumsy, too forceful. He thought about making sure promises were kept. Wondered what he could say to make this woman agree. "Yes, ma'am. I got the call this morning."

"What does this mean? They can't have changed the plans this quickly."

"There's a new push to get this done."

Angry red colored the woman's cheekbones. "Mr. Nightingale you, and your cohort need to leave now." She slammed her hands on the table and stood. "I thought you were here in good faith. I see that once again I misjudged you and our new governor."

Nightingale saw his chances slipping but refused to give in. "I'll find out details and come back later. The governor is upset about Posey." He didn't know how much to say, but he knew he'd rather be in a gun fight than in this verbal back and forth that left him with no cover.

"So, she has some ability for emotion. I wish she had such compassion for me."

"I'll see you to the door," Faulkner said. He'd been in the background and now stepped forward, sounding like a guardian.

Garrick looked at Nightingale, flipped his hands in a nothing-else-to-do move. They put their hats on. Faulkner motioned with his head, and both men walked in front of him to the door.

Nightingale stopped at the front door and looked at Faulkner. "I'd appreciate it if you could help the lady to see our side," he said. He felt like he had rocks in his mouth. He swallowed and didn't know how to regain his momentum.

"She listens to her heart, not me," Faulkner said. "I thought the state only needed about five hundred acres."

"I got word this morning of the new proposal," Nightingale said.

Nightingale and Garrick walked side by side to their trucks. "Who called you?" Garrick said.

"McGowan called and said something had come up. Time is getting more crucial. Posey's death looked suspicious. He said make her an offer, he didn't care how wild, to try and get her off dead center. This needed to end. Made an offer. Didn't work."

Garrick stood at his truck and craned his neck toward the

pastures in front of the house. "I think I'll stay in town a little bit. This is getting interesting."

"What'd she tell you?"

"The land has been in her family since her great-granddaddy. Talked about how hard it is to farm now. What brought this change?"

"Don't know," Nightingale said. "McGowan said tell her we want the whole thing."

"Garrick climbed into his vehicle and leaned out the window. "That's brutal.

"That's politics," Nightingale said.

13

C onstance watched Nightingale and Garrick as they walked
to their vehicles. Nightingale didn't look like a bad man.
But then, how would she know what a bad man looked like? He
played the part well enough.

Her gut ached. Her bones throbbed. She wondered if
childbirth hurt this much, like someone had yanked her insides
out. She leaned with one hand on the window frame, thinking of
her father.

What ached more—her heart or her pride? She didn't have to
look over her shoulder; she knew Hank Faulkner was staring at
her. She sensed his distance because in the past few months he
had been moving into her space, and now that had changed.
She'd been acting like a naive schoolgirl in not admitting to
herself that Hank Faulkner wanted more than she did out of their
—their what? Not friendship, not relationship. It was not
something she had faced until yesterday's argument.

She didn't turn around, but straightened, still looking out the
picture window, while Nightingale and Garrick drove away.
"Thank you for coming today."

"You don't have to thank me," Faulkner said. "Do you have

work for me, or would you rather I leave?" His voice was stiff, his words stilted.

Still pouting, she guessed. She couldn't help a sarcastic half laugh. "Looks like work might be a lost cause. I've got to think, Hank."

"All right. I'll leave."

Anger washed over her. She jerked around, venom overpowering good sense. "Look, right now I need someone to talk to who understands what's happened. I need ideas. Can you understand that?"

He stood statue-still, his face reddening, his words measured. "I'll be glad to talk," he said. "But I won't be yelled at. God help me, I can see why you don't have friends." One vein pulsed at his temple.

Constance bit her lip, immediately regretting her words. "Okay, that's fair. I'm sorry, but I'm desperate. Do you have any thoughts about how to save this ranch?"

His features softened. He walked back to the kitchen. "Why don't you cool off and write down your options? I've wondered why you don't get a lawyer."

She drew in a deep breath. There it was—what she knew most of the people around here wondered. Breathe out. Start some strong coffee. "You know my father was a lawyer?"

He nodded. "Everybody knows that."

"That about says it. I grew up thinking he could do no wrong. He was one of those go-to-church zealots. Told me if I ever got pregnant to not come home. Men—people—like that can twist words however they want."

She lost count on the coffee she had added, so she poured it back and started again. "To put it simply, I don't trust lawyers. They've called here, offering to work for free if they don't win, when they know they can't win but it would look good on a resume to fight the state of Texas."

Faulkner had rooted a notepad and pen out of the junk drawer. "Okay, for number one, we'll write down 'get a lawyer.' No need to put down reasons. Number two could be that we board the place up and have a stand-off. We might be able to get those ELF guys to help if we promised no guns."

"You can't be serious." She turned from the coffee pot. "I don't want a thing like Waco on my conscience."

"I said no guns. I'm not crossing that off yet."

"I dreamed last night that I blew the whole farm up."

He looked up from writing. "How?"

"Just got some dynamite and blew it all to kingdom come. The thing is, with that idea I'm left homeless and I've helped their project along by my stupidity."

"Think of another angle," Faulkner said. "We can send some of these articles to Dallas and Austin TV stations. TV Stations love human interest. You are the helpless widow, and the state is running roughshod over you and the family farm. You could write letters or call, go there?"

The idea—as crazy as it seemed—offered hope. "Do you think anyone out there would listen to me?"

"I've watched enough news that I think you have a shot, but we need to hurry. Where are the newspaper articles?"

While she looked for the articles, he put down his pen and looked up phone numbers. She spent about ten minutes calling the Dallas TV stations. She got the same response from all four: someone would call her back. She made sandwiches, and while they ate, they continued to gather articles from the Internet and print them off.

She had started calling the Austin stations when his cell phone rang. He took the call and looked over at her while he talked. When he hung up, he said, "It's late. My sister needs help with the chores tonight."

Constance let out a long breath. Her hands shook from the

caffeine. They needed to break. "You've been a big help." She patted a stack of paper, then looked at him and saw his anger was now mixed with affection or fear, but she couldn't tell which.

She didn't look in his eyes when she spoke. "I know part of my problem is me. My neighbors don't like me, so they won't help. We'll go ahead and do the repairs around here that I had planned. I need your help. I'll be in touch." In her ears, she sounded like her sister, prissy and goody two-shoes.

Faulkner looked like he might be reading her mind. "You know, you can't keep sloughing people off when they might get too close for your comfort. Makes for a lonely life." He walked out, slamming the door behind him.

Reality washed over her. She yelled his name and ran.

Outside, she stopped short of touching his arm. He didn't turn around, so she talked to his back.

"Wait, you're right. This thing with the state is driving me crazy. I'm still numb from Christopher's death. I need time."

A long silence filled the air before katydids started chirping.

Faulkner didn't turn around, but she heard the sarcasm in his words. "Mrs. Dearborn, we all need time."

14

Garrick loved to give advice, but Nightingale was in no mood to listen. He walked toward his own truck while Garrick climbed into his.

The problem was, and Nightingale recognized this weakness in himself, he was no good at lying. The only thing to do was play his cards and hope he could live with what was dealt. When he'd gone about a mile, Nightingale pulled onto the grassy side of the road and picked up his phone.

"How'd it go?" McGowan asked.

"'Bout like you expected," Nightingale said. "It's kinda like hittin' a mule upside the head with a board. She was stunned."

"You sound like you're on her side."

"I don't like being the bad guy. She had no warning."

"She can worry about it for a day or so." McGowan drew in a muffled breath, then exhaled.

Probably smoking.

"Damn the traffic," McGowan said. "I'm on my way up there."

Good, a face-to-face meeting would get clarity.

"Meet me at that bar where you met Posey—the Laughing Cow—isn't that it?"

"Yeah, what time will you be here?"

An hour later, Nightingale drove into the parking lot of the Laughing Cow. The rear door of a black suburban opened and McGowan rolled out.

As long as Nightingale had known him, McGowan had dressed well, but this man looked like a reprobate. His shirt was wrinkled, as were his jeans. The boots shone, but when Nightingale neared the car, the odor of a feed lot made him wince. Something brown had caked on the side of the fancy boots.

"Did you do that"—he nodded to McGowan's feet—"on purpose?"

"No." McGowan pulled a cigar out of his mouth and kicked against the car. "No wonder the driver wasn't talking. I thought something wasn't right with the cigar. I stopped at my place before I came up here. Had to check on one of my cows."

He smiled and scuffed the boot in the gravel some more. "The boys won't know what to think when I tell 'em to clean the truck." He nodded toward the bar. "Let's get some cold beer, and you tell me about what's going on here."

The bar seemed smaller and darker than Nightingale remembered. Paint flaked off the window frames, and the floor squeaked as they walked across it. The inside looked like something out of a bad TV western. Nightingale counted five men, including the bartender, who, he'd found out on the last visit, was also the owner. Rusty motor oil signs and 1940s advertisements for hair oil, which seemed also to promise it worked as an aphrodisiac, served as the décor.

At the bar, he waited for two bottles of beer, then joined McGowan at a table in the back. He hadn't asked McGowan for his preference in brew, and noticed the raised eyebrow when he saw the beer.

Nightingale put the beers on the table and sat down before he spoke. "Why're you here, Roy?"

"It looks like the medics up here drew blood before they sent Posey's body to us. They're saying there was enough alcohol in him that the disconnect of the pump killed him. You didn't tell us about that."

"Didn't know. Guess they did that when they put me out of the room. So what's the conclusion?"

"The governor's upset. We're getting our own tests, but Posey had some run-ins with drugs. Makes me wonder."

"You told her this?"

"Didn't have to. She knows."

Nightingale took that as a "no." Posey's foibles would remain undiscussed. The thing was, Nightingale thought Posey might be a lot of things, but he was not a drug user. "What now?" he asked.

McGowan stared at Nightingale like he had to read him.

Nightingale returned the stare, figuring it meant nothing good.

"I meant to come up here and tell the woman that this has to be done, but with this Posey thing, the governor wants you to finish it. We've got to have the woman's agreement."

Nightingale didn't breathe, didn't move, didn't let his eyes leave McGowan's. "I'm not a dealmaker."

"The governor likes you. She likes honesty."

"I signed on to watch out for Posey, and he died. If you think Posey was killed, I'll find the man who did it. I can find out about the explosion. Something went wrong—I know—and I can find out what happened. But I'm not a salesman."

McGowan's face hardened. His eyes became dark voids of anger. "We don't have time for you to be a salesman. You can take that however you want to, but that woman has got to see that we mean business." He leaned over and whispered, his fists clenched, his breath smelling of beer, the dark anger of his eyes replaced by hatred. "If she won't sell half, we can take the whole damned thing. She's got to see that this state is more important than her little half-assed desire to keep a family farm."

Nightingale realized that he'd been wrong. He hadn't seen how far it could go. How much of it involved politics no longer mattered, even though it might be beyond politics. The water deal translated to power—all over the state.

"She can always bring in a lawyer. I'm surprised she hasn't yet. What then?"

McGowan scooted back in his chair, recoiling from his outburst for a moment. "Yeah, I thought about that. She doesn't have money for a luxury lawyer, but somebody may take it just to say they fought the state. All the more reason to push her for an answer. What about these environment nuts?"

"The sheriff won't tell me if he thinks they were responsible for the explosion. You need to pull some rank here."

McGowan looked at him sideways and took a swallow. "You don't have a clue about politics, do you?"

Nightingale leaned in and whispered, "I know enough to say you should lower your voice in here or the whole county will know what you're up to."

McGowan frowned. "Let's get out to the parking lot." He threw a twenty on the table and ambled to the door like he had all the time in the world.

Outside, he went to the Suburban and leaned against it.

"I need a day to go back to Broken Rock," Nightingale said. "My fiancée is sick. I've got to check on her."

McGowan looked at him like he'd said he was going to the moon. "We've got five days to get this settled. I'm sorry she doesn't feel good, but we've got to move on this. Trust me."

McGowan knocked on the door to the Suburban, and the thud of doors unlocking filled the air. He opened a door, turned, and pulled his sunglasses down on his nose. "Oz, you *can* do this if you want to." McGowan paused and looked away. "If you decide not to, well, call me. But one way or another, this is gonna happen." He turned to the car, then swung back. "But don't forget our deal."

Nightingale didn't move when the vehicle sped away. The taste of bile filled his throat. Dust filled his nostrils, and when he unclenched his jaw, grit scraped on his teeth.

He pulled off his hat, smacked it against his leg, and started toward his vehicle. Anger knotted his stomach. He was not a political animal, but even he could see that underneath this someone craved power or money. Posey's death deserved an investigation and that, obviously, was secondary to the water plan.

He sat in the truck a minute, waiting for the A/C to pull some of the dampness and heat out of the air. As he started the engine, his father and mother came to his thoughts. Without a doubt, much of his current problem came from his hatred of eminent domain and the power of people he didn't know.

He still remembered his father's face when he heard that the railroad wanted his land. His father had grayed and aged ten years in a few months. His mother and father had talked long hours into several nights, considering whether to fight the railroads or take the money and live with the consequences. In the end, they had no choice—they'd never had a choice. Just like Constance Dearborn.

15

The next morning, while Nightingale showered and got dressed, he thought about his history with Roy McGowan. Nightingale had never been one to think about fate, but McGowan had always turned up when the time seemed to be convenient for each of them. They were first friends in elementary school, and after second grade, Roy's family left town. He came back in fifth grade and left again after sixth. By then, they had visited each other's homes. Roy's father wore a uniform, so Nightingale guessed he was military. The family was poor, like all of Nightingale's friends, and when Roy showed up, they picked up where they'd left off, like McGowan had been gone for only a few hours.

Then in eighth grade, McGowan simply showed up at school one day after a history class when slavery was mentioned. Outside of the classroom someone said, "Look how dark Nightingale is. Sally Hemming was probably his great-grandmother." McGowan stepped between Nightingale and his attacker, but not soon enough.

Nightingale went home with a bloody nose, suspended from

school, and his father sat him down for a talk. "You know from history that a lot of different people settled America, don't you?"

He was in for one of his father's teaching lectures. He nodded.

"Well, I'll tell you right now that I have some Irish blood, some Cherokee, and some German. Your mother has some Scottish and probably some flat-out Tennessee hillbilly. Her great grandmother was a slave, but she and her husband got their freedom. They left farmland to your family."

At that point, Nightingale went to a mirror. He was dark, but he'd also blistered and tanned. His eyes were green.

His father continued to talk. "I would bet that most of those youngsters you go to school with have a mixture akin to us, if they know at all. You can't be an American and not have a mixed heritage. Ignore the bullies."

"But they call me names."

"Try walking away. Boredom is a great peacemaker."

The next day at school, when Nightingale turned his back on the catcalls, Roy McGowan stepped up and walked beside him.

Nightingale never knew what caused McGowan to choose to walk with him. The name-calling changed to, "McGowan, you're an Irish spud lover." The comments never seemed to bother McGowan, and that was a trait Nightingale had admired, but never questioned, until now. As an adult, Nightingale realized that childhood years gave clues about adult years. And now Nightingale wondered how that granite exterior translated to the man who had been a good friend for so long.

McGowan had not been a good-looking kid. He was what Nightingale's mother called a "towhead" because of his fair hair. But young Roy was already almost six feet tall and had the self-confidence of a kid much older. And he liked playing the hero. Nightingale needed rescue. McGowan's confidence rubbed off on him and, after a few months, school became enjoyable.

McGowan disappeared at the end of the year and came back for the last two years of high school. He walked in like he had never been gone. Soon after picking his desk, McGowan ran for class office. Poor children still formed the basic student population, and they were the core of McGowan's voters.

Other people waited to be nominated, then usually acted humble when someone had put their name forth for election. Not McGowan.

Nightingale smiled at the memory.

"I'd be a good Treasurer of the junior class," McGowan had said. The classes were small—twenty-five students—and about ten of those looked at him in surprise. A few had met McGowan anew, and others remembered him from two years before.

Someone in the back of the room said, "Nah, he ain't been here long enough."

"Ain't is not a word," the English teacher said. "It's time to vote."

McGowan was elected Treasurer. He took the office seriously and began organizing bake sales and cleaning crews. The bake sales usually fell to the mothers to orchestrate. The cleaning crews went around offering to wash windows and cars, do chores, or babysit, and the money went into the class coffers. Half way into the next year, the junior class had money set aside for a class trip and almost half enough for the next year's trip. That next year, McGowan was president of the senior class.

McGowan rose in popularity, and Nightingale became more analytical, the quiet sidekick for McGowan. During the time that McGowan was gone, Nightingale had become more of a loner, a transit that fit well in his life as a Ranger.

Each time he looked back on his life, he considered his acquaintances many but his true friends few. He considered McGowan a friend, but he wondered if McGowan felt the same.

He reached for his hat as his phone rang.

"Nightingale?" The voice of Sheriff Patterson answered his hello. "You heard anything from that autopsy?"

"No," Nightingale said. "I was hoping you had news for me."

"Come on down here, and we'll see what we can talk about."

Puzzled, Nightingale hung up the phone. McGowan had not had time to get back to Austin, but he might have called the sheriff. Nightingale never saw a good outcome to withholding knowledge, but that's the way things sometimes worked in law enforcement. He'd been guilty of it, and it always came down to trust. He grabbed his hat as someone knocked on the door.

Without an invitation, Cayden Shepherd walked in. He walked all the way to the desk that held the laptop. "So why don't you want me back?"

The boy's voice cracked, and Nightingale didn't know if it was due to age or emotion. He only knew he didn't want to say the wrong thing. "You did a great job. I've just run out of time to explore the town."

Cayden swiped one hand across the hair falling in his face, but his eyes didn't leave Nightingale. "My grandma doesn't know what's important now."

Nightingale sensed more going on than the boy was saying. "And that would be?"

"I can help you. My grandmother hates the Dearborns, and you need help." His voice rose in frustration. "A woman went in that man's room. I can help."

"What you're saying doesn't tie together. What does it matter that your grandmother hates the Dearborns?"

"It matters because someone is trying to take our land, and it's not right. And it's not right for someone to die for it."

"Whoa, *our* land? Why our land?"

"Because Judge Alexander was my father. That's what pisses off my grandmother. He never acknowledged me, at least not to the world. So I got nothing when he died. I don't care, but

Grandma does. I'm going to make it on my own. I'm smart enough. And I like Mrs. Dearborn. She doesn't deserve to be screwed."

Nightingale thought of a wise retort, but the kid was too serious. "Let's go back to what you said about someone dying for the land. You want to clear that up for me?"

The boy's defenses melted a bit at the question. He cocked one eyebrow cynically. "Don't you wonder who went into Mr. Posey's room? And then he died?"

Nightingale walked to the window. Did this kid know something or was he desperate for attention?

"He didn't die that first night," Nightingale said. "And no one else has mentioned him having a visitor."

"I know that." Cayden jerked his head and rolled his eyes. "And I wasn't here the second night. But don't you see the similarities?"

"In other words, you don't know," Nightingale said. No need to try to be philosophical about gut reactions. "I'm not arguing with you. Tell me again about who you saw."

"I thought it was a woman," Cayden said. "She was dressed in a long black skirt, had on a hat, and a ponytail showed at the back. She tapped on the door and nobody said anything. The door opened, and she went in."

"What about her face? Would you know her if you saw her?

"I never saw her face."

"I haven't told anybody about this yet," Nightingale said. "Until we can prove something, it's best to leave it be. I've got to go now."

"Can I go?"

"No, you go back home. Your mother will be worried."

Cayden nodded. They walked downstairs, and Cayden went down the steps while Nightingale stopped on the porch. A shiny blue truck was parked by the curb.

"Nice truck," Cayden said.

From the top step, Nightingale saw Garrick's grin as he stepped out of the vehicle.

Nightingale said, "Garrick, did you want to see me?"

Garrick looked up and grimaced in the sun. "Be there in a minute." He shook the boy's hand and muttered something that Nightingale couldn't understand. The boy went on after Garrick gave him a friendly pat on the shoulder.

At the sidewalk, Nightingale told Garrick about the boy and the phone call. "You want to go with me to see the sheriff?"

"I'm game. Will he still talk with me there?"

"We'll see. I'm thinking I need to have somebody who can testify for me. This one-Ranger business sometimes needs edits."

Sheriff Patterson was waiting in his office. "I didn't know you were bringing backups."

"Garrick decided to vacation up here and offered to tag along. We used to work together."

"Yeah, I did a little checking on my own," Patterson said. You've been the one-man band of West Texas Rangers and then had the brass balls to quit. You gonna level with me about what's going on?"

"I think you know more about this than I do," Nightingale said, "but it started with me coming along to keep Posey from getting his tail in a crack. Now he's dead, and I'm wondering if he was murdered."

"You guys got the body."

"But you got blood before he left."

The sheriff had a sly grin. "Right." He pushed back from his desk and blew a breath of disgust or bravado. Nightingale couldn't tell which.

"Nobody likes to have other law enforcement come into an investigation—am I right?"

Nightingale nodded.

"Usually fucks up everything," Garrick said.

The sheriff laughed. "Right. My guys said they thought Posey didn't die natural. One of 'em said they smelled the odor that a diabetic body sometimes gives off. It's a fruity smell, they said. Then we sent the body to Austin, so that's what we know."

"What about that explosion?"

"That could have been the work of the environmentalists—although they haven't owned up to it, or it could have been Hank Faulkner."

"Mrs. Dearborn's hired hand?"

"One and the same. He was an explosives expert in the service. He's still got some side effects—PTSD, maybe. He came back and laid low. Lives with his sister and works pretty well full time for Mrs. Dearborn. There's two young fellows who showed up at Mrs. Dearborn's house and scared her to death. They said they were from ELF. She called here to report it. Said Faulkner roughed one of 'em up, but I never heard from them."

"Are they still here?"

"We don't know. We've got a lot of tourists in town. So, you got anything for me?"

"Posey was sent here to get Mrs. Dearborn to agree to sell," Nightingale said. "Some important people need a water plan in place."

The sheriff frowned, and a low growl came from his throat. "That's all?"

Nightingale put his hands out, palms empty. "That's all I know," he said. "I hate that I can't help more. If I hear from the autopsy, I'll call, but they're leaving me out of the decision-making."

The sheriff stood. His cheeks puffed as he blew out air, reminding Nightingale of an angry long-horned steer. "Right." The sheriff didn't sound convinced. "I guess you all can find the way out."

Garrick was already out the door. In the truck, he was his usual chipper self. "Sounds like neither one of you have anything to go with. What're you gonna do about Posey?"

"There's something all wrong about this whole thing. I'm waiting to hear from McGowan. If he says Posey was poisoned, then I'm finding who did it. I owe that to the man. Till then, I'm going over to Mrs. Dearborn's house and tell her that she's got to sign that agreement—no matter what she feels. I hope she sees my way of thinking before Roy McGowan comes back.

Nightingale stopped next to Garrick's truck to let him out.

"I'm staying down the road a piece at a Holiday Inn Express," Garrick said. His boots hit the ground and he turned back to give Nightingale a significant look of, "You know what I mean; leave me alone." "Hunting up some old friends tonight. Don't call me. I'll call you."

Nightingale wondered about the friends but didn't pursue the matter. Garrick knew people all over the state. "Sure. Try to stay outta trouble."

"I'll stay close to some good food."

Nightingale headed his truck toward the B and B. He didn't want to talk to anyone at the moment.

A different person sat at Mrs. Jackson's desk when he walked in. The young man, who reminded Nightingale of Emma Jackson with his dark hair, thick eyebrows, and skin that looked like tissue paper, stood to greet Nightingale and stuck out his hand. "I'm Silas Jackson. Mother told me we had a lawman here. I've been away at school. I'm sorry I missed the excitement."

Silas's voice wavered, like he might need more practice being in charge. But he looked to be nineteen or twenty.

Nightingale wasn't in a cordial mood, but he shook the man's hand, then started for the stairs. "You didn't miss much."

Silas raised his voice. "If I can help in any way, please let me know. Mother said you might like a tour of the town."

Nightingale already had a tour. He guessed Silas was offering his services, but he didn't want a tour with Emma's son, so he mumbled as he went to the stairs, "Probably won't have time."

Nightingale went to his room. It was late in the day, but there were some things he needed to know about ELF. He called Bob Gilbert, who had replaced him as officer in charge and had a sense of humor. Gilbert readily agreed to do some digging into the organization without pushing Nightingale too hard about why he needed the information.

Before he hung up, Nightingale asked, "How you enjoying the job?"

"Piece o' cake," Gilbert said. "Shoot a few Indians and the odd Mexican or Negro, and everybody stays in line."

Gilbert was half Apache. Most of his jokes were about minorities.

"You've still got your scalp and sense of humor. Reckon you could find out about land sales in the last few months?"

"Anything in particular? You don't mean houses?"

"Right. Just land around the park north of Broken Rock and where the state is getting ready to do water projects. I'll call back in a few days."

"Sounds good. That'll get me out of the office."

Nightingale ended the call smiling and missing his job. Or maybe not. He hated to admit how unsure he was about so many things. Hell, he might as well admit he'd like to be a hero and get a secure water source for Broken Rock. Maybe, if he could do that, Josephine Holly would come around to marriage. No, that was a fantasy. In the middle of all of that, there was Posey's death and McGowan acting weird. Frustration ate at him, causing his stomach to knot.

He needed a plan. He needed concrete evidence, a clue, but in his past career action usually happened so fast he put clues together into a pattern as he went. He'd taken care of matters as they happened. Posey, on the other hand, had not been a great salesman, but he'd had documents. "I've got a contract with me. Already has the legal description filled in. All she has to do is sign," he'd told Nightingale. From that he knew the next step.

He had to get into Posey's room. The key Mrs. Jackson had given him for his room had a long stem and a curlicue handle. He guessed it had some sort of chip in the head, but the door locks sounded inadequate. He went out to his car and dug out a thin set of tools—his burglar kit—which he stashed under his jacket.

Coming back inside, he saw no one at the front desk, so he stepped into the dining room. Silas appeared from a side door.

Nightingale clutched one arm tight to his body and backed toward the stairs as he talked. "Sorry if I seemed short a few minutes ago. I was wondering if anyone has taken the other room upstairs. I have a friend in town who would like to stay here."

"Actually, I think Mother has it rented toward the end of the week, but I'll ask."

Nightingale thanked him and headed to the steps. The silence that had been alluring became a troublesome thing. From the downstairs, he heard a door slam and the telephone ring. He tiptoed to Posey's room, where he tried his room key first. Nothing. Then he inserted the skeleton key from his kit. With some jiggling and a credit card in the right spot, it clicked. He tenderly pushed the door open and stepped inside, his palms now sweaty and his chest tight. Even though he was a cop with a good reason, he was still breaking and entering. No amount of analysis helped. Crime was crime. Was this what a burglar thought about?

The room looked as he remembered. First, the closet. Posey's clothes hung neatly with colors together, and there was no sign of his briefcase. Nightingale picked his way to the perimeter of the room, then checked under the sink in the bathroom.

Voices from the hall broke into his concentration. Mrs. Jackson and someone. He quick-stepped toward the bed as a key rattled in the lock. The door swung open.

He rolled under the bed. Dust bunnies swirled. Can't sneeze, don't breathe.

"I can't imagine why you want to stay up here where a man died," Mrs. Jackson said.

From under the bed, Nightingale saw Silas Jackson's boots and Mrs. Jackson's low black patent heels.

"It's bigger than my room. When do you think the sheriff will let you use it again?"

"I don't know. I'm going to call him now. Don't you want to wait for a new mattress? I've got to paint the place." She seemed to be talking to herself as her feet turned a full circle.

Her son's boots walked to the closet. "Nice clothes."

Mrs. Jackson's feet followed. "Silas, close that door. What if they do fingerprints again and find yours? We're not supposed to be here."

"Okay, calm down. Look at this shirt—silk."

"Put that back."

Hangers rattled against one another.

"I'm putting it back. It is a little creepy up here. Like somebody is still here." His boots turned away from the closet. Side by side, the feet walked to the door.

In the silence, Nightingale took shallow breaths, not moving. Under his ribs, something metal poked him. After the lock clicked shut, he sucked up his chest and pulled out a silver circle bracelet, about half an inch wide. He counted to sixty slowly and rolled from under the bed. It was a woman's jewelry. He held it gingerly by the edges, memorizing the scroll work on the side, and slid it back under the bed. He'd never make it as a thief. At the door, he listened, then stepped into the hall and pulled the door shut, relocking it. Once he was a few feet down the hall, he lengthened his stride and got back to his room. That was lucky. Posey's car could wait until after dark.

Back in his room, Nightingale knew he needed a plan but he felt blank. If he found nothing in the car, he'd have to figure out some sort of plan.

He paced and looked out his window. He had a view of the cottages behind the B and B. A cart sat outside one loaded with linens. He saw a figure, maybe it was Cayden, carrying a stack of towels. He didn't want to see the boy right now. Cayden stirred too many memories, shadows of his own teen years, of some bad decisions.

He went downstairs, got into his truck, and drove away from the city. The sky was clouded over in gray mushrooms. At a small market, he bought an RC and a bag of redskin peanuts. In the truck, he ripped open the peanuts and poured a few into the bottle, watching the satisfying fizz of the salty snack in the cola. After two gulps and some satisfying crunches, he poured the rest of the bag into the bottle and took his time driving back onto the pavement. He'd forgotten how good the salt and the sweet was, the crack of the nuts, almost erased his need for a cigarette.

He drove slowly, like his father used to, looking at the fields. Side roads that veered off into the fields were only paths with grass in the center. He turned down one bumpy lane and stared at the receding water line of what used to be a lake, wondering why the governor put Jack Posey in this environment that was so foreign to him. Was she really doing a favor for a family friend?

Something whimpered. He opened the truck door, and a stringy-haired, dirty puppy of unknown heritage stuck its head under the door. The whimper grew along with the wagging of a scraggly tail.

Nightingale cursed through his smile. Whoever had dropped this animal out here to be hit by traffic or starve to death needed a good stomping. Nightingale leaned down from the seat and picked up the puppy. It fit itself into the curve of his arm. He put it on the seat, and it wriggled to his lap. "Hang on, buddy, we'll get you some food." The pup squirmed closer to him. He could feel its ribs under the matted fur. "Hang on." A lump formed in his throat.

It was after five, but Nightingale had seen a sign on his way out of town that advertised a veterinarian, and all the vets he knew worked late, so he hoped this one did, too. Like so many of the businesses in town, the sign was low-key. On his return, he looked for the cottage, rather than the sign, and saw both at the same time. Two cars filled the drive. Another sign, smaller and tattered, pointed to more parking in the back.

Nightingale carried the pup into the front office, where he explained his dilemma to a prim-looking woman whom Nightingale guessed to be at least sixty-five.

The woman frowned. "We're about to close, but I'll tell the doctor what you need." She disappeared through double doors, while Nightingale held the puppy close, scratching his tummy.

A short, silver-haired man walked out behind the receptionist and stuck out his hand to Nightingale. "I'm Raymond Elliott. My wife tells me you've saved one of our throwaways. There are some cruel bastards in this world."

He took the puppy from Nightingale, talking to it as he led the way to the back. "He or she"—he turned the animal slightly —"he will need some food, shots." The vet stopped short. "You brought him here as an owner, right?"

Nightingale hesitated slightly. *Egad, no, I don't need a puppy in the middle of this, but what's the alternative?* "Yeah, I'm the owner. I'm staying at the Sycamore B and B."

The doctor asked his wife to make a bottle of goat's milk then led the way into an examination room and shut the door. "Emma Jackson won't let you have a pet."

"I thought not. I'll need to board him for a few days."

The doctor stroked the puppy, talking while he checked its ears—"no mites"—then its feet and rear end. "He's hungry. Probably has worms. Here's the bottle. You feed him, so he'll bond with you. If he gets sick you get to clean it up."

Holding the bottle and the puppy, Nightingale looked to both sides, as if someone might see him. Poor critter needed help. The sides of its stomach expanded and warmed as he suckled.

The vet peered at Nightingale over his glasses. "You with the law?"

"I used to be. Still am in some ways."

"So how's your job going?"

Nightingale didn't like the way this conversation was moving. He took a quick look at the vet, who was beaming.

"Look," the doctor said, "everybody in town knows there's a Ranger at Emma's place. They also know you've been out to talk to Mrs. Dearborn about selling some land to the state."

"Leaves me at a disadvantage."

The doctor nodded. "You need to find the Sarah's Vacation restaurant and get there about 6:30 in the morning. 'Course, it won't do you no good. Nobody'd talk with you in there. A few regulars stop in for breakfast every morning, including the sheriff. So how'd that young fellow die?"

Nightingale stared at the old man, pissed off at his disadvantage and no longer bothered that his face showed it. "What else have you heard?"

"Not much." The vet grinned, and Nightingale remembered

his father telling tales when he had a captive audience. "So how much do you know about Alexander and his daughters?"

"Very little," Nightingale said.

"Old man Alexander was a prominent judge. His wife was a prim Southern belle. Growing up, Emma and Constance had real different personalities—still do."

"Hard to believe they're sisters." Nightingale forgot what he was doing, and the puppy yelped. Nightingale corrected for his error.

The vet grinned and nodded. "Constance was like she is now, kinda standoffish. Emma had a wild hair that most folks have forgot. Anyway, the momma died when they were teens, and the old man just about lost his mind. Long story short, he had an affair with a really young Mexican girl that produced a child. Smart kid. You've probably seen him around here. The girls had hissy-fits while their daddy was running around, and then when he up and died, he left the farm to Constance and the B and B to Emma. Emma accused her sister of some shenanigans to get the farm, and they've not spoke since then."

"What about the kid?"

"Constance says he's a half-brother. Emma, well, Emma is better than most of us." He winked and shook his head. "People are so damned strange."

"Would Emma do anything to stop the sale of the land?" Nightingale asked.

"Not to my way of thinking."

"She's a widow?"

"Don't know. Her husband disappeared when their son Silas was five or six years old. It was strange. Nothing much said out loud in town. She was upset when Silas didn't inherit something from old man Alexander."

The puppy had almost finished the bottle when Nightingale's phone vibrated. The puppy flinched awake. The doctor frowned.

"Sorry," Nightingale said as he pushed the phone onto off and further into his pocket. He picked up the puppy, enjoying the squirming animal. "I've still got some work to do. Can I leave him here a few days? I'll leave a credit card number."

"We'll take good care of him, but you'll need to stop by and see him some," the vet said.

Outside of the office, Nightingale smiled at the memory of his father that the old doctor had caused. But he realized that was a small thing compared to the happiness he felt with having a new dog.

In his pocket, the phone vibrated again.

In all caps, a text ordered, "Call me. Have news." Roy McGowan demanded attention.

17

I t was getting close to dark, and Nightingale still didn't want to talk to anyone, so he kept his phone turned off. When he got back to the B and B, he parked and started walking downtown for supper. Posey's big car still sat in the parking lot, sun-screens up, now with the slightest powder of dust covering it.

The first restaurant was closed. He meandered around the town square, gave up the idea of vegetables, and strolled back toward the Sycamore deciding to drive a piece and get a juicy, delicious burger.

As he neared the B and B, he noticed that street lights shone on only one side of Posey's car. The darkened side was also closer to the shrubs that formed a partial fence for the establishment. He knelt and, reaching around under the car, found the undercarriage covered in mud. No sign of a hidden key. Annoyed, he swiped his hands together to get rid of the dirt while noting that Jack Posey was not a man who loved hard work. He'd put the key in an easy-to-find place. Nightingale walked to the driver's side, felt under the front fender, and there it was—a magnetized key holder. One push of the open lock symbol and all of the doors gave the satisfying thud of unlocking. He was in.

Just then, he heard the screen door open and footsteps on the porch. Nightingale's heart raced, despite his head telling it that he was in the clear for checking the car.

Sweat formed at Nightingale's temple, and he reached under his jacket, barely touching the handle of his service weapon. He pulled open the driver's door and slid into the car. It smelled like new leather.

The porch was a few feet off the ground, so Silas stood above. His white shirt was out of his pants, fluttering like a Klansman's robe.

Nightingale drew a long breath. He could concoct a story, but he wanted it to be something that Silas couldn't easily check. He turned on the engine and lowered the window. "Did you need me?"

"No. Just heard the car start." Silas's suspicion came through his voice.

The young man's face was shadowed so that Nightingale couldn't read him, but his gut told him that, despite the ominous look, this boy was relatively harmless.

"I'll be inside in a minute," Nightingale said. He continued to rev the engine, turn the lights off and on. When he got out and looked at the blinker, which was working perfectly, Silas went inside. Nightingale went to the back and checked the cargo area. A suit bag lay folded to the side. Under that was a small suede case that might hold a thin laptop. He picked it up and folded the garment bag over it. Then he locked the car and dropped the key into his pocket.

Inside the B and B, there was no sign of Silas.

Standing at the dining room door, Mrs. Jackson spoke. "Mr. Nightingale, I didn't know you had a key to Mr. Posey's vehicle."

Silas pushed the dining room door open and stood beside his mother, looking like the cat with the canary.

"The governor's people called and asked me to check on the car and Mr. Posey's belongings, in my capacity as a Ranger. There was only this empty bag in the vehicle, and I haven't been allowed in the room. I guess his clothes are still there?"

The conversation turned on his question. The lady blushed. "Yes, I believe so, but I'm caught between you and the sheriff. He told me to stay out. Do you need the clothes?"

"I don't think so. I'll let you know when the governor's office contacts me further." He gave a tiny tip of his hat and started up the stairs with the garment bag.

"Would you like to leave the bag in our safe?" Silas hurried to the desk that served as the sign-in station for guests. He pointed to a wall behind him.

Nightingale detected a smirk of smart-ass superiority in the younger man. "No, it'll be safe with me." He remembered himself at that age. It was not a pleasant memory, but he hadn't felt superior. He repeated his good-night and went to his room. As he walked, he added lying and theft to breaking and entering.

His phone showed one more call from McGowan, but no message. He wasn't surprised when his call was not answered. In a few minutes, the phone rang.

"Why haven't you been answering?" McGowan said.

"I've been busy."

"I was beginning to worry." He gave a half-hearted laugh that Nightingale didn't try to interpret.

"You have news?" Nightingale asked.

"I got a report that leans toward saying Posey was murdered."

"Leans—what kind of half-assed assessment is that?"

"We don't know if Posey undid the pump himself. We may never know. With the drugs and liquor in him, the lack of insulin finished him off."

"What does the governor think?"

"She doesn't know about this."

Nightingale waited a minute for both pieces of news to sink in before he told McGowan how bad the situation was. Obviously, McGowan had no idea how a cover-up would ruin the governor's credibility, if anyone found out. But that was his job. There had to be more. Nightingale blew out a long breath and went to the window. "You want to enlighten me as to why she doesn't know?"

"Nightingale, she's mature in age, but not in politics. She's not mean enough, either. If she thinks Posey was killed intentionally, she'll make that her focus. That can't happen. We've got to get this water deal completed."

"So, you're ready to ignore the 'leanings' and say his death was accidental. Why the hurry?"

"It's economics."

Did McGowan really think economics was more important than people? "I think we need to find who killed Posey, and then we can get Mrs. Dearborn's signature. Reckon she's behind him dying?"

"Who knows? More to the point, I don't have time for you to go off and investigate something that may not be true. I know you're still a Ranger at heart, but if you can't stay on task, I'll have to find someone who can. Call me tomorrow and tell me your progress."

McGowan didn't bother with goodbye. He simply hung up.

Nightingale made some decaf coffee in the tiny pot next to the television. While he waited for the coffee to brew, he stashed the garment bag in his closet and opened the suede case onto the bed. No sign of a computer or memory device. However, a stack of papers was stapled together, and each page had a separate address under the title "Notice of Appraised Value."

Under the papers, he found a map, which showed the area for

the proposed reservoir. Lines around the reservoir area were in thick, dark blue. Posey had made some rough lines in black magic marker around the acreages belonging to farmers and ranchers. At least that was what the outlines seemed to be. And, with enough shuffling, Nightingale found land and appraisals that matched, at least in ownership. He recognized two names. Faulkner land touched the Dearborn property on the northeast boundary. The vet owned land on the opposite side. None of the other names were familiar. But the kicker was that none of this information was secret. Anybody could find this stuff in courthouse records or on line, if they wanted to go to the trouble of looking.

He went to sleep still frustrated. McGowan was right that the state needed a water plan, but Nightingale didn't know in his heart that he could sacrifice his integrity in order to make that happen.

18

S till groggy with sleep, Constance Dearborn reached across the bed and came awake when her hand touched the flat coolness of the sheet. She had not dreamed. It just seemed so natural that the warmth of Chris would be there, but he was not. Tears swelled in her eyes, but she staunched them. "Silly female weakness. Christopher, this is your fault—again."

She went to the shower, still aching with loneliness. She had cried enough, and had repeated this scene too often.

She forced her thoughts to the media plans that she and Faulkner had discussed. They had agreed quickly on the TV stations as being an efficient place to plant the ideas they hoped to sell.

They'd considered radio, too, but she knew nothing about the local stations, though she'd sometimes listened to NPR out of College Station. The local newspapers might also help, but she needed something quicker. And there was the Internet—but she knew even less about that. No, the people she needed watched TV. Then again, maybe an environmental-leaning website would be the answer.

She dried off, put on some clothes, and headed for the kitchen.

In the back of her mind, she noticed that her dead husband had left her thoughts. That was good.

She took in the stacked papers, the lined tablets with "To Do" across the top. Her laptop was closed, but the PC in the corner had come on, as programmed, at 6:00 a.m. The time was almost 7:30.

The phone rang. It was a Dallas area code. Someone named Edward claimed to be a producer at the TV station. She felt a chill. "How can I be sure you are from the station?"

He didn't like the question because his answer was clipped. "Look, Mrs. Dearborn, you called and talked to one of the staffers. Is the state trying to take your farm?"

She could see her chance at telling her side of the story slipping away, so feeling totally unprepared, she started.

"This land has been in my family for generations," she said. "Six months ago, I received a letter telling me that the state had a new water plan and to be a good citizen, a good Texan, I would have the privilege of selling some of my land to make a reservoir for people in other parts of the state. I grew up here. Taking my land is like cutting off my arm." She heard her voice tremble and stopped for a minute. "Then came the bullying."

"The state officials deny that they have 'bullied' you," Edward said.

"Sure, they say that, but they've got people trying to make me sell." Her voice got louder into the phone. "People need to know this." Her hand cramped because she was holding the phone so tight. She loosened her grip, knowing she'd said too much.

"I'll send someone over to see you," Edward said. "We've got information from the governor's office. We'll listen. That's all I can promise. Crew will be there in two hours."

Constance hung up the phone. Her hands were sweating, but

she'd quit shaking. She looked around the kitchen, trying to think of how to cast her argument. She had not done a good job so far. She wanted sympathy from viewers; instead, she felt stupid. She'd not been prepared. She'd almost told Edward that she didn't want to supply water to his rich friends.

How could she explain the threats from the state officials? The maps had to be the answer. If they could take her land this way, they could take someone else's land. She'd show them the maps.

When the TV truck pulled up, Constance looked around for Hank Faulkner. She needed a coach, but she had not asked for help. Too late, she regretted not calling.

The woman who interviewed her simply asked her to tell her story. When she talked about her father and his love of "this land that had my granddaddy's blood and sweat and tears in it," she cried.

The interviewer was young, a journalism student, she guessed. A pretty blond who had done no homework.

"Aren't you getting paid for your land?"

"You're not from Texas, are you?" The words were out before she could think. She sounded bitchy, so she tried to regroup.

"I don't see how that's important," the girl said.

"I didn't mean to be condescending." Constance leaned toward the girl. "It's just that people who own land here have usually worked hard for it. If it's a family farm, it's probably been in the family for years and came at great cost. Money can't replace that kind of value—the kind you can't touch."

"What about people who need water to drink? Some of them have to live in the city."

Constance tried to look pleasant while holding her temper. "Most Texans will understand totally what I mean by love of the land and family heritage. Someone else can give up their land."

Her voice rose, and she felt the heat in her face. "The state had lakes; they let the reservoirs around here go dry."

A man standing away from the camera made a motion with his hand cutting across his throat.

The reporter nodded. "Thank you, Mrs. Dearborn."

The camera now concentrated on the pretty face, and the smile continued until the cameraman turned away.

The reporter looked at the camera and pulled off the microphone. Her lack of interest came through the monotone in her voice. "We have to get back and edit this if we plan to make the evening news."

Constance looked at the woman's worn at the heel shoes and felt offended that her story was not important enough for a real reporter.

They began pulling cords, lights, cameras. Everyone had turned away from her. At this rate, they'd be down the driveway in twenty minutes. Constance put a hand on the young woman's arm. "I'm sorry if I sounded rude. I need help, for people to know."

The pretty face took a long look at the hand on her arm. "This is good. We may come back."

Abruptly, she walked away.

Constance knew they would not be back.

When they were gone, she called Hank Faulkner. "Did you know the TV people were here?"

"No, what happened?"

She didn't tell him she had wished for moral support. He didn't seem too concerned, and she guessed he was still sulking. She filled him in on her take on the interview.

Faulkner offered no opinion. "You got any work for me today?"

"Only the regular chores. If you could come put some feed out for the horses and cows, I'd appreciate it. We could talk over these media plans." Again, she regretted that she had no close friends to bounce ideas off of. Nobody cared about the rich, unhappy woman who rarely came out in the community.

"Sure, I'll be over after I do what Ava needs. Did they say when they'd air your interview?"

"No. It may never see the light of day." She laughed, though she hoped the segment would be broadcast, wondering how it would be edited. Would viewers see her as a nut case?

She was in a tizzy when Faulkner showed up. "I blew it, Hank. I wanted sympathy, and I came off as a bitch."

"You're seeing the bad side of it all. Hell, you said they may not even air it, so don't get in the dumps yet."

She wondered if she should just let it go. She hated this urge to talk over what had happened in the interview. He was probably right, and anyway, what could she do about it at this point?

She walked with him out to the stables. Together they fed the animals and checked their water supply.

They didn't talk until they were headed back to the house and the tension caught up with her again. "What will I do if I lose?"

"You'll survive, just like your dad and granddad did," he said. His words were bitter. He didn't look at her. "I've got to go back and help my sister. Have you decided to stop calling the media?"

"I hadn't thought it through. I feel like I've been under attack for years and I hate the people who caused this."

They walked into the dining room. The stacks of newspaper articles, lists of local radio stations, and folders about water around the state lay where they had left them.

"What do you want to do with all of this?" He leaned against the kitchen counter that divided the dining room and kitchen. "I guess the better question is: what is your next step in this war between you and the state?"

Constance looked at the papers, trying to face the question.

She had said no for six months. That was her gut reaction. Everything had been a reaction to the state's moves. "I'm backed into a corner. I'm calling a lawyer and the bank. I'll get a second mortgage. I'm not going down without a fight."

When she didn't see the story on the ten o'clock news, she told herself it would be tomorrow. She went to bed but watched movies late into the night.

19

A car honked at Nightingale's slow pace and passed him as he drove to Constance Dearborn's farm. He hardly noticed; Posey's death haunted him.

His gut feeling was that Posey had been murdered, probably because of his role in the water deal. Nightingale's sense of justice made him want to find a killer, but a killer might not exist. Without information, the scenario existed on quicksand.

The needs of Broken Rock made his choices even more important because those people were friends and family. Broken Rock had to be a part of a water plan. Otherwise, the town would literally dry up and be covered with West Texas dust. The governor's threat to bypass the little town was not idle. Big cities like Dallas and Lubbock would get water, no matter what. No one would miss the tiny places like Broken Rock. Certainly, very few votes would be lost.

Leaving the town without water would be "the thing we must do for the larger good." He'd seen it with railroads, with toll roads, and with industry. And the population, everyone who got water and considered themselves part of the larger good, would gladly take their good fortune, no matter what brought it about.

He hoped that none of them ever knew of his bargain with the governor.

Slowing the truck for a rabbit to cross the road, he considered Roy McGowan. Nightingale had never been one to see the big picture on the scale that Roy did. Roy looked at events and tried to decide how they would affect the future. In comparison, catching criminals was something made up of a series of fairly short-term events. The big picture now was very different because Nightingale had a stake in the game.

Roy had turned into a pure politician. "Whatever it takes" was his motto.

"Ah, hell," Nightingale muttered to himself. "Roy's right—this state needs water." But it seemed beyond coincidence that the man who'd come to finalize the water deal wound up dead.

Every day counted when it came to foul play. Clues became stale. But Posey had been dead over a day now, his body moved to a different town.

Nightingale forced his thoughts back to Constance Dearborn. Truth might be the tactic to throw her off balance.

Lost in his thoughts, he parked the truck and, in the August heat, trudged toward the house. Mrs. Dearborn opened the door before he knocked.

"Mr. Nightingale, what an unexpected surprise." Her sarcastic tone went along with her stance in the doorway. "Have you brought more bad news?"

Nightingale held his hat. "I want to apologize for the earlier meeting. I'd like to talk, not as a person sent by the governor but as a private citizen with a stake in the future of the state."

She didn't smile. "You can say what you want to inside. No need to be without good manners."

She crossed her arms as he walked in, and he sensed her suspicion, as if she expected him to belittle her at any moment.

The thought of her unease toward him was appalling. He

turned away from the thought, trying to clear his mind with a view of the cattle in the pasture across from the house. When he looked at her, he hoped for some empathy.

She waited a minute, then walked over to the couch and asked him to sit down.

It was not a totally encouraging moment, but he took it. "You know that Posey died," Nightingale said, "and I'm not sure of the circumstances, but I came here to talk about my hometown." He told all of his story, except he didn't say that the governor had promised him water if he got her to sell her land. He tried to convey how dry and hot and hard it was out there, how Broken Rock was his home, and how he didn't want it to disappear.

When he was done, she stared out the front window a few seconds.

"I have no help for you," she said. She looked at her hands clasped in her lap. "I'm sorry your town is dying, but I don't feel like being the sacrificial lamb right now."

Nightingale drew in a deep breath as he took in the view of pasture and cattle and peace.

The woman worked her jaw.

He could see her stubbornness fighting against the female softness of her heart and knew he'd been partially right about her.

"You've met my sister?" She asked and smiled sardonically.

"Yes, ma'am."

"I'd be better off to be like her, claiming religion for every thought and deed, but the truth is that I'd hoped the governor or some soul out there would relate to my plight and change the plan."

"I don't think that will happen," he said.

"I was interviewed for a news story yesterday," she said. "I'm going to watch the news tonight," she said. "You watch it, too. Call me tomorrow, and we'll talk again."

20

Nightingale headed for the Holiday Inn Express and was rewarded when he saw Garrick's truck. He parked beside it.

Once inside the lobby he called Garrick. "What's your room number?"

"I don't need company right now."

"Garrick, have you . . ." He didn't finish the question because he didn't want to know what the older man was up to. "Call me later," he said.

Nightingale went back to the Bed and Breakfast. In his room, he pulled out the map that had been in Posey's briefcase. He checked the television to find the news channels and was staring at the map when the phone rang.

"What the hell are you doing coming to my place? I told you I'd call when I got back."

"Your place? It's a damned Holiday Inn. You told me that you were visiting. How was I to know you were having afternoon dessert?" By the word dessert, Nightingale started smiling. "Sorry I interrupted."

"Guess it's just as well. Is something up?"

Just like himself, Garrick still wanted to know what was going on with the investigation. Was it curiosity? A sense of duty? Nightingale wondered what motivated a man to leave sex to go find a killer. Then, maybe he just woke his former partner from an afternoon nap.

"I wanted you to watch the news tonight. One of the Dallas stations came and interviewed Mrs. Dearborn. I thought we could compare ideas later."

"Well, I could tell her right off that those people are likely to make her look foolish."

Nightingale silently agreed. He, too, had eaten the proverbial crow over misinterpreted remarks. Reporters, unless he made the rules, were not his friends.

"I've still got some visiting to do," Garrick said. "I'll call you in the morning." The last sentence had emphasis.

Nightingale went back to the map and made a list of the names around the black line that Posey had drawn. The line would, supposedly, be the edge of the reservoir, land that now included part of Mrs. Dearborn's farm.

Nightingale considered himself in possession of neither a particularly depressed nor upbeat personality, but he didn't like flailing at problems. He leaned back in his chair, considering how he would explain the situation to his best friend.

The knock on the door surprised him.

"Nightingale, it's me, Garrick."

Despite the voice, he looked out the peephole and then opened the door. "What're you doing here? I thought you had places to go and people to see."

Garrick came in pressed and unwrinkled, even though it was the end of the day. "My friend who I wanted to see is dead. Hell of a note. You said something about a TV show."

In the last few years, the thought of mortality had been poison to Sutton Garrick. The way Nightingale saw it, for most of his life, Garrick had flirted with death, but his sensitivity after he entered his sixties made the subject off limits. It couldn't be discussed. It had to be avoided. He changed the subject when anyone mentioned it; if he couldn't do that, he either made fun of it or cursed it. But right now, Nightingale was in no mood for Garrick's sensitivity.

"How'd he die? Were you close?"

Garrick threw his jacket into the eighteenth-century chair at the desk and began pacing. "What's so goldarned important about a TV show?"

"Mrs. Dearborn was interviewed by one of the TV stations. Told me to watch tonight and call her tomorrow."

Garrick sat up straighter and pulled a small bottle of whiskey out of the pocket of the jacket. "Got any cola? We can talk over drinks."

Nightingale went into the hall for ice and two bottles of cola.

Silas Jackson stood outside what had been Posey's room. He had pushed the door open but not entered the room.

Nightingale expected a greeting, even a grunt, from the younger man, but Silas looked stricken, like he'd just touched poison.

"Anything wrong?" Nightingale asked.

"No."

In the darkened hall, the moonlight coming from Posey's room looked spooky. Leaves on trees outside the window moved in the breeze, causing a strange rustling noise, as if a life force remained in the room.

Silas seemed hypnotized. "Do you believe in ghosts?"

"Can't say either way," Nightingale said.

"I know this door was locked. When I touched it, it swung open." Silas turned, his eyes huge with fright.

Nightingale thought he had locked the door when he left, but

Silas was clearly upset. "Maybe the sheriff was up here and didn't tell you."

Relief washed over Silas's face. "I'm sure that's what happened." He pulled the door shut. "But I don't think he wants anybody staying here, so I'm not spending the night, and you can tell your friend that Momma is not letting anyone stay." He turned and walked rapidly down the hall.

Garrick was standing in the door.

Nightingale nudged him back into the room and pulled the door to, giving Garrick a brief summary but leaving out his earlier visit to the room.

Garrick snorted, reached for the ice, and went to the desk to pour the promised drinks. "Here, let's see what the lady says." He had turned the television on, and the ten o'clock news promised "more about the drought and the state water plan as it affects all of us," after the lead story.

Constance Dearborn's story was the last segment before the weather report. Nightingale tried to figure out where the story had been edited, but it was impossible. In an effort to be unbiased, the reporter interviewed a suburban Dallas family who was already rationing water.

The commentator ended the piece by pointing out the dilemma the state faced. He went into detail about the plan working in steps that the legislature had planned and now criticized. Mrs. Dearborn's property was an integral part for water going to the Dallas area, as well as for cities to the south. She just happened to be on the right longitude and latitude to serve all purposes. That answered some of the nagging thoughts Nightingale had about why her property was the only fit for the project.

Nightingale had the TV control and hit "Off" at the commercial.

Garrick turned toward him, a wry smile on his lips. "You

know that old saying, 'Whiskey is for drinking, water is for fighting'?"

Nightingale nodded.

"Well, I think we've got us a regular range war in the works. Ms. Dearborn doesn't know about hard times until she takes on those big city people with money."

"I'm gonna try one more time tomorrow to ask her to sell," Nightingale said. He drank deep of the bourbon, enjoying the tang of the oak against his tongue, knowing he would not be this relaxed except for the liquor. "You want to go with me tomorrow morning?"

Garrick drained his glass and stood. "Might as well. I always enjoy watching you pissin' in the wind."

21

Emma Jackson poured Murphy's Oil into a bucket of water, dipped a rag in, and squeezed the mixture out. She loved the smell of the oil cleaner. She stared at the floor, knelt, and started scrubbing the stairs. The small places between the railings were the hiding places of dust.

She stretched up the stairs, staying on her knees, pulling the muscles in her arms and sides, keeping her eyes on the chore in order to avoid thinking.

Silas had offered to help. He was such a good child. Really extraordinary. She thanked God every day that his father's leaving had not affected him. When he was five, he had asked about his father, and she'd explained that he worked odd hours out of town.

Her final lie had been telling Silas that his father had been in an accident on a train and he was dead. By then, Peter Jackson had been gone for eighteen months. Silas was six and barely remembered his father. He accepted anything his mother told him. Having such a close church family had made all the difference, but now, now Silas had been away to school. Something had changed. She worried that he would become like

Constance, wild and unruly. Could that untamed disposition be inherited?

She had not spoken to Constance in several years, but she became worried when she heard about the explosion and her sister's resistance to the state's water plan. It was in the newspaper, probably would soon be on TV. Constance was still as stubborn as she always had been. Daddy had always said that she got it from her mother. Emma swiped the back of her hand across her forehead and sat back on her heels. She'd reached the top of the stairs. Holding the dirty rag in one hand, she went back downstairs, picking up the bucket of water to pour out the back door. No, she'd have to reuse it. The stairs had not been that dirty after all.

She rinsed and twisted the rag again and started around the edges of the room, wiping the hardwood and baseboard. The only customer she had at the moment was the Ranger. Mr. Posey's death sure had stifled business. Might as well clean while she had the opportunity. She took a break and went out to the two cottages behind the B and B.

"Isabel, where are you?" The girl usually had a good work ethic, but lately something had been hindering her.

"Yes, ma'am, I am in the blue one." Isabel's voice, but it was the boy, Cayden, who opened the door to the cottage and nodded a greeting.

Emma didn't like the way his gaze stayed with her. He had no fear, no deference, and she didn't like it. He thought he was related to her. Well, it would be a cold day in hell before . . .

Oh, my goodness, the very idea that the boy could get that much anger going in her heart brought heat to her face. She brushed by him as he held the door open, gave a cursory look into the cottage where Isabel was working, and flounced back to the big house.

She'd prayed. She'd begged for tolerance. That was why she

was paying the woman to clean the cottages, paying retribution for her thoughts. That boy could not have come from the seed of her father. Such nonsense.

Silas walked into the living room at the same time she did. "Mother, is anything wrong? You're red as a beet."

"Nothing that I can't handle. Why don't you go check on the cottage cleaning and tell the girl to go home. I'll mail her a money order. No, on second thought, she probably wants cash." Emma grabbed her purse and handed him a wad of twenties. "Ask her what time she got here. I pay eight dollars an hour."

Silas rolled his eyes. "If she did a good job, I'll give her ten. I made a spice cake. Go get a piece with some iced tea."

Emma started to protest but instead waved a hand and turned away. Cooking again. He never had a girlfriend, not that anyone here was smart enough to deserve him, but that was something else to pray about. 'Course, she'd prayed a plenty through Silas's life, especially after his daddy left. She dragged her tired self into the kitchen, following the warm cinnamon and clove aroma of the cake. There it sat, like a picture out of a magazine, glazed with brown sugar icing. Emma stared at the cake, the tears aching in the back of her throat. She was fighting the devil for Silas's soul.

She knew he dated girls; he just hadn't found the right one. She held that thought as she poured tea.

She heard the heels of his boots click against the tile and felt the warmth of his body as he sidled up beside her. "I've been thinking about your offer, and I guess I'll just stay in my room. Have you asked the sheriff about using Mr. Posey's room?"

She smiled when his shoulder nudged her. "I've left messages, but he hasn't called back."

"That's okay." Silas pulled out a china saucer, put it beside the cake, and cocked his head to one side as he stared at the confection. "By the way, Mother, where were you the night Mr. Posey died?"

He turned slightly and looked directly into her eyes.

The air moved as if a fan had been turned on. Emma laid one hand on the counter. She placed her tea glass on the napkin, her mind racing, then moved her hand to the edge of the granite to grasp something substantial. "I was asleep in bed. Why would you ask me such a thing?"

"Because, when I went to your door to say goodnight, you were not in bed."

"That's ridiculous. I must have been in the bathroom."

"I was worried that you'd started sleepwalking again, Mother." He sliced into the cake with a decisive whack. "Maybe I need to stay here—not go back to school in the fall."

With a mother's wisdom, Emma saw that her son didn't believe her at all.

"Nonsense," she said. "Be sure and clean up your mess." She left the kitchen and went to her bedroom. Why did Silas say she wasn't in bed? Probably teasing. He loved to gig her.

Constance used to do the same thing. She'd tell her lies and she, dumb bunny that she was, would confront friends or parents with some tale of peeping toms or hobos stealing chickens that Constance put in her mind. Some of Silas's ways were uncanny, they were so like his Aunt Connie's. Just a touch of cruelty, sometimes.

In her bathroom, Emma pulled out a rag and the can of Ajax and began scrubbing her tub. For years, she had been able to pretend Constance was dead. Suddenly, she was alive and stirring up news. Disgusted, she threw the wet rag in the tub, dried her hands, and went to the phone.

The phone rang twice. Emma almost hung up, regretting her foolishness.

"Hello," Constance said. Silence filled the phone. "Hello."

Emma drew in a breath. Now that she had called, words left her. "Constance, this is me. Are you okay after the explosion?"

Constance also waited before replying. "Yes, thank you for asking. Why are you calling?"

"I was worried about you." Emma's hand hurt from holding the phone so tight. She still worried about her sister's health. "I had hoped your bitterness after Daddy's death was gone."

Silence again. Constance had never lacked words. Emma wondered if her sister was still listening.

"I guess you've prayed enough for me that bitterness has just melted away."

Emma closed her eyes, one hand knotted in a fist, as she ignored the goading in Constance's voice. "I know you don't like advice, but I thought I'd tell you the whole state is going to hate you if you keep going with this ridiculous plan to stop the reservoir." Emma rushed on. She knew if she stopped she'd never finish. "I know you love the farm. Daddy would want you to put up some sort of resistance, but this has gone far enough. You can't win against the government, you know."

"Really."

"I think since you lost Christopher you're holding on to your hurt. You need to think of the younger generation, like Silas, the people who will need this water."

"Oh, and Cayden, too. Right?"

Emma shivered. That boy again. "Please, focus on one subject. I'm trying to help."

"Emma, I don't need your hyper-religious philosophizing to know what I need to do. We both know it will thrill you for me to lose some—or all—of the farm."

A pause in Constance's words warned Emma of the taunting before she heard it.

"By the way, I saw Silas in town the other day. He didn't

know me, but he was with some other young men. Such a handsome boy. Does he date much?"

"I can see that you haven't changed," Emma said. She slammed down the phone and uttered a prayer. "Please, dear Lord, get my sister out of my life."

22

True to his word, Garrick woke Nightingale. "Why the hell are you calling this early? It's five o'clock."

"I'm awake, and you should be."

"All right, you win. The vet told me about a restaurant called Sarah's Vacation. Ask your desk clerk where it is. I'll pick you up in an hour."

Garrick stood outside the hotel, looking dapper in a crisp blue shirt and jeans with a starched crease. Nightingale had ironed his clothes, too, but he didn't have the benefit of starch and a dry cleaner.

When they walked into Sarah's Vacation, Nightingale saw the veterinarian sitting at a corner table. Dr. Elliott waved and motioned for Nightingale to join him. Nightingale walked over, where he declined the invitation and introduced Garrick.

As Garrick and the vet shook hands, Nightingale asked, "How's my puppy doing?"

"Gaining weight. Needs to go home with you."

"Soon," Nightingale said.

Nightingale and Garrick settled at a table by themselves, with Garrick muttering about Nightingale's habit of adopting strays.

They ordered sausage and eggs with biscuits. Garrick added gravy.

"Probably means indigestion, but it'll be worth it. Remind me to buy some antacid."

Other people drifted in, all men. The little banter and exchange between tables came in spurts, but the atmosphere was several decibels quieter than the doctor had described.

Garrick and Nightingale kept their conversation low and talked mainly about how good the food was.

Dr. Elliott stopped by their table on his way out. "People won't talk with you here, but we all saw Constance last night on the news."

Nightingale grunted and pushed away from the table. "What are they saying?"

"You ought to come and walk the pup. We can talk, and you can take him to see Emma. She might like him." The doctor laughed like he'd told a great joke and walked out.

Garrick nodded toward the vet's back. "So this is where the politics of the town is decided."

"That was insinuated. You ready? We're not going to get anything here. I'll stop at the vet's later."

They got in Nightingale's vehicle and headed toward the Dearborn ranch.

Garrick reached over and turned the radio off. "After that speech Mrs. Dearborn made last night about Texas ranchers loving their land, I expect she'll have some supporters. Reckon?"

Nightingale grunted. "She's got the personality of a cactus. Don't know."

"Some of the folks I know up here lost land to her old man for taxes. They were uninformed, slow, I guess, if you be honest. He took advantage."

"Hadn't heard that part. Sounds like the family pissed

everybody off. She hasn't asked for help. At least not that we know about. But this idea of taking her land—that's hard to swallow because everyone knows it might be them next. I think the kid is the only person who likes her. I still don't think she'll sell, but I'm gonna ask before I give it all up."

"You need to get home to Josephine."

Nightingale looked sharply at the old man. "I've talked to her every day. She tells me she's doing better. Said she didn't need me there."

"You've never had a woman to worry about so you're ignorant. Women are funny. They say one thing and mean another."

Nightingale swallowed hard. He cared about Josephine more than he realized. She'd always been honest and forthright with him. That was one of her qualities he loved the most. Sometimes she was too honest. And as he got closer, Josephine Holly shied away. She said she needed space. Nightingale was sure of one thing—he was totally confused. He sometimes thought she didn't love him, and as soon as the thought occurred, he denied it. But in his darker moments, the question remained. He was glad to see the Dearborn driveway ahead to put his thoughts on a different track.

The gate was open. No vehicles were in front of the Dearborn house. It was still not 8:00 a.m., but he'd expected Faulkner to be there. He parked and walked to the front door with Garrick following. After knocking and ringing the doorbell, he tried the door handle. The door opened easily. The quiet bothered him.

"Hold on," Garrick said. "This ain't right."

Nightingale shook his head and frowned, motioning Garrick to be quiet. He pulled his weapon and stepped into the living room. "Mrs. Dearborn, are you here?"

The clock ticked. The coolness of a fan washed over him. His heart slowed, his senses livened; he heard a mockingbird, Garrick breathing, and smelled blood. He raised his voice again.

"Constance Dearborn, are you here?"

Garrick had turned his back to Nightingale, watching the hall, the doors that might hide someone.

Nightingale found her on the floor of the kitchen.

A puddle of blood ran onto the tile. "Damn. Mrs. Dearborn, can you hear me?" Even as he spoke, he knew the answer. He knelt to touch her throat for a pulse.

A key rattled in the back door and Garrick swung around. He had a Sig Sauer trained on the door as Cayden pushed through.

The boy froze for a minute and stared at the body. "Connie?" He paled under his dark skin. He bit his bottom lip and dropped to his knees, crawling to her as tears began to run down his face.

Nightingale reached over to stop him, but the boy tore away from him. He screamed and fought, kicking as Nightingale pulled him up off the floor. "No, I love her. Not her, please, God."

Holding the resisting boy around the waist, Nightingale steered him into the living room. When the boy continued to shout, making no sense, Nightingale shook him.

A brittle silence followed.

Nightingale glanced at Garrick, who stood in the kitchen door. "Call an ambulance and the sheriff."

Garrick nodded.

Nightingale stared at the boy. In the depths of sadness, he looked younger than fourteen. "Cayden, how long have you had a key?"

"Since last year." He sniffled, took the tissue that Garrick offered. "What happened to her?"

"How long have you been outside?" Nightingale asked.

"I just got here."

"Did you see anyone?"

He straightened, his voice filled with bravado. "If I had I would've done something. She taught me how to shoot." Then he seemed to melt. "She knew I would protect her—but I didn't, did I?"

"Let me see your hands." Nightingale sniffed the boy's hands. "What's that odor?"

"Rosemary. I brought a big piece with me. She used it in bouquets."

Nightingale drew in a huge breath of frustration. "I can't protect you if you're lying."

"I'm not lying. It's at the back step."

Garrick walked closer. "The sheriff won't be nice. Stick to the truth, and we'll get whoever did this."

"You think I did this?" Cayden's eyes glistened with fear, shifting from one man to the other. His voice shook as he tried to control it. "I loved her. She was my sister." He knotted one fist, swung, and hit Nightingale in the stomach.

Nightingale doubled onto the fist and twisted the teenager back against his own body. "If you'll listen, instead of acting like a juvenile—"

Just then, Sheriff Patterson walked in, touching his sidearm like he felt just enough unease to pull it at any provocation.

Cayden stilled. He inched closer to Nightingale. Maybe he'd finally realized which side he should be on.

"What the hell? What's he doing here?" The sheriff asked.

Nightingale continued to grip the boy's arm, afraid that Cayden would run. Nightingale looked over the sheriff's shoulder. "Let those guys in." He nodded to the medics standing behind the sheriff, and pushed the teenager onto the couch.

Garrick moved over to sit beside Cayden.

"The body's in the kitchen." Nightingale walked back with the sheriff, explaining what had happened, including Cayden's arrival.

At the sight of the dead woman, the sheriff pushed aside a medic and groaned. "Oh, no, Connie." He knelt by her body for a minute, touching her hand. He stood, seeming to be lost in grief. "We were cousins, you know."

Nightingale remembered that Mrs. Jackson had mentioned the kinship earlier. A tough investigation would be even tougher.

The sheriff shook his head, suddenly all business. He faced Nightingale. "Guess I've learned life goes on. You said the boy came in after you got here."

"Yes, he had a key."

"I want to question him, but we've got to get crime scene people in here." He paused and slid his eyes to Nightingale. "You're not gonna give me grief are you?"

"This is your territory. I'm a visitor."

"Very gracious of you." The sheriff's skepticism leaked into his words. "I'll get crime scene folks from the county office."

"We'll bring the boy to your office," Nightingale said.

"Now," the sheriff said. "Bring him now." He barked orders to another deputy about securing the scene.

Garrick and Cayden walked behind Nightingale to the truck. Garrick muttered something that Nightingale couldn't hear, and when Nightingale glanced back, Cayden was looking gratefully up at the older man. The boy got in the back. He was shivering but looked stubborn, his jaw clamped tight.

They'd gone a mile when Garrick leaned closer to Nightingale and lowered his voice. "I nosed around in her bedroom. She had another computer in there. Wish we could see the things that were on it." A folded piece of paper stuck out of the pocket of his jacket.

"What's that?" Nightingale pointed at the paper.

Garrick whispered, "Nothing, what are you expecting?" He pulled the paper out and squinted at it. "It's my dry-cleaning receipt. I swear you're acting more like a guilty man every day."

Nightingale rolled his eyes. "You and I both know that crime scene has to be squeaky clean, especially since we found the body." He didn't add that Garrick might preach precision but he often practiced fuzziness. He tended to grab whatever was at hand.

23

At the sheriff's office, Nightingale walked Cayden inside to the lobby. The sheriff appeared down the hall but only waved and disappeared into a room as the sound of hammering testified to the ongoing construction. The place had the air of an unfinished house. To Nightingale, it didn't seem quite as menacing at the outset. One glance at the boy told him different.

Cayden's huge, dark eyes brought a stab of empathy. Nightingale tried to convey support through a touch on the shoulder and partial smile.

Deputy Howard showed them to a small room that needed paint and smelled of frightened men with over-ripe underarms.

The deputy leaned against one wall, arms folded across his chest, still wearing his sunglasses.

Patterson swung the door open with a short command. "Nightingale, you sit back there. This young man is one of our own. He knows we've got his best interest at heart—don't you son?"

Nightingale took the chair behind the teen, figuring the best way to keep the boy out of a cell was to keep the sheriff happy. He'd seen children thrown in jails; he remembered one boy in particular. Detention maybe, but adult jail brought no good end. He kept his mouth shut and let the sheriff talk, trying to avoid conflict.

The sheriff spoke into a tape recorder, naming those in attendance, then supplying the date and the purpose of the meeting. He glanced at Nightingale and cleared his throat.

"Okay, Cayden, I want you to tell me everything about your visit to Mrs. Dearborn's house this morning."

Cayden squirmed, straining back toward Nightingale, and then he seemed to realize how alone he was. He became very still and looked at the beefy sheriff.

Like the other boy, who hadn't had a chance to answer questions, at fourteen, Cayden was about five feet nine, but his frame was still thin. When Nightingale touched Cayden's shoulder or subdued him during an outburst, he felt his bones. Cayden was not yet filled out with a man's muscles and promise of strength.

"You know, son, this looks bad. You could almost look guilty, but we know you. We'll be looking for a weapon in the area surrounding Mrs. Dearborn's house. You'd help yourself and us if you saw anything or anybody, or you know anything about how this horrible thing happened. Maybe it was an accident?"

"I . . ." his voice faltered on the first words.

Dry mouth, Nightingale thought. Scared to death. 'Course, no one would offer water when it was so easy to bully a kid. Nightingale fumed, knowing he was prejudiced.

"I didn't see anyone."

"Why were you up there? Why did you have a key?"

The door opened, and Garrick poked his head in. "Guess you all wouldn't mind an old Ranger joining the party?" He stepped inside. "For a minor citizen." He took his hat off and shook the deputy's hand.

"We said that on the tape, that's he's a minor," the deputy said. He exchanged a look with the sheriff, who shook his head.

"We know and you know that this kid has to be questioned. He may have knowledge he's not aware is important," Patterson said.

Nightingale stood. "Mr. Garrick just wants to be sure no one can say the youngster was coerced." Garrick went to Nightingale's chair, and Nightingale stayed at the door so that Cayden could see him. "We had cases with minors, as I'm sure you have, Sheriff, and they can get thrown out on technicalities."

"Sure, sure," the Sheriff said. "Let's just settle down, so I can get some business done." He blew out a long breath. "You were going to tell us about this morning."

"I go there during the summer on Thursdays to help with chores. I've been going since I turned thirteen. We, my momma and Connie and me, decided it was safe for me to cut through the woods from town."

"Do you hitchhike?"

"No."

"How did this arrangement happen?"

The boy cut his glance toward Nightingale, who nodded. Cayden's next words seemed easier, more confident. "I don't know for sure. It was after Connie's husband went into the army, but before Mr. Faulkner worked for her."

"You went every Thursday?"

"Not when school was in. Then I went on Saturdays, if I wasn't helping Mother."

"Industrious young man," Patterson said. "How are your school grades?"

Cayden grinned slightly. "Not real good."

"Back to this morning. Did you call first?"

"No, sir. Never have. No need to start now."

"You'll need to show us."

"No problem. There's a path that the deer have used."

Nightingale could see that Cayden had warmed to the sheriff. He wanted to help. Such trust could get the kid in trouble.

"Why did you have a key?"

"Connie wanted me to get inside if she wasn't home and it was raining."

"Did you knock?"

Cayden looked at Nightingale, his eyes suspicious. "No. I usually just went in, and she showed up from inside the house or from the barn."

"Did you see or hear anything this morning that was different?"

"No, sir. It was quiet. I didn't pay much attention. I walked across the yard and went in. Oh, I left the rosemary limb outside."

"Rosemary?" Sheriff Patterson squinted at the boy and then the Rangers.

"I told Mr. Nightingale that she liked it."

"Okay, let's talk about some other things. Did Mrs. Dearborn ever say anything about being afraid of anyone?"

Cayden shook his head.

"For the record, the witness is shaking his head no." The sheriff interrupted, then continued. "And you saw nobody leaving the property? Did you see anybody on the road at the house?"

"From the way I came in, I couldn't see the driveway."

"Where did Hank Faulkner usually park?"

"Mostly in the back, but he usually didn't come 'til late on Thursdays. He helps his sister."

The sheriff nodded as if he understood and cared.

Nightingale gave him high marks for the empathetic role.

"What was your relationship to Mrs. Dearborn?" the sheriff asked.

"She was my half-sister."

"Who told you that?"

Cayden started to fidget. He glanced at Nightingale, no longer secure with the questions. Nightingale said nothing. The boy had to get through this by himself.

"She told me. About six months ago, she told me she suspected it, because of something her father said."

"What was that?"

"I don't know. She said it didn't matter. She showed me pictures of him as a boy. We look alike." Cayden grinned at this, like he had passed a test of which he was proud.

"Can you think of any reason why anyone would kill her?"

The happiness left as quickly as it had come. "No, I don't think many people liked her—except Mr. Faulkner—but she was a good person."

"You think Faulkner liked her?"

Cayden looked at his hands and then at the sheriff. "Mr. Faulkner loved her, but she didn't love him."

24

The sheriff had stopped the interview after Cayden said Faulkner loved Constance Dearborn. Nightingale tried to hear what was said between Patterson and his deputy, but couldn't. He figured Faulkner had just risen in the ranks of suspects.

"Get him outta here," the sheriff said, pointing to Cayden.

Garrick herded the boy out of the room and into the hall with Nightingale following. They barely said howdy to the girl deputy at the front desk. The bright noon sunshine outside looked almost like a good omen.

"Get in the truck," Nightingale said. "We'll take you home."

Cayden climbed into the back seat. As soon as they cleared the parking lot, he slid up to the edge of the seat as far as he could. "They think I killed her, don't they?"

Nightingale glanced at the boy's fingers digging into the upholstery. "You're a person of interest because you had a key and showed up at the house. Are you buckled up?"

"As far as suspects, Nightingale and I might fit the bill," Garrick said.

"How?" The boy sounded hopeful as his bravado thinned.

"We weren't invited, and he"—Garrick pointed to Nightingale—"was trying to get her to sell part of her land, which she didn't want to do."

"I wish I could help." Cayden slid back in the seat. "Grandma will pitch a fit."

No one said anything for the rest of the short ride. Garrick undid his seatbelt as they pulled into the driveway. "I'll go in with you to explain, but if I were you, I'd do a lot of things to make Grandma happy in the next few days."

The front door opened, and Cayden's grandmother walked out. Nightingale listened from the truck as Garrick explained what had happened and that the boy should stay close to home for a few days.

"Just till we get a few details ironed out," Garrick said. He started back to the truck, then stopped, and Nightingale heard him ask her out for early dinner.

Garrick looked smug when he opened the truck door.

"Where you gonna take her?" Nightingale asked.

"Away from here. That lady is classy. We'll go to Lark Springs. There's a good wine selection there. Then, too"—Garrick glanced sideways at Nightingale—"maybe she can shed some light on the boy and this dead woman."

Nightingale let Garrick out at his hotel and drove to a shady spot down the street, where he pulled the truck in and dialed McGowan.

There was no good answer to McGowan's terse, "What's up?"

"Constance Dearborn has been murdered."

"The woman who wouldn't sell?"

"Right. Sutton Garrick and I found her this morning. She'd been shot."

"Hell, I wanted her to sell; I didn't want her dead. Any idea who did it?"

"No."

"Guess we better find out how we can get that land."

The words hit Nightingale wrong. "Roy, the woman is still warm. Reckon compassion is totally out of politics?"

"I guess it will look bad," McGowan said and sighed. "I'll call you back later."

The force of McGowan's words brought Nightingale back to his thoughts of why he quit the Rangers. Too many people insinuated themselves into murders or robberies or kidnappings. Too many people threatened him with harm. But he had known Roy McGowan for years, and this push and shove for winning was not the McGowan who had been his hero in middle school.

His phone rang, and it was McGowan again. "You're right. Forget what I said. Is there any hope that the sheriff can handle this quickly?"

"What do you think? He's out of his league."

"Keep me informed," McGowan said.

Nightingale's sarcastic answer was lost to the dead phone. He wanted to know what the governor said—how she reacted to Dearborn's death. He wanted details about Posey's death. He needed McGowan's help, but the man danced around the issues. He'd never run into so many roadblocks in a case for the state. As he approached the B and B, he wondered if Emma Jackson would be waiting for him.

When he stepped into the house, he heard sounds from the kitchen. It was just past noon, and he didn't know how much Mrs. Jackson had been told by the sheriff. He had pulled the front door shut and started toward the stairs when Silas opened the door to the kitchen.

"Mr. Nightingale." His voice had a sureness that had not been there before. This was a man in charge. "Some neighbors are bringing in food for Mother and me because of this tragedy. You're welcome to join us."

"I need to make some calls, but thank you all the same."

Silas stepped closer. "We need to talk to you. We have visitors now. We'll come to your room later."

Nightingale put his hand on the bannister, pushed his hat back a bit. "I've got some business to do. I'll come down in a few minutes."

Let them think what they wanted; he didn't want them in his room. Sure, Emma Jackson owned the place, but he had moved in with his stuff. Sure, someone cleaned and made the bed, but mentally, he didn't want to bring a case—especially not murder—into his bedroom.

He placed his hat on the desk, hung his jacket in the closet, and put his Sig Sauer in its holster in the chest of drawers. He changed shirts, glanced at his image in the bathroom mirror, and wet and plastered one piece of hair that stood out on the side of his head. As he looked in the mirror, he wondered about the people in Mrs. Jackson's kitchen. Might not be a bad idea to see who these folks were and what they thought.

People still milled around in the kitchen, talking and drinking coffee. When Mrs. Jackson saw Nightingale, they all seemed to work off of telepathy, moving to the exit door, murmuring condolences, offering to help.

Some of the former effervescence had left Emma Jackson. For a woman who said she and her sister had not talked in several years, she seemed to have shrunk and gained lines in her face in the few hours since Constance's death. Nightingale had known other strong Southern women who possessed the ingrained politeness of a Southern belle. He was not surprised when she walked and talked with each of her visitors as they left her kitchen.

When she turned from the doorway and faced Nightingale, she reminded him of a wilted flower. "I want to know what happened to my sister," she said.

Silas touched her elbow. "Mother, let's go to the living room." He guided her out of the kitchen and toward the couch.

Emma perched on the edge of the sofa, her red-rimmed eyes belying the strength of her words. "Did someone kill her over the land? Has anyone considered that man who worked for her?" The words were a tumble of thoughts. "He had problems since he came back from the war."

Nightingale sat across from them, wondering about how the sheriff would look at this "talk". "I guess the sheriff has already told you what he could. I don't know any more than that."

"He did call. Said she was dead. He had nothing to tell us, but he said he'd talk with us later," Silas said.

Mrs. Jackson interrupted her son, her voice urgent. "I need to know who did this. Why aren't you out investigating?" She stood up, her arms stiff at her side. "What if someone is trying to kill me or my son?"

"Mrs. Jackson, no one is out to kill you." Nightingale talked slow and low—the voice he used to comfort people and pets. "But I need to know if you and your sister talked lately." It was a stab in the dark, but Nightingale hoped that if they had talked, something had been said that might give him a clue about the reason behind Mrs. Dearborn's death.

Mrs. Jackson looked down, then to both sides before she sat back down. "I called her—a bit after the explosion. We didn't say much. I was worried about her making so many people mad. She told me to mind my own business, which is what she usually told me."

"Nothing else? Was she worried?"

She shook her head. "She didn't like me, or Silas. She mentioned that child, you know, what's his name?"

"Cayden. What did she say about him?"

"Something about inheritance, but she was just trying to bait me and be mean. She knew Silas is the only heir in our family.

You've got to understand that Constance hated me. I couldn't hate her, because that is not the Christian thing to do. She's hated me since Daddy died. But that has nothing to do with this." The words sounded practiced.

Silas reached over and patted his mother's hand. "He knows that, Mother. Why don't you lie down a bit? Take one of those pills the doctor gave you."

She looked at her son, her eyes glassy, but she nodded like she understood. "I do feel overwhelmed."

Silas stood and walked out of the room beside her.

When he returned, Silas lowered his voice. "What will happen now with Aunt Constance's land and the state wanting it?"

"I don't know." Nightingale stood. "You got any iced tea in the kitchen? Who were those people here?"

"Just folks from the church. Mother gets her strength from her faith and the church."

"What about you?"

Silas looked down the hall and waited until they had the kitchen door closed before replying. "I don't have her faith. And I don't believe this town is the center of the universe."

Nightingale looked at the younger man with a degree of thoughtfulness. "Do you have any ideas about who would do this?"

"I can't see it as deliberate—I'm too naive. The church group says this is God telling people they'd better change their ways."

Nightingale shook his head in dismay, thanked Silas for the tea, and went to his room. The young man surprised him with his frank answers—a heathen among all these Christians. How did he get by with such an attitude?

25

Some habits stayed longer than others. Garrick still switched on Ranger mode too quickly and realized it when he found himself driving around Audie Louise Shepherd's neighborhood looking for he didn't know what except some clue about her grandson, Cayden. Who were his friends? Where did he go to school? How did it feel to be raised by two women? Who was his male hero? Part of the answers he would find out from Audie Louise.

The town of Beulah was like any other that had bloomed after the wars and then cratered in the last few years. He guessed this little section of three-bedroom brick homes had been built about forty years ago when brick was expensive. He imagined the town back then thriving from the river traffic and surrounding prosperous farms.

How did a widow woman pay her bills? Maybe the daughter made more money than he imagined. Audie's pride might be a problem if she felt like her daughter was supporting her. Then again, her husband might have left her some money for everyday survival. Didn't matter; he just always wondered how people paid their bills. Money, or lack of it, was always a critical factor to him in an investigation. Nightingale tried to find out about home life and, Garrick had learned, that was just as critical as money.

Garrick liked the idea of a meal with a good-looking woman. He kept Nightingale under the impression that he still had an active sex life, but the truth was he longed for an intelligent conversation. He missed having a smart woman in his life. Why was he like that? He'd been his happiest when Nancy was alive, and he hadn't had the good sense to appreciate her like he should have. God, he missed that woman.

His own yearnings translated to telling Nightingale to call Josephine Holly—to show her more attention. He knew what companionship could do for a man. Sounded like a myth, but it was true—men needed women to give them a reason to act like humans.

Cayden's grandmother reminded him that women could be smart and beautiful past sixty. He wondered what her age was, but he wouldn't ask. She'd probably tell him. Women who still had that hourglass figure and held themselves straight and proud often liked to brag about their years.

Garrick pulled into the driveway, went to the porch, and knocked. Audie Louise came to the door and didn't ask him inside. He smelled tortillas. She slipped out of the door and quickly pulled it shut. "I don't want Cayden to talk to you right now."

He opened the truck door for her, and as they drove away from the house, she explained.

"Cayden has a bad case of hero worship for you and Mr. Nightingale right now."

"What's wrong with that?"

"Oh, not that you're bad people, but he doesn't realize how much trouble he's in. He is a suspect in Constance Dearborn's death." She turned and stared at him as he drove. "Isn't he?"

"Yes—but so are other people."

She folded her hands primly in her lap, as if she had made a point. "Well, he doesn't need to be rewarded with talking with you and seeing this truck. He likes good-looking vehicles, preferably fast ones. He's got to realize how serious this is." She looked out the window. "I still remember when being a Mexican or a black man meant you were guilty. Still does to some folks up here. He's got to be more careful."

Garrick already didn't like the way this was headed. "How 'bout we talk about something besides our worries."

The widow smiled. "Truly a good idea. Let's talk about food."

So the conversation went from food to weather as they drove to the restaurant. Once they were inside, Garrick asked for advice on what to order. Audie Louise asked about family, and after Garrick said his wife was dead and they had no children, he eased the conversation back to Cayden.

"I don't think you have to worry about the boy. His only problem may be that he wants to work too hard."

By then, they were on the second glass of wine. Cayden's grandmother mellowed. "You care for him, I think, and that makes me feel better. Why are you here?"

"I was bored. Retirement is not that grand. I have old friends up here—or I did—so when Nightingale came, I just drove up too."

"Friends?"

"Alice and Mason McClure. Mason died last year, and I didn't know 'til I went to their house. Neighbors caught me up. Alice has moved away to stay with her kids."

"Oh, I see."

Garrick noted Audie Louise's look down at her hands and away when he mentioned his black friends. "You knew them?"

"Alice worked for me once. I didn't know her husband. She was a good woman."

Garrick filed the look and comment to think about later.

"So, had you planned to help Mr. Nightingale?" Audie Louise asked.

He paused and thought a minute. No need for her to know everything. "We're friends from way back. I didn't plan to help; it just seemed natural to fall in with him on some things. Now this thing has come up with the murder. He's glad I'm here. Did you know the lady?"

"I knew her when she was young. Constance was the bratty younger sister. Emma and I were friends back then, although you wouldn't know it now."

"This is all very strange," Garrick said. "They didn't talk, right?"

The food arrived, and the waiter filled their glasses again. "When Mrs. Alexander died, the judge came back from the funeral and didn't come out of the house for a month. Emma and Constance took turns going to visit him. Emma was already turning strange. Her religion took over her life. The sisters clashed.

"My Isabel had her own business, cleaning offices and houses for extra money. She had been cleaning for the Alexanders before the wife died. When Emma and Constance's visits became fewer and fewer, I worried. Finally, they stopped going to see him. I guess he was hard to deal with. Isabel tried to avoid being alone with him for a while, but he talked to her. She felt sorry for him." Audie Louise chewed a bit of bread and washed it down with the wine.

When the waiter tried to refill her glass, she placed a hand over the top and asked for water.

Garrick had heard bits of this story, but Audie Louise presented the picture from a different angle. He waited for her to continue.

"Somewhere in that time, Isabel became pregnant." Audie

Louise looked across the vacant tables in the restaurant and sighed. "Then the judge died and left the ranch to Constance and the B and B to Emma. It wasn't six weeks later that Emma's husband disappeared. That was about the strangest thing." Audie's drawl thickened as she got deeper into the story. Her narrative moved easily away from the subject of the judge and Isabel.

"Rumors had it that Emma drove him to the river bridge, they argued, and he jumped. Patterson was the sheriff then, too." She stopped and looked at Garrick. "You know they're cousins, don't you? Yes, well, nothing came of his disappearance. Seemed like the whole town was in shock from the judge dying, and then with Emma's husband vanishing, people just whispered and shrunk inside their houses. Guess they were afraid the family was cursed."

"So, Isabel was pregnant," Garrick said.

Audie Louise straightened and leveled a cold stare at him. "There was no question that the child was Judge Alexander's."

"Did your daughter tell Constance and Emma about the baby?"

"We went to them. We had to see them separately. It was humiliating, especially with Emma Jackson." Audie Louise drew a long breath. "My daughter is proud. After visiting Emma, she said, 'I will speak to them no more. This baby is mine. I will take care of it.'

"She told me early on that she loved the old man." Audie Louise's tone softened, became a mother's voice. "It's funny, isn't it—what love will do? She's not a dumb girl, but she believes that the judge will take care of Cayden somehow, even though he's dead."

Garrick couldn't help a wry smile. "What do you think?"

She shrugged. "I don't believe in fairy tales, another reason why Cayden needs to know how serious this is. If he gets tainted with accusations, it could ruin his life. Small towns are cruel that way."

Garrick agreed. He suggested they leave and knew he'd not ask the widow to spend the night, no matter how much he wanted to try that new pill.

26

The next morning, Nightingale thought about his conversation with Silas as he drove to the Dearborn ranch. The young man seemed to enjoy the role of being a stranger in this community that his mother loved.

A fog of humidity filled the air. Nightingale's clothes stuck to him. The air hung heavy and hard to breathe. The truck air conditioning smelled like mold and wet leaves. He put the windows down, hoping to drive the stale air out. He almost stopped to take the puppy with him but thought better of that plan. He'd be distracted, trying to keep the little critter out of trouble. He'd play with him tomorrow. And when they got home, he'd train Bandit to be a guard dog. He smiled to himself, feeling foolish that a dog could brighten his outlook on life.

He wanted to be back in Broken Rock so badly he could taste it. He wanted to find Constance Dearborn's killer, but his primary goal had to be completing the job for the governor. He figured Posey's death was part of the equation. His gut told him that the two recent deaths were related, but he didn't know how.

He kept reacting with Ranger-like thoughts and deeds, even though he tried to control that urge. He kept telling himself the job for the governor couldn't be done well with a murder hanging over it. The two dilemmas were separate. And much of the problem was brought about because of his desire to be in control.

Even if the sheriff was smart, he was related to Emma and Constance and no telling who else in the town. But Patterson did seem to be affected when he saw Constance. He would try. He'd probably do an okay job of finding Constance's killer, especially with Nightingale doing what he could to help an investigation along. Quietly, of course.

So he would leave the dilemma of the murder to the sheriff, and he would continue his job for the governor. In the back of his mind, he knew he was pitching so much horse hockey to his conscience, but he could live with it for a day or two.

At the Dearborn ranch, two county cars sat out front. A Ford 150 truck that he thought was Faulkner's had pulled to one side and parked on the grass.

Nightingale climbed out of his vehicle and started toward the house.

Faulkner headed toward him from the direction of the barn.

Nightingale stepped up his pace to meet the man.

Faulkner's hat shaded his eyes, but his face seemed older. His shoulders drooped. When he got closer, Nightingale saw that sadness pulled the corners of Faulkner's eyes down. Someone had told him, and either he was a good actor or he had nothing to do with Constance's death.

Faulkner put out his hand. "Sheriff came by to see me last night."

Nightingale looked at the icy hand as he shook it.

"Neuropathy," Faulkner said. "The shrapnel damaged some nerves, so my hands are usually cold."

"Sorry." Nightingale stifled a "thank you for your service." Seemed off color when he considered the man a suspect.

"I came today to take care of the animals. They won't let me get over the yellow tape."

"No need for us to be inside the house," Nightingale said. "Can you tell if they've found anything?"

Faulkner shook his head. "Nope, they're acting like I'm not here."

They'd walked to the back of the house. Three men in brown uniforms paced back and forth, covering every inch of the back yard for any clue. Another man at the edge of the woods waved and yelled something that Nightingale couldn't understand.

"What happened?" Faulkner asked. "Sheriff said she was shot. Rest of it is rumor, and it's driving me crazy."

"When did you get here?" Nightingale asked.

"Over an hour ago. No one will tell me anything. Said I'd have to answer questions." He jerked his hands in the air and then pointed to his own chest. "Me. Answer questions. That's bullshit."

Nightingale shared the frustration, but couldn't say it. "Did the sheriff question you?"

"Asked me where I was yesterday morning." He stopped talking, cleared his throat. "I want to help."

Nightingale had not dealt with a soldier, but he figured he'd seen several hundred traumatized relatives during a variety of murder investigations and there had to be similarities. "You could help right now by going on home. Calm down. There's nothing you can do. The sheriff will call."

"Right. But I want to help." He stared at the men still walking, their heads down, oblivious to his trembling emotion.

"I can drive you home, if you want."

Faulkner stared at Nightingale. He nodded and reality settled over his features. "No, but thanks. Call me when you hear something."

Faulkner walked to his truck without looking back.

Nightingale shook his head. Another suspect who didn't act guilty. 'Course, his idea of a suspect and the sheriff's idea might be totally different. When Faulkner was out of sight, Nightingale walked round the edge of the yellow tape.

The backyard area ran the width of the house. It ended a hundred yards away, where the trees and undergrowth began.

A familiar-looking officer yelled hello to Nightingale. "Guess I knew you would be here," Amon Toohey said. "We can't let you in."

"Yeah, I know. Just one question: does your search go into the trees?"

"Right. Sheriff Patterson is bringing in an expert from Dallas to get more details, but he's thinking it was someone on the edge of the woods." Toohey cast a worried glance toward the house and then, as if he'd forgotten that Nightingale was there, turned away.

Nightingale shrugged and started back to his vehicle. He and Garrick had arrived at 9:00 a.m., and Mrs. Dearborn's body was not cold. He thought of the boy sauntering though the woods, unaware of how close to death he was.

He almost ran into the sheriff as he rounded the corner of the house.

"Why are you here?" The sheriff wore anger on his sleeve. "Since you've decided to show up, I need to talk some more to that boy, and you can bring him to me."

"Sure. We left him with his mother."

"Yeah. By the way"—the sheriff turned to stare at Nightingale —"did you and Garrick mess with anything while you were here?"

"Course we didn't. Why'd you ask?"

"Nothing that I can say for sure." Patterson moved his gaze to the men as they walked across the back yard, then he turned and closed in toward Nightingale. "The lady left a will on her computer. We found it as soon as we opened the files, and we're not computer nerds, but I wondered about a printed copy."

Nightingale looked at the men, then the sheriff, thinking about Garrick roaming through the house. "Is it valid?"

"Depends. If she signed a print copy it is. But it has to have witnesses. If she just wrote one by hand, you know Texas law counts that. I don't know about one just sittin' on the computer." Once he shifted away from accusations, he cooled in tone.

"I've never dealt with that," Nightingale said. "When can you share what was in the will?" The vision of the piece of paper sticking out of Garrick's pocket as they left the Dearborn ranch gave no comfort.

"I'm talking to two different attorneys first. I'd just as soon you didn't tell the governor's people yet. I'll call her."

Nightingale nodded agreement. Didn't take a genius to understand that the sheriff wanted the commendations from the governor, and a smart person would not cross that.

"What about the shooter?" Nightingale asked. "Anything new?"

"Probably used a scope. Had some thought to it. I need an expert to help with details. You guys have that, right?" Patterson's stare bored through Nightingale.

"Headquarters is pissed with me. They'll probably send somebody if you call." He could see that was not the answer the sheriff wanted, but it was the truth. He didn't try to explain.

As he walked away, he stuck his hand in the air in farewell. "Call me when you hear anything. I'll do the same if the governor's office calls with anything definite about Posey." He wanted the sheriff to keep Posey's unsettled death in mind. Who knew—it might lead to information he needed in other matters.

Professionals would decide what weapon killed Constance Dearborn, and he would find out. But he had other issues to worry about. For one thing, he wanted to see what had been in

Garrick's pocket. Sweat trickled down his back. If it was the will, he knew what would be best, and it was too late for that.

In the truck, he turned on the A/C but still needed breathing space. Slapping off the A/C, he rolled down the window. Damn Sutton Garrick and his conniving ways. He hadn't gotten a mile down the road before he yanked the truck off the pavement, pushed autodial on the phone, and waited, too angry to talk while driving.

"Where the hell are you?"

"I'm at the hotel. Me and Audie just got back. You sound mad."

"Tell me that you didn't take a copy of a will out of the Dearborn house."

"Well, you're headed this direction, right?"

Nightingale couldn't tell if that meant Audie Louise Shepherd was still with him or not, but he had his answer.

All the way to the hotel, Nightingale tried to figure out how to tell the sheriff that Garrick, a former Ranger, had taken a major piece of evidence. There was no good way. Garrick would have to go in and confess that his curiosity got the better of his judgment. But damn, a lawyer in a courtroom could make hay of the deed.

Chain of evidence, duty, honesty, truth, all those words that had been part of his DNA for years had been thrown aside in the last few days. What had happened to the man who lived by the letter of the law? Couldn't blame it all on Garrick, even though he was handy.

And why did it rub him so raw? Because he was there on the governor's job, not to solve a murder. He'd been sent to get a water agreement finalized. Despite his aggravation, he had to keep that in mind.

Garrick walked outside as soon as Nightingale pulled into the hotel driveway. He opened the door before Nightingale cut the engine. "What the hell are you so riled about?"

Garrick held the door open, waiting for an answer that didn't come. He slid in and fumbled for the seatbelt

Nightingale growled, smashed the accelerator, and left the hotel, turning toward the bar on the outskirts of town. "I'm riled, as you succinctly put it, because you stole evidence in a murder case. You have the will—right?""

"I'm gonna ignore the fact that you waited until now to say anything."

"What do I tell the sheriff? We're supposed to be law-abiding citizens, lawmen. Plus, we don't need to jeopardize that kid's future." Nightingale's voice seemed loud, even to his own ears.

"I didn't take anything." Garrick had balled one fist on his lap and wrapped his other hand around the seatbelt. "But you don't have to explain my actions." Garrick said. "I'm a grown man—still a Ranger in my heart—and I'll live or die by my own decisions."

A heavy silence filled the truck.

27

Three vehicles sat outside the Laughing Cow, none of them familiar. At three in the afternoon, every bent fender and dust covered hood looked dull from the heat.

Nightingale rolled out of the truck, gearing up for an argument before they got inside of the bar. "Has it occurred to you that we've not followed the letter of the law in this case?"

Garrick stopped abruptly. "Is that what's in your craw?"

"Me? You used to make me fill out more forms than a damned government informant."

"Yeah, and I think I overdid it. You turned into a real prick." They stood facing one another, and Nightingale watched the old Ranger's face, but could read nothing.

"You still want a drink?" Garrick asked.

Nightingale nodded, welcoming the upcoming battle.

They walked into the bar and settled at a back table.

After their beer arrived, the silence began to grate on Nightingale. Hell would freeze before the word "apologize" slipped into the conversation.

"The way I see it"—Garrick leaned into Nightingale's space—"you got here way before I did. I don't know what you've done except for that stunt under the bed. You've always gone by the letter of the law, even when a slight twist would have served better. I don't know if you've robbed a bank or stole something, or if shooting that boy years ago is itching at you, but the only thing I've done is tag along and have a wayward piece of paper in my pocket. I ain't been here long enough to get bitched at. So what's your problem?"

Nightingale looked over his shoulder, blew out a deep breath. "It's the way things are going—they're not. If I needed help on a case, I asked for it. Patterson needs help." He lowered his voice to match Garrick's. "Constance Dearborn was killed deliberately—not by some freak hunting accident. I think her death and Posey's are tied together, but I don't know why."

"You're wrong about Posey."

"Why do you say that? You never even met him."

Garrick sat back. "Hell, you're not even thinking like a Ranger."

Nightingale took a long drink, so he wouldn't show how the goading bothered him. "How is that?"

"You're assuming too much," Garrick said, "because they both had an interest in the water issue. And they knew each other, but my God, they just met. Something else is in this thing, and I'm not asking you what it is, but you used to be analytical, even when you went with your gut. Something is bothering you. You're not keeping the crime separate from yourself."

Nightingale hated it when the old man was right. It brought back way too many memories of being handed his hat, accompanied by Garrick's smug "I told you so" expression. "Okay, let's analyze, since you think I need help with that.

"We know most murders are motivated by greed, love, or hate, so we start by looking at family, friends, and business associates. As far as I know, Posey's family was tight with the governor and he had no friends. Why would state government kill Posey when he was hired to get Dearborn's land bought? That leaves an accident or natural causes, which are obviously *your* two most likely possibilities."

"What about Dearborn? Faulkner claims to have loved her, and so does Cayden," Garrick said. "Her sister appears to have hated her. We don't know about Silas or the locals. Nobody I've met liked her or her daddy."

Nightingale nodded and stared at Garrick. "The value of her property would be motivation enough to corrupt a preacher. State government has all the incentive they need, but that's a stretch. Bureaucrats are too sloppy, and they'd get caught. How's that for analytical?"

"The boy could have done it." Garrick almost whispered the words.

The noise in the room seemed to mute. Nightingale's heart pounded so hard he was sure Garrick heard it. A darkness settled around him. "I'm not believing that."

"Truth hurts." Garrick poured the rest of the beer into his glass. "Is this about that boy you killed?"

Nightingale leaned forward and tapped the table with his forefinger, trying to contain his anger. "You may be old and think you're wise, but this is not about that boy. And in case you've forgotten, *this* boy is innocent until proven guilty. It's about a murdered woman, shot through a window in her house from ambush by some lowlife snake in the woods. She deserves justice."

"Bullshit. You've always spouted that crap. What's next?"

Like two old hounds with years of snarling and snapping at each other, neither of them had to have the last word. With stress akin to hatred, they simply quit speaking.

They each threw a ten on the table and walked out.

28

Garrick knew he was right. He also knew that he had to let his anger with Nightingale smolder while it burned to an ash. He grunted when Nightingale dropped him at the hotel. As he walked by his truck, he glanced into the truck bed. Normally empty except for his snake stick, the truck bed now had a lumpy blanket wadded next to the cab. Garrick reached for the knotted fringe of the fabric and pulled. The blanket pulled back.

"Mr. Garrick, please don't." Cayden's dark hair stuck out at one end and his tennis shoes at the other.

Garrick peeped under one corner, then looked to his left and right. "Okay, just so everyone will know I've lost my mind, I'm gonna stand here and talk into the air."

"No, please," Cayden half-whispered from under the red and orange wool. "What's your room number? I'll come in when it's safe."

Garrick didn't argue. He said the number, went inside, and called Cayden's home. Audie Louise answered. He mentally congratulated himself that he had not asked her to come to his room. "Your grandson is here with me. Is it okay with his mother for him to stay tonight?"

Audie Louise spluttered and cursed. "Bring that child home. He can't run away from every disagreement." In the background, he heard another voice. The voices became muffled. Audie Louise returned to the phone and delivered an icy, "We'll see you in the morning."

At the first tap on the door, Garrick jerked it open and stood aside. "I ought to turn you in right now. Get in here."

"Did you call my mother?"

"Yes. Parents don't deserve to worry when there's no reason."

The boy stood in the middle of the room, a beat-up backpack in one hand, his brown eyes darkly circled with worry.

"Are you hungry?" Garrick asked.

"Yes."

"Let's go get a burger, my treat."

"I don't want to go inside." Cayden held out his shirt. "I'm kind of stinky."

Garrick didn't argue when the odor of sweaty male adolescent hit him. "Why don't you take a shower? Any clothes in that pack?"

"A shirt."

"That's enough. Put on your same shorts, clean shirt. Then we'll eat. You'll feel better after the shower."

In under an hour, they were in Garrick's truck and headed to the Dairy Queen. Once inside, they ordered their food, shuffled awkwardly at the counter until it came, and then slid into a booth with black faux-leather seats and silently took bites of fries and burgers.

As Garrick bit into a clump of fries, he said, "You want to tell me why you left home?"

The boy laid his burger on the paper wrapper, taking his time. "I didn't think about it much. I knew when I walked in that Grandma would be accusing me, not wanting to listen, and I was right. I did what you said, and I was polite. Momma said we would talk later. Then Grandma started telling her how wrong she'd been to let me go to Connie's house." He wadded up his fists and leaned toward Garrick. "Why does it matter?"

"How'd you get out?" Garrick asked, ignoring the defensive tone in the boy's voice.

"Window."

"Why'd you come to me?"

"I figured you wouldn't tell me how I'd screwed up." Cayden gave a half-grin. "Or if you did, you wouldn't be yelling at me. And I didn't know how to get to Mr. Nightingale's room. Where is he?"

Garrick knew this was coming, but he didn't want to give details about Nightingale. "In a minute. First, I want you to tell me about your walk to the Dearborn house. Just go through the motions, and tell me what you did from the time you walked out the door of your house."

The smile left. Cayden crumpled the greasy hamburger paper, then gave Garrick a piercing stare. "I didn't lie." His gaze shifted to the door, like he might run at any minute.

Garrick wiped his mouth, took his time. "I didn't say that you lied. I think it might be a good exercise to go through without the sheriff and deputy standing over you."

A light of understanding seemed to wash over Cayden and he continued. "Okay, I left the house and got to the path pretty quick"

"Describe this path. Wide, narrow?"

"Narrow, next to the vet's house. He keeps cows and horses out there sometimes. There's an opening in the trees. I guess two people could walk on it. It leads up to the top of the hill, kinda follows the road. I know the way from there. It's an hour or so walk."

"You said there wasn't anything different during your walk."

Garrick said. "As you got close to the house, what was the first thing you saw?"

Cayden closed his eyes. His eyelids moved as he revisited the scene. "I saw the roof of the house. I was looking for the rosemary bush. It grows at the edge of the woods. Connie said there had probably been a house up there on the hill, way back before she was born. When I got to the bush, I bent down to get a big limb. I didn't want Connie to see me; I wanted to surprise her. I could see through the big window into the dining room, and I didn't see anything. I thought Connie might just be waking up, or she might be out looking after the cattle, but usually they mooed and carried on if she was out there. The birds weren't singing. It was really quiet."

"Could you see the road the whole time you walked from town to the house?"

"No, just when I was walking out of town. I recognized all but one of the cars I saw."

Garrick had hoped the boy saw a vehicle turn down the road after it left the ranch, or something to give some clue about the shooter. But he couldn't force it. And he didn't like the change in the boy. Nightingale had described the teen as confident, but now he was uneasy, skittish. "What do you do as a pastime?"

"I dream about how to get out of this place."

"That's a harsh statement."

"It's not easy here. Have you told Nightingale that I'm here?"

"Not yet."

Cayden stopped slurping the milkshake. Fearful, worried eyes stared back at Garrick. The boy had invested his hope in Nightingale, and he was stuck with this old man. "Are y'all related?"

"What makes you ask that?"

"Well, you aren't in love, but you argue when you're around

me. You don't want to be a bad influence on me, but when you don't get along you both get tense."

Garrick sat back and stared at the kid. "Who are you —Dear Abby?"

The boy blushed. "You asked." He shrugged and smiled at the ribbing.

"Y'all are like my mom and grandmother. They have a lot they disagree about. But they try to hide it from me. Mom has a pretty good way of dealing, but she has a hot temper and sometimes she says things she doesn't mean. You're like that." The boy shook his head.

Garrick didn't like this degree of analysis. "So, why did you run to me?"

"Because, I think I can learn a lot from you."

"That's the biggest pile of horse . . . manure I've ever heard." The words con artist came to mind and Garrick tamped them down. "Let's get out—"

Before he'd finished the sentence, Cayden had slid out of his seat, rushed to the door, and disappeared into the night.

29

After Nightingale dropped Garrick at the hotel, he kept thinking of the years of off-again-on-again time he'd worked with the older Ranger. Part of the problem was that Garrick did what he thought he needed to do in order to catch a murderer. And he could be outlandish out of pure cussedness. Nightingale expected the worst. In this case, he had accused Garrick of taking the will before he gave him time to tell the truth or create a lie.

Garrick had worked with him when they were both on the Texas Ranger payroll. Then Garrick's wife was murdered, and the man went into a fit of depression and drinking. Finally, he resigned. When the old man came to himself, he had not mellowed.

If anything, he was pushier, more braggadocious, a risk-taker. But through it all, Garrick was still a Ranger. He would never mess with evidence. Nightingale regretted his accusation. He'd have to apologize—eventually.

Right now, he had to decide how to approach his more current problem. And when he walked into the living room of the Sycamore B and B, Silas and Emma Jackson sat there, in matching Queen Anne chairs, as if they were waiting for him. Nightingale saw how they favored each other. Silas had his mother's round face, her tendency to be a little heavy, and her small, sour mouth.

Nightingale took off his hat and smiled like they were his best friends.

"Mrs. Jackson, I have a strange request," he said. "I have this puppy that I've adopted." He went on to ask for visiting privileges for the dog.

"This is highly unusual." Her face became stiff, unmoving, as she glanced at Silas. She walked to the desk, sighing like she was suddenly tired.

"Mother, this is good," Silas said. "A lot of the more modern hotels are allowing pets. They charge a non-refundable fee up front and then more if there's damage. The cottages have tile floors. This will be great for business."

"He'll be in a kennel a lot," Nightingale said.

Mrs. Jackson leaned against the desk, the wrinkles around her eyes and mouth etched deep. He wondered if she took some kind of medication.

"You can move to a cottage at a higher price." With a fountain pen in her hand, she pointed and lectured. "If the animal does damage, you'll have to pay."

"That sounds fair," Nightingale said.

Silas slid to his mother's side and scrambled in the desk for keys.

Nightingale went upstairs and began folding shirts into his suitcase. His boots had been moved in the closet and some of the pants were not as neat on the hangers as he had left them. He'd left nothing incriminating for a nosy body to find—again old habits served him well.

Silas met him at the bottom of the stairs. Two cottages occupied the yard to the right and slightly behind the B and B. Huge pin oak trees gave shade over the two cottages, one with forest green trim and front door, and the other with navy blue trim and door. A picket fence finished the scene. Nightingale figured the puppy would love the green lawn surrounding the small house, where he could sniff and pee at will.

As they walked to the cottage, Silas gave a commentary. "Mom had the cottages built after she inherited the Sycamore. You get the one with the green door. We have folks coming in next week, so you'll have neighbors." He unlocked the door and went inside, giving a brief glance to the bedroom and opening the refrigerator. "Better get yourself some food," Silas said. "You can still have breakfast at the B and B, but I always like to have snacks."

Standing in the bedroom, Nightingale didn't reply. He heard Silas again. "I'm leaving the keys on the table by the recliner." Then the door slammed.

Nightingale set his bottle of Jack Daniels on the kitchen counter and went out and moved his truck to the parking space for the cottage. Walking back to the door, he took in the lay of the tiny yard and picket fence shared with the cottage next door. He felt good in the new isolation. The Sycamore remained close enough for Mrs. Jackson to spy on him, but somehow this felt better. He poured himself a drink, with one cube of ice, and turned on his laptop, leaning back in the recliner that replaced the Queen Anne nightmare, to check news and weather. A few showers had hit Texas, but the rest of the West remained arid.

He remembered comments that Posey had made about a worldwide water shortage and started an Internet search. After reading that a billion people around the world lacked access to safe drinking water, he closed the laptop, deciding that he couldn't worry about the planet. He closed his eyes and dozed, to be awakened by a knock on his door.

Still groggy, he stood and walked to the door, noticing that the porch light was out, which seemed odd. He took one step out, still holding the screen door, and peered to his left. It was darker than it should be, and with wariness setting in, he glanced up to see why the street light was also out.

He heard the step of a boot behind him and tried to pull the screen door closer. Something banged against the base of his head, followed by a flash of white pain. A fist hit his middle, knocking his breath out. He doubled over and retched into a black void. Voices mumbled. He fought for consciousness and knew he'd been pushed away from the cottage. He fell against two legs that felt like tree trunks and staggered, pushing himself halfway up. From there, he ran headfirst into an opponent who was only shadow.

In the darkness, he swung and got lucky, feeling the hardness of bone, hopefully covered by soft flesh.

Someone grunted. "God damn you."

He moved slowly, but his attackers moved slowly, too. He couldn't see them except for white covers over their heads.

Gloved hands dragged him upright and held his arms.

He braced on their arms and kicked forward, glad to hear the crush of his foot into bone. He smelled beer and sweat as someone rammed a fist into his gut.

Then the numbers overcame him.

"Go home, hombre."

Someone else pounded his stomach.

When they dropped him, he curled into a fetal shape, which got several kicks into his back. Finally, blackness surrounded him.

≈

A SENSE OF DAMPNESS WOKE HIM. PAIN THROBBED IN EVERY part of his body. He had been shot before, he had been hit before, but he had never been beaten. Each breath hurt. He turned his head to look up and saw a few stars. It occurred to him that one eye would not open. He rolled his head and shivered from the cold. Several thoughts piled into his head, among them the thought of shock.

The porch light was still not on. He couldn't believe he'd walked to the door, right into the hands of three or four thugs. A chill came again. He could remember later, but he needed to get into the cottage while he had some wits and strength.

He rolled to one side, assessing damage as he moved. Probably a few broken ribs. He didn't think limbs were broken, but inside, oh my God, his insides hurt mightily.

Slowly, he pushed onto hands and knees and crawled onto the porch. He pulled the screen door open and leaned against the door frame. Holding onto the door frame, he stumbled inside, aching with every move.

Inside the cottage, he assumed his tormentors were gone since he'd made his way inside without another attack. He winced at the pain from the busted lip. There was no safe harbor. His only friend was Garrick.

He looked for his cell phone and spied it on the table next to the recliner. Some outside sense wondered why they had not come inside, but he was too tired to care. Once again, he crawled a few feet, pulled the phone into his hands, and became still. He moved so his back rested against the recliner, where he allowed himself to gently fall to one side and rest.

He slept. When the clock chimed, he slowly got to his knees and locked the door. From there, he lurched to the kitchen counter for the whiskey, then, hanging onto the wall, went to the bathroom, where he took four ibuprofen and a large drink of

Jack. From there, he sat on the edge of the bed before gratefully falling onto the covers and scooting up to touch a pillow.

At five, he awoke again, repeated the pills and Jack, and hit auto dial on his phone. When no one answered, he went back to sleep.

30

After making sure Cayden was asleep, Garrick pulled the Scotch out of his suitcase and poured a good-sized drink. The boy had waited at the truck after running out of the Dairy Queen. Garrick just meandered out to the truck and said, "Get in."

He told himself to let it go, everything was fine, even though nothing was fine. Later on, he'd ask questions, but for the moment, he let it go.

Back at the hotel, he hitched the phone to the charger and turned down the volume. At the window, he shoved the heavy drapes aside and looked out over the partially filled parking lot.

Light posts stood sentinel, making every move visible as people returned from dinner or went to the car for a forgotten item. A slight breeze moved the trees. The boy slept on.

How could people be cruel to children? Somebody in this town had made life hard for the skinny kid. Sure, kids could be a pain in the ass, but they usually outgrew it.

He didn't want anyone to know that he had softened after years of being a Ranger. It seemed to him that early on he puked a lot when he saw a man gut-shot or a woman dead after a rape.

There were years when he became so callous that he didn't react except to feel disgust.

Then he met Mary Nightingale. She changed him. He liked to think he changed her some, but he didn't know. Mary was like fire and ice. She was wild and wise. Good thing that she threw him off, 'cause then he met Nancy and fell in love for sure.

The boy slept on, bringing to Garrick the thoughts of Nightingale as a boy, the boy he wanted to call son but didn't know for sure, and sometimes the best things in life were left unknown. The boy brought other memories, the ones about a dead boy that Garrick knew Nightingale needed to forget.

He got up to pee and refilled his drink.

Taking the refilled glass to the desk, he made a list of things that had to be done. He had to talk to the sheriff. Maybe "talk *at* the sheriff" was a better phrase.

He had more faith in the lawman than Nightingale, but he also had sympathy. The man was voted into his job—what a curse. And this guy seemed to be related to just about everybody in town.

He planned to see the sheriff early the next day when he would tell the man his opinion, which the sheriff would ignore, and that would be that. He didn't care if the sheriff paid attention or not, but he needed to be told that if he wanted to be on the winning team, he'd better change his ways.

THE AUTOMATED CALL FROM THE FRONT DESK CAME EARLY. Cayden, apparently a morning person, lifted the receiver and put it back down before Garrick had his eyes open. They took turns in the shower. Garrick was pleased to see Cayden sitting on the bed, ready to go, when he finished dressing.

"Don't you wear a gun?" the boy asked.

"When I need to," Garrick said. He left the gun, holstered, wrapped between his t-shirts and boxers in his luggage. Didn't need the tie but brought along his jacket. They didn't have far to go to get the boy home. "I'd offer breakfast, but I've got things to do, so you'll have to eat at home."

"That's fine. Tell Mr. Nightingale I said hey."

When he stopped the truck, Garrick touched the boy's arm. Some invisible understanding held him in his seat. "You need to know that this is serious. The sheriff is going to talk to you again, so stay home. Say 'yes sir' and 'no sir.' Don't be a smartass."

Cayden's mouth quivered almost in a smile. "Are you and Mr. Nightingale staying 'til they find the real killer?"

Garrick let go of his arm. "Yep. We'll be here."

The boy grinned and jumped out of the truck.

GARRICK SAT IN THE TRUCK AND SURVEYED THE TRUCKS AND two cars occupying spaces in the parking lot at Sarah's Vacation and Eats.

Couldn't take the boy in there. Someday though, that young man would come back and the old codgers would rue the day they'd been so prejudiced. Hell, Garrick caught himself before he climbed too far on his inner soapbox; this was murder—for all he knew, Audie Louise Shepherd had done the killing.

He'd noticed the missed call from Nightingale. He figured he had two things to do before calling Nightingale: eat breakfast and see the sheriff. But there was no hurry. The smell of sausage and bacon and coffee made his mouth water. Nightingale had been really moody lately, but he didn't like people noting his dispositions. So Garrick listened to his own growling stomach and headed inside. If he was on death row, he'd probably want a good breakfast before dying. His tasks could wait.

White men occupied five tables in the back corner. He knew one person, Dr. Elliott, from the visit earlier.

The doctor waved but didn't invite him to join him.

Garrick was not surprised. He swung one leg over a stool at the front counter. To the waitress, he said, "I don't need a menu. I want sausage and gravy, scrambled eggs, and coffee. And if Miss Sarah is here I'd like to say hello."

Garrick had met the proprietor at another time he had been in the restaurant. He admired her and wanted to know her better, but she also might be a source of information to out-of-towners.

In a few minutes, Sarah Valentine, a voluptuous blonde at least thirty years younger than him, sashayed out. "Good to see you again."

"I came back for your biscuits and gravy, and I've got a serious question."

Sarah's dark eyebrows rose, and she put one hand on her hip. She leaned in, matching Garrick's teasing voice in a whisper. "What question would that be?"

Garrick pulled back a bit, not enamored with the air in his ear. "How come you named this Sarah's Vacation? You're working —this is no vacation."

She looked at him and giggled, deep dimples in her cheeks. "I am having the time of my life, darling. This is a vacation to me. Sometime I'll tell you the whole story, but that's the truth." She patted him on the back and let her hand drift all the way to his waist before moving to the table behind him, pouring coffee and leaning close to get orders as she went.

Dr. Elliott stopped and shook hands as Garrick's food arrived. The vet mentioned the puppy. Garrick assured him that the puppy would soon have a permanent home.

Garrick left a ten-dollar bill under his plate but paid with a credit card. He planned on coming back.

Sated with protein and cholesterol, he headed to the sheriff's office committed to telling him the truth because he was tired of tip-toeing around it and having to be so careful about what he said.

Deputy Howard was not there, but a girl deputy directed him to the sheriff's office.

"Coffee?" she asked.

The sheriff nodded and turned to Garrick but didn't ask him to sit down.

"What brings you here so early?" The sheriff's squint looked more suspicious than surprised.

After the coffee arrived, Garrick quietly pushed the door to and sat across from the sheriff on the only other chair in the room.

The sheriff motioned toward the door with a flip of his hand. "Gets stuffy in here with it closed."

"Maybe so, but it's about to get downright warm." Garrick pulled a crumpled piece of paper out of his shirt pocket and handed it to the sheriff. The man's face turned a bright, angry red.

"What kind of smart-assed move is this? Why are you showing me a cleaning ticket?"

"You asked about a copy of the will. You accused us of tampering with evidence. Nightingale thought I found something, which I didn't. To set the record straight, we have all the authority we need. We're Rangers, and Nightingale is working for the governor. You want to keep threatening me or do you want to talk like grown men?"

The sheriff leaned in closer on the worn desk. "You're gonna give me some line of bullshit—right?"

"Damn, man. I'm trying to help. I guess you're saying there was a will. Did you find a paper copy?" Garrick asked.

"No. But why would she have a copy on the machine and not have it printed and signed to make it legal?"

"Maybe she didn't plan on dying so soon," Garrick said.

Obviously, the sheriff had begun speculating and surmising based on not much more than hunches like a lot of cops Garrick had known over the years. "How you conclude that we're the reason you can't find something you *expect* to be sitting, already printed, on her desk is beyond me."

"You two were there before us, smart-ass. We looked all over the house."

"It's the only place you looked that *we* had access to, which puts us in your spotlight. Did she own anything else of significant value?"

"Just the machinery on the ranch," Patterson said. He'd cooled down and still seemed to be going over facts in a scenario that only he saw. "There's a hell of a lot of it on a spread that size. I figure this makes several people possible shooters. If they knew about this, the kid or his mother could have killed her for the ranch."

"I see a whole passel of prospects, including her sister, her nephew, and the hired hand," Garrick said. He walked to the door.

"Bring Nightingale by here when he decides to be in an accommodating mood. I got something to tell him." Patterson looked pleased.

OUTSIDE THE JAIL, GARRICK CALLED NIGHTINGALE, AND just as he was about to leave a message, Nightingale answered.

Prepared to give a smart greeting, Garrick hesitated when he noted the strange tone in Nightingale's voice. "Is that you? Are you ailing?"

A long pause filled the phone with the smacking of a dry mouth trying to gain moisture. "I had visitors last night."

"What kind? You hurt?"

"I'm gonna take a hot shower. Get me some of that arnica that you say is so good for bruises—about a gallon should do it. I'm in the cabin with the green door, not a room. I'll leave the door open for you."

Nightingale heard Garrick's hello and said, "I'm in the bedroom." He'd swallowed three ibuprofen with coffee earlier but still hurt all over. "Be there in a minute."

He'd waited on bending to get on shoes or boots. Faced with the final decision, he chose the tennis shoes. Deciding the soles of his feet didn't hurt, he had maneuvered his right foot into the shoe when he heard Garrick.

"God almighty. How many were there?" Starched and creased, Garrick stood in the doorway with a brown paper sack in his hand. "We better get you to a doctor."

"Maybe later. May need my ribs taped, but I want that stuff to smear on first."

"So how many were there?"

"Probably three. Two guys held my arms, and I got a good hit in on the one in front of me before he came at me. I guess that kick got me these busted ribs."

"Reckon you got a good enough lick on any of them that they'll show up hurt today?"

"I doubt it. They surprised me." Nightingale grimaced and

stood, lurching to the mirror at the dresser where he began patting the cream around his purpled eye. Then he smeared it on his torso, flinching at his own touch. "This shiner is gonna show."

"Yeah, no need to try and hide it. The sheriff wanted you to come by. Might be a good time to ask him about vigilantes in the neighborhood." Garrick took the tube of cream from Nightingale and continued to talk. "I figure you didn't see any faces."

Nightingale moved away. "Careful, that hurts. No, they had on white hoods."

"No imagination," Garrick said.

"They told me to go home. Called me 'hombre.'"

"Probably a good idea to get out and let people see what some of their friends and neighbors can do."

Nightingale buttoned his shirt; even his fingers hurt as he pulled the buttons through. "I guess it might be interesting if anybody cares. There's been a murder—two, in my books—and I don't know if anybody cares."

"Don't get cynical—that's my job," Garrick said. "I better drive. You're moving like you're eighty-nine years old."

Movement helped loosen the soreness, but Nightingale couldn't seem to pull himself up straight. Lord, he was slow. Maybe the vet could prescribe something for the pain.

Garrick opened the truck door for him and had the engine revved and the A/C on when Nightingale pulled his foot into the passenger side.

Silas stood on the porch and watched, much like a child watching a circus. He kept squinting, leaning against the rail.

Nightingale spoke. "Tell your momma I had visitors wearing sheets last night."

Garrick backed the truck out before Silas could reply or question.

"You look pretty scary," Garrick said.

"I know. Wish I could see his momma when he tells her what I said."

Garrick drove to the jail. "I told the sheriff that we didn't take anything from the murder scene. Showed him my cleaning receipt, how it stuck out of my pocket."

Nightingale remembered his accusations, his acid words. "Why didn't you say that when I asked?"

The older man shook his head. "You're supposed to know me and not have to ask."

"What'd he say?"

"Wasn't happy about it, but he just has to be pissed. We're the law, too, even though he doesn't like it. I think he chalked it up to a doddering old fool's interference."

"I think he's smarter than you give him credit for. He knows that people throw around all sorts of misinformation in a case like this. What about the boy?"

Garrick filled him in on Cayden's visit. "The kid is a smart-assed teenager with a chip on his shoulder."

Nightingale shook his head and blew out a frustrated breath. "He's gonna keep screwing around and mess up big time."

"You need to get over this. You can't save him without his help. This isn't the boy that got shot twenty years ago."

"I don't want to talk about him. Quit the arm-chair psychiatry."

Garrick said no more, but he couldn't help replaying the scene as he was sure Nightingale had done in the last few days. He and Nightingale had gone to a house on the outskirts of Lubbock. Rumors had it that LSD had been brought in. That was the drug of choice back then. Looking back, Garrick didn't know what happened, but a sixteen-year-old boy had come around a corner out of the kitchen with a gun in his hand. Nightingale shot to protect Garrick. The gun the boy carried was not loaded. The family had a stash of marijuana.

At that time, Nightingale had been a Ranger for two weeks. He continued to come to the office, but he looked like a ghost. There was no counseling, just guys talking about bad luck, and telling him to try to forget about it. For several years afterward, Garrick thought Nightingale was too cautious to be a good Ranger. But over the years since, he had proven to be one of the best men they had for investigations of murder, felony, theft, and kidnapping.

When they arrived at the jail, Garrick went in. Nightingale stayed in the truck, trying to forget his various pains and hoping for some flash of inspiration that might help him find the men who had beaten him. His eyes were closed when he heard the door to the truck open.

The sheriff had already left the office. "The girl said he'd gone to the Dearborn place," Garrick said. "She offered to call and find him. I told her to not bother. She probably called anyway."

"Let's go up there and see if he's found anything he'll share. I need to walk out some of this soreness." He looked sideways at Garrick. "And we can see what he says about guys in white hoods."

The gates were open at the ranch, so Garrick drove up as close to the house as feasible.

"You're a good nursemaid," Nightingale said, "but I'll walk at my own pace. Slow and sure."

Faulkner's truck and the sheriff's car were the only vehicles in sight.

The sheriff came out of the house, wiping sweat off his brow. He looked at Garrick and then Nightingale, who was coming up behind the older man.

Patterson did a double take, taking a few steps closer to see the damage. "What the hell happened to you?"

His surprise seemed genuine.

"I had visitors last night. Some guys in white hoods told me to go home and emphasized their feelings with their fists."

"I hate that. You shoulda called me." The sheriff's face blossomed redder. He was a head shorter than Nightingale and stood rocking back and forth in his space, shifting his eyes from Nightingale to Garrick and finally settling on Nightingale. "Silas told me that you'd been in Posey's car. Find anything?"

Nightingale's neck stiffened. Raw and aching all over, he resented the easy dismissal of the attack on him by the sheriff.

"I didn't know Posey's case was a criminal investigation." The pain in his ribs took away his breath, so he waited a second. "Is that why someone went through my belongings at the B and B?"

"You're probably paranoid. Anything taken?" The sheriff looked toward the horizon.

Nightingale didn't grace him with an answer. "Have you found out anything about the guys from the environmental group?"

"They're in an RV park outside of Longview." The sheriff folded his arms and stepped into the shade. "So, you rifled through the car."

Enough. The silence ballooned into the surrounding air. Nightingale felt Garrick's hand on his shoulder when his fury took him forward. "Yeah, and I also got my ass whipped by three or four men, who I'd wager you know. I'll bet they're some of the fine citizens of Beulah." Anger was a balm to Nightingale's pain as he inched closer to the sheriff.

The sheriff stepped back. "You know as well as me that I can't find out who decided to beat on you unless you want to file papers and have me leave this investigation to see if I can find out whose fist might match your wounds. They may be citizens of Beulah, but I don't know. I've got a full plate, so suck it up. You're still a Ranger and he"—here he pointed to Garrick—"says he is."

Patterson stood taller and wiped sweat off his forehead. In a milder tone, he said, "Why don't you go talk to those ELF guys and let me know what you find out. I can let you know details about Mrs. Dearborn later. Meet me at my office this evening."

Basically, Nightingale agreed with the sheriff, but he felt the need to strike out at someone. But this was way too convenient. The sheriff was throwing them a bone after his outburst.

Garrick touched Nightingale's arm and nodded his head toward the truck. "Sounds sensible to me. We been trying to help and didn't know how."

"Five o'clock at your office," Nightingale said.

The sheriff turned away and grunted what could have been yes or no.

When they were in the truck, headed toward Longview, Nightingale spoke. "That's the first time I've been disgusted with the law. What's wrong with this picture?"

"He wanted to get rid of us," Garrick said. "You wanted to talk to those boys anyway. And if you didn't, I did."

Nightingale pulled his hat over his eyes. "Wake me when we get there."

Garrick didn't need to wake him. A cattle guard was the welcome mat to the RV Park. The wheels bumping over the metal grid brought him up, cursing and drawing in breath to fight the pain.

Garrick slowed the vehicle, and they looked around. Nightingale stuck his head out the window at the first person they saw and asked for Jason Keel, the name the sheriff had given him. They drove a short distance and pulled in beside a jeep with Montana plates. Nightingale pulled out his badge and knocked on the door under an awning that provided some shade to the RV. A young man opened the door.

Nightingale had always had better luck with honey than vinegar, so after introducing himself and Garrick, he said, "We heard you visited Constance Dearborn. We wondered who you were and what you were doing there."

The young man had a dark beard and black hair.

Nightingale guessed the beard was there to make him look older.

"We work for an environmental group. We went out to talk to Mrs. Dearborn a few days ago. Harry got beat-up by some man named Faulkner. Looks like the guy got you, too. Come here, Harry." A blond, skinny guy shuffled from the darkness.

Both men squinted despite the shade. Harry moved like a man twice his age and sported an eye with the shades of purple and yellow from a recent battle. He stepped forward. "I didn't file any charges, but he damned near killed me. Where were you guys when I needed you?"

"You were trespassing," Nightingale said. "You're lucky he didn't shoot you. Did Mrs. Dearborn or Faulkner ask you to come up here?"

"No. And why should we tell you if they did?"

Nightingale waited a minute. "There's been a murder at the Dearborn place. We're questioning anyone who has been around in the last few days."

Keel's eyes grew big; he stepped toward Nightingale. "We're trying to help you people before you destroy the earth. Why would we kill anyone?"

"Right." Nightingale didn't budge. He felt Garrick move closer. "Let's not get into a discussion of who's saving who," Nightingale said. "Can you account for where you've been in the last few days?"

"We've got people who saw us here every day since Harry got beat up."

"You carry any weapons?" Garrick asked.

The two men looked at each other and laughed.

"We probably need to," Jason said. "That crazy bastard with Mrs. Dearborn scared the shit out of us. Is he who got killed?"

"How long you been here? And when did you plant the explosives?" Nightingale asked.

The two men exchanged a look that gave Nightingale his answer.

"I don't know what you're talking about, explosives. We've been here about a week." Jason Keel's short temper kept running awry of his declaration for nonviolence. "What does it matter?"

"Just wondered," Nightingale said. "Don't plan on leaving 'til you check with the sheriff in Beulah."

"The hell you say." Keel turned his back and pushed Harry to the side as he shoved his way into the RV.

Nightingale nodded to Garrick, who had written the license plate numbers of the men's truck and trailer in a pocket notebook. On their way out of the little enclave, they saw a woman walking from one of the RVs to a car.

Garrick stopped the truck. "I'll see what she knows." He knocked on the woman's car window as she buckled her seatbelt.

She didn't look amused.

"Ma'am, I'm a Texas Ranger. My partner and I wondered if you know the two young men, Jason and Harry, who live near the back of this group?"

"No, are they in trouble? We need to get them out if they're trouble-makers."

"No, ma'am, we just wondered if they've been out in the last few days. Do you all notice each other's comings and goings?"

"They stay to themselves. Went out a few times, I'm guessing for groceries."

"Thank you, kindly. No need to worry."

Garrick returned to the truck. "One of us needs to check with the feds about these boys and maybe come back and see if anyone else noticed them—especially Thursday morning. I think that look was our answer about the explosives. Guess we'll have to talk to them again."

"Yeah, but right now, I want to find out why the sheriff wanted to get rid of us," Nightingale said.

Garrick turned the truck in the direction of Beulah. They were already late.

32

"Guess I didn't have to worry." Nightingale leaned closer to the windshield, staring at the lone car in the parking lot. The sheriff was not there.

"Don't know where he is or when he'll get back," the deputy had told Garrick.

"It's after five," Nightingale said. "The doc closes at six. We can get the pup and then go eat."

"You sure you want to leave him alone in that cottage?"

"Yeah. After talking to the sheriff and Silas seeing us, I don't think anybody will come back. Bandit will be okay. Doc said he's already crate-trained. If you're worried, we can pick up food and come back to the cottage and stay with him."

Garrick loved women and food, and Nightingale didn't know which came first. He wasn't surprised at the answer.

"We can go over to Sarah's Vacation. Breakfast was fine, so I'm sure the supper will be good."

"I accept. Your treat."

Garrick turned the truck into the vet's driveway.

Nightingale swung his long legs out and immediately stopped. Pain cut through his side where a fist had landed. He ground his teeth, popped three pills with a drink of water, and shook his head.

"I'm going in with you," Garrick said, ignoring the groans of his partner. "I've got a question for the doc."

Doctor Elliott's wife had a typed sheet of instructions for new pet owners.

Nightingale stood back, moving slowly because of his pain.

The vet stood aside while his wife read cautions and suggestions. Then he walked out to the truck with the kennel. Garrick had a bag of dog food and treats.

Nightingale walked slowly, grimacing sometimes when the puppy jerked on the leash.

They stood under the large oak tree, watching the happy pup as he sniffed and peed and pulled against the leash.

"I'll bring him back for boarding in a few days."

"You still working on getting the Dearborn land for the governor?" The vet didn't hide his stare at Nightingale's moves. He had told Elliott about the vigilantes and mentioned pain meds.

"Yes." Nightingale started to scratch Bandit's ears but stopped when pain hit his ribs again.

Garrick waved one hand to the field surrounding the clinic. "Did you see Cayden Shepherd cross your field on Thursday morning?"

The doctor had watched Garrick's talk with his wife and didn't seem comfortable with the meandering lawman. "My wife might have. He was regular in his visits to Constance. Never bothered the animals in the field like some of the boys, so after he trekked across a few times, I forgot about him."

"How do you feel about the water plan?" Nightingale asked.

"I don't talk politics with my neighbors or anybody except my wife." He looked around like he thought someone might be listening behind a shrub. "Whatever I say has to be between us."

He stared at Nightingale and then Garrick, eyebrows raised in question.

"No problem being mum on my part," Nightingale said.

Garrick nodded.

"People up here are conservative and honest. They'll vote for the man or woman who is honest with them before they'll vote for a crook. They don't think the governor was honest when she campaigned up here. She said nobody would lose land. People may not love the Dearborn family, but the governor is taking their land. That's probably why you got beat on last night. People up here don't like being used."

"You haven't answered my question."

"Let's put it this way. I voted for the governor the first time, but I don't know what a few years will bring."

"Do you have ideas about who might have killed Mrs. Dearborn?"

"I thought about Faulkner, or Silas, but Silas is too wimpy. Might have been an accident."

The doctor's wife stuck her head out and said supper was ready.

"I'll call you in some pain meds if you want," Dr. Elliott said.

"I'll stick with the Ibuprofen and soak in the tub."

"Call if you change your mind." He smiled, gave them a small salute, and started toward his house.

"Supper sounds good," Garrick said.

They returned to the cottage, where Garrick led the puppy around the fenced back yard. Garrick fussed and grinned all in the same breath.

After noting that his eye was less swollen, Nightingale coaxed the pup into the kennel, turned on all the lights, and locked the door.

At the restaurant, Garrick asked for Sarah. She had gone home for the evening.

Nightingale squinted at a familiar figure at one of the back tables. "We need to sit closer to the back," he told the waiter.

As they weaved their way through the tables, McGowan stood and offered his outstretched hand. "Nightingale, what happened to you?"

"Had visitors. And why are you here, Roy?"

McGowan didn't answer. He scooted chairs, dragged his table, and finally, with a nod to the waiter, they settled at a larger space, menus in front of them. McGowan finished his beer and ordered a beer for his friends. He called for fried green tomatoes, but as soon as the waiter was out of sight, an uneasy silence settled over the table.

Nightingale had no interest in food. Something inside had knotted up. All of the goodwill of the doctor and getting on with the job drained right out under McGowan's ostrich boots. Nightingale stared at the beer in his mug. Beside him, Garrick took a long, slow drink like he might be on the verge of starvation.

"I didn't expect to see you here," Nightingale said.

"I thought I'd come up and see what was happening," McGowan said. He cleared his throat and muttered about allergies. "Look, Oz, I didn't know how things were going, and I thought I could scare the sheriff into moving things along. I can't believe somebody attacked you."

"I don't want your help." Maybe this was a run of bad luck, but he knew better. Nightingale didn't like McGowan's condescending tone, nor that he was obviously checking on progress of the case.

"I know that. Don't get touchy." McGowan finished his beer and called for the wine list. The waiter didn't see McGowan immediately, and when he did, tension filled the air around the table. After uncorking the wine, he poured a sample for McGowan.

Nightingale could no longer contain his aggravation. "When did you decide to come up here, Roy?"

"I needed to get out of Austin." McGowan tasted the wine before asking for glasses for each of them. "I like my job, but politics is high pressure." A gallows laugh followed the words.

"Driving back tonight?" Garrick asked.

"There's a house about three blocks from the B and B. I rented the whole darn thing for a week." His words slurred a bit.

Nightingale wondered if he'd been drinking before coming to the restaurant.

"My son's coming up here in a few days. We're going fishing. Need to spend some time with the boy. His momma is not too fond of me right now."

McGowan had married a Houston debutante after he'd been in politics for a couple of years. At the time, a Ranger in Austin who knew both of them told Nightingale he'd give the marriage two years. Some of Roy's fights with his wife were legendary since they usually took place in the best Austin restaurants. McGowan's tempestuous marriage had not improved, but the couple had a son, so apparently, the union had continued. Nightingale didn't like nosing into McGowan's personal life. He figured Roy McGowan did not return the courtesy.

Food was delivered to the table, and McGowan brought up tales of their high school years.

"Nightingale practically was my guardian after that little history class flare-up. Did you ever find out if you had some black ancestors?"

"My great-grandmother had some black relatives."

"You weren't so proud of it then," McGowan said.

Nightingale felt the heat of a blush run up his neck as he remembered taunts of the children and McGowan standing up for him. "Kids can be mean. Now people are searching for ancestors. Then, it was a different story."

The conversation lulled again. Garrick picked it up. "Did you ever hear any more about Posey's autopsy?"

"Just what I told Oswald. It was all I could do to keep it low-key. You just don't want it publicized that the governor's pick to put together the land deal is a drug addict."

"You said it was insulin and you weren't sure of the drugs," Nightingale said. He wondered about McGowan's choice of facts. Did he truly not remember, or was Posey a convenient scapegoat?

"I've dealt with the press, and they always choose the worst possibility," McGowan said. "Even if it's not true. It would stink, mark my words. So, what's your next move, Nightingale?"

"I'm finding the killer of Constance Dearborn."

McGowan cut his gaze toward Nightingale and carefully placed his wine glass next to his plate. "I thought the sheriff was doing that. What about your agreement with the governor?"

Nightingale swirled the wine in the glass, almost tipping the liquid out.

He owed the people in Broken Rock, even if the promise was to himself. They needed water.

He took a deep breath and his head cleared. He turned on McGowan, almost growling, holding the glass still. "You mean you don't want me to do what I've been trained to do?" He leaned closer. "You'd deny water to the people of Broken Rock if I don't follow through on this cockamamie sale. We don't even know who may wind up with the Dearborn land."

McGowan narrowed his eyes at Nightingale. "Forget the Dearborn spread. Forget the woman who died. Find out who owns land to the east and west. Let the sheriff do his job." McGowan reddened, delivering his own growl. "We need that deal finalized. Somebody will sell. They're human; they need money. When something this important is hanging in the balance, the needs of the majority outweigh the desire of the deceased. I don't want you acting like a hero. The woman probably got shot accidentally by a hunter."

Nightingale drank a sip of wine. "A woman has been murdered, Roy. A civilized society owes her a search for her killer. That's the way I was trained, and in the past, that's one thing you wanted, honesty and a search for the truth. That's what I want."

Garrick glanced at both men, his bushy eyebrows raised. "You boys need to eat and talk about this later. People are staring."

Nightingale looked around. "There's only one couple here."

Garrick pointed his fork to the door where the wait staff hurried in and out. "Those people can hear, and they love to gossip."

Nightingale's last bite of steak hung in his throat. He swigged the wine dregs.

Garrick's knife scraped his plate as he sliced another morsel off his T-bone.

Nightingale put his napkin beside his plate and stood. "I'm leaving." He looked at Garrick. "You riding with me?"

Garrick nodded and pulled out his wallet.

McGowan shook his head. "I got it." He glanced up, knife and fork still in hand like someone out of *The Godfather*. "This is for your own good, Oz. Garrick, talk some sense into the man."

33

Nightingale barged out of the restaurant, gritting his teeth with each step. When the muggy night air hit him, he braced both hands on the sides of the truck bed and stared at the star-sprinkled sky. Behind him, he heard footsteps on gravel. "You weren't a bit of help."

"What'd you want me to do, tell him we're the law—the rest of the state be damned?" Garrick sounded pissed.

"For once, I want you to stick up for me." Nightingale thought anger at Garrick might be a permanent way of life. "I should be finding a killer."

"We need to talk." Garrick's voice was low in the middle of his own venom.

"I'm going back to the B and B." Nightingale felt the pinch of pain in his ribs and slowed his moves. Some friend McGowan was—didn't care if he got beat or kissed. Then he was glad he hadn't said anything.

"You sound like a kid having a tantrum," Garrick said.

They exchanged a glance, sheepish, struggling under the weight of years of knowing each other. Nightingale had embarrassed both of them.

"Don't you say one God-damned word about me and that dog," Nightingale said.

Garrick shook his head and climbed into the driver's seat.

At the B and B, Nightingale hobbled into the cottage and brought the puppy outside.

A honeysuckle vine grew on one side of the cottage, and the fragrance filled the night air.

Garrick had stepped off the small porch. The puppy went over to him and smelled his boots. "You want me to walk him?"

Nightingale handed the leash to Garrick, a weak apology but as close as he could get. He stood behind the rocking chair at the end of the porch. His hands fidgeted, closing back and forth over the wooden slats.

Garrick walked off the side of the porch into the back yard under a big oak tree. A wooden fence draped in tiny LED twinkle lights surrounded the yard. Garrick unclipped the leash and urged the pup to go pee. The lights shone enough for the men to keep their eyes on the puppy while they talked about other things.

"First time I've wanted a smoke in a while," Nightingale said.

"Do you know how mad you got back there?" Garrick's voice came at him out of the shadows.

Nightingale gripped the chair back so hard his fingers hurt. "I've got this. Don't piss in my boots."

"You may think you've got control, but with your anger that close to the surface, you don't need to be looking for a killer or a suspect.

"I don't need a shrink."

"What you need is time," Garrick said.

"What are you trying to say?"

Garrick's silhouette stood at the tree, unmoved.

Nightingale rubbed his temples, trying to clear his thoughts. A wash of rage and sadness fell over him. He couldn't nail down what he thought or felt for certain. He knotted his fist. "I quit a job I love; I want a woman who doesn't love me; I can't help my friends and family like I want to. So, you shot that man who killed your wife. If I knew who beat on me, I feel like I could shoot them and never regret it."

"Killing that man didn't help. I got depressed. Drank enough to sink a ship, and a year later I woke up and said, 'No more.'" Garrick walked into the light, the puppy in his arms.

"These murders seem unimportant to everyone except us. Murdered people deserve justice," Nightingale said.

"You've always said that." Garrick smiled and looked up to the sky. "Maybe you've been too cool all these years."

"That's a crock. You're going to your hotel. Tomorrow I'm checking who owns land on the west and east side of the Dearborn acres. The governor will have to settle for what she can get."

After Garrick left, Nightingale settled in the recliner with the puppy asleep next to him. He tried to view the anger eating at him as a force separate from him. Anger was not an emotion he felt accustomed to.

He was angry because Josephine Holly didn't want to marry him. He felt humiliated, rejected. That had never happened. His heart hurt. Even more than that, he was angry at himself for retiring from a job he loved.

Now he'd been attacked for simply living and breathing. In his job, he'd been shot, strangled, and knifed, usually by someone who wanted to save his own skin. That motive he understood.

But in this case, he saw other motives. And standing back, separating himself from the anger, he knew he had let his guard down. He'd been caught by surprise, so his pride hurt, too. He was beaten to get him away from the murder investigation or away from the water deal, or because of his darker skin, or all of the above. But basically, he'd let his guard down, and now he was living with the results.

His aching muscles fought for attention, shifting it away from finding a murderer to considering how many pills he should swallow to relieve his pain.

34

Getting ready for bed, Nightingale turned down the covers. He and Garrick had not talked in philosophical or medical words, but Garrick, in his usual bluntness, made Nightingale think, and he needed to slow down and go over what was happening to him.

"Nancy used to chastise me by telling me men could do with some examination of their souls," Garrick had said.

Nightingale didn't want examination. And yet, in his years with the Rangers, the methods of therapy for officers involved with violence had gained his respect. He regretted quitting the Rangers. He would tell the governor that and tell her he wanted his job back. Yet another hold she had on him. Damn, he shook his head.

The ache for revenge was the worst part. Other people had it —not him. He had never encountered such vitriol in his thinking. This was what he saw in bad cops, men who tasered or used their weapon before they thought. Granted, sometimes that was necessary, but this had come from an attack he couldn't understand.

Trouble was, he had work to do. Staying busy usually saved him from bad situations.

He patted the pup's head, scratched his ears, coaxed him into the kennel, and climbed into bed.

The drive back had mellowed him somewhat. He narrowed his problems to simple human pride, as with Josephine's refusal to marry. Except for the death of his parents, his life had been good. And now everything he touched seemed tainted with bad luck.

This emotion that he thought was love caused more hours awake at night than asleep. Whiskey didn't help, just added to the anger and to the regret that he'd waited too long to find a woman for his life. But he hadn't cried; maybe he just wanted his way.

He had avoided wine until the meal with McGowan. Finally, he got up and went to the window, wondering about a destitute ghost town named Broken Rock.

The next morning, he stayed in bed after the alarm rang. This amount of reflection led to hysterics and crying jags in women. To hell with that. On the other hand, he felt that he'd sorted out part of his problems.

He threw the cover aside and reached for the Tylenol and water. Moving slower, he put the pup on a leash and took him outside.

He didn't call Garrick. They'd settled the night before on what to do.

He drove to the vet to leave the dog and got directions to Hank Faulkner's place, where he would find out if any of the ranches around the Dearborn property might consider selling to the state.

At breakfast at Whataburger, his mind went back to Garrick. The old Ranger had lived in his own version of hell during the years it took him to get over Nancy's death. Nightingale pushed the darkness to one side and started toward Faulkner's farm.

Narrow roads and no signage made him wonder about his directions. His truck compass showed him moving northeast, but the cloud cover confused him. Trees canopied every small road, wrapping him in a dense silence. Moisture hung in the air and didn't fall.

In the quiet, his thoughts jumped to the night his mother died. He didn't need that kind of distraction. Any apparition was his mind's feeble try at coping with his heartache. But, and here he almost stopped the truck in his realization, his mother had been precious to him and marriage already seemed like a dream he had missed. Maybe he didn't love Josephine as much as he loved the idea of marriage.

So he pushed his thoughts to the man he was visiting. As he topped a small rise, he saw the Faulkner house. It occurred to him that he and Hank Faulkner had little in common. He knew the former soldier lived with a sister. Usually, he had the background and family situation memorized when he talked to anyone who might be a suspect. In this instance, he'd not had time or resources to examine the man's life—his own problems had interfered. And, as he reminded himself, he was not investigating a killing. He was trying to find owners of land around Mrs. Dearborn's property.

He decided he could do both and Roy McGowan would never be wiser. He'd give information to Garrick to pass on to the sheriff for the investigation. Hopefully, the man would do the right thing.

When he stopped the truck, he glanced at his watch. He hoped he wasn't too early. The time was 8:30, and sunshine peeked over the roof of the Faulkner house, which sat prim and proper like something out of an English novel.

Aged red brick, a cedar shake roof, and ivy around one shutter reminded him of his cousins in Obsidian, though their house did not have the fairytale look of this one. A lush grape arbor occupied one side of the yard. Poppies, bachelor buttons, begonias, and roses nodded in profusion around the edges of the house and bedded around two large oak trees.

Nightingale stood by the truck for a moment, smelling honeysuckle, wondering if this house reflected anything of Faulkner, or only his sister. Nothing stirred as he took his time walking up the gravel drive onto a path that wound to the small front stoop.

He knocked on the door, waited, and knocked again. Hank Faulkner answered the door. A ragged towel draped over one hand. The other hand was covered in oily dirt, and he swapped the towel back and forth, all the while scrubbing on the grime. The noxious odor of turpentine hit Nightingale, and he stepped back, assessing Faulkner's grease-covered hands in the pristine surroundings.

"You sure pick weird times to show up," Faulkner said. "I thought Sue Nell would answer the door. That black eye shows you're not welcome. What're you here for?"

Nightingale took his hat off. He didn't bother to smile. "You're not subtle, are you?"

"Sorry, I guess it's my drugs kicking in. Sometimes I remember my manners, and sometimes I just don't give a damn. It's kind of freeing to say what you think."

Nightingale enviously considered the concept. It would never work for him. "I need to talk to you about the land around the Dearborn farm."

They had walked into a tile foyer. A large dining room hosted a wall of windows directly in front of them. Beyond that, a line of trees marked the back yard.

"Why didn't you go to the county courthouse?"

"It was easier to come to you."

"That's true. You nosing around the courthouse would set the local wags to notifying the sheriff." Faulkner emitted a low chuckle. "He's not fond of you."

"I know."

"I guess we can sit in the living room. You go on in. I'm gonna wash the final layer of skin off, and I'll be in to see if I want to answer your questions."

Nightingale walked around the room, staring at the art. He didn't know a lot about paintings but noted an original of blue jays by Ralph McDonald and a print of a Texas flag by Trudy Sween.

"So, do you approve?" A woman's voice came at him from the hall doorway.

A chill ran up his back. He didn't usually miss it when people walked in behind him. He turned and looked at her, noticing bare feet.

For some reason he couldn't assess, he felt embarrassed. "I was only looking."

"I know, but people try to figure out too many things by looking at a person's art and the books they read." She walked to him, her hand out to shake, but not smiling. "I'm Sue Nell Faulkner, and you are?"

She stood almost six feet tall, with a head full of thick auburn hair that she had tamed into braids—one on each shoulder. She wore a gauzy drop-waist dress that had small dollops of mud and mulch stuck in a few places on the skirt.

When he said his name, she stepped back, and the cool air of welcome became icy. "My brother told me about you. He's suffered enough for this country. He didn't kill Constance Dearborn. I hope you're not here to ask about that."

"No, ma'am." Nightingale admired her fierce defense. At the same time, he wanted Faulkner to return. Things didn't seem conducive to a casual conversation with hostility from both brother and sister. At the sound of footsteps behind him, he turned. "I just had a few other questions."

"So, I'm glad you've met my sister," Faulkner said. "Constance's death has us both in dark moods."

Nightingale sat on the couch.

Hank and Sue Nell pulled chairs closer to him. Sue Nell crossed her legs and settled back in her chair, giving all the signs of a participant in the conversation.

"Why did you want to know about land surrounding the Dearborn property?" Hank asked.

"I think the state has decided that they may have to take a different route to get the reservoir."

"They can't pay me enough money to sell." Sue Nell leaned forward, deep frown lines creasing her brow. "The very idea that someone who cares nothing about the land and doesn't even know my family wants to buy this land and cover it with water. . . ." She threw up her hands and started toward the kitchen. "I've got to have coffee."

Faulkner smiled at his sister's back as she huffed out of the room. "We don't have secrets. Sue Nell owns this land. Her property borders the Dearborn land."

"You own any of it?"

"Nope. My Daddy and I had a falling out. Sue nursed him through cancer and death while I was overseas. It's hers."

"I take it she won't sell?"

"Not from what I've heard. She's got a fortune in timber, and if she handles it right, it can be something for future years. It'd be criminal to cover all this good land and trees with water. None of those cities that need water understand, nor care, about what we have here."

Sue Nell returned with the coffee service rattling on a silver tray. She vehemently continued. "No, I will not sell, and I will give them hell if they think they can take this land. Have you told him what your Constance really thought?"

Faulkner sipped his coffee. "That was something she told me privately."

"I imagine the lawman needs to know."

The dynamic between the brother and sister confused Nightingale. Sue Nell's last comment had the prick of a mean-hearted tease. Something was wrong.

"Let's get out to the workshop. I'll show you where I got this grease," Faulkner said.

Sue Nell shook her head. "Leave your cups in the kitchen. I'm going to the garden."

Nightingale took a quick drink, grateful for the caffeine.

Faulkner led the way. They walked through the kitchen, which gave Nightingale time to admire the tiled floors in a kitchen that looked too neat to be usable.

"Sue Nell is a good cook, but she doesn't get inspired too much. A baloney sandwich is as good as a filet mignon to me."

Faulkner seemed to try to be comfortable, but Nightingale sensed the tension. He'd known men who'd been shot, or those who had killed someone, or men before a gun battle, scared, anticipating death, and almost welcoming the peace if they could get though the pain. They were raw, flinching at the slightest noise. That was the rawness that Faulkner carried.

The workshop sat back in the trees with barns and a fenced pasture on the side. Surrounding it all was the timber that Faulkner had mentioned. "So the timber—you can treat trees like a crop?" Nightingale asked.

"Sure. It's not a quick return. Not even in our lifetime, but you take care to cut only mature trees. I don't know anything beyond that."

Once inside the workshop, Faulkner went to a small fridge and pulled out a cola. "Need more caffeine," he said.

He offered one to Nightingale, who took it, popped the tab, and set the can to one side.

Work benches lined two sides of the shop. In the middle, an old Studebaker sat with its engine in various pieces around the shop.

Faulkner slammed a screwdriver and wrench into a tool box. "You know, I resent the hell out of you coming up here to pump information out of me. I know I'm a suspect in Constance's murder." He popped open the cola and took a long drink. Then he glared at Nightingale. His voice grew louder, and his face glowed a warm pink. "Why are you here? It's sure as hell not about timber." He leaned back against a work bench.

Nightingale looked over Faulkner's shoulder, let his gaze fall to his side and the floor, hoping he wasn't obvious in his search for a weapon should he need one. "I'll be honest with you."

Faulkner nodded, a slight smirk obvious in his disbelief.

"I wanted to find who shot Mrs. Dearborn. I was told that the sheriff would do that and I should stay out of it." He swallowed, forcing down the urge to say more, to defend his desire to find a killer. "I've been told to find whoever owns land on either side of Mrs. Dearborn's property."

Faulkner's slit-eyed glance slid to a rickety stadium chair. "Sit down," he said. "I'll sit in the car. You can pull your weapon out if you think I'll blow up. I'm sure you've heard of my temper, or was it PTSD?"

The car door creaked when he opened it. "Bent in a wreck," Faulkner said in the way of explanation. "Sue Nell thought I should tell you that Constance didn't really think she'd have to sell the land."

Nightingale eyed the tiny stadium chair, where he envisioned his butt dragging the ground, and didn't sit. He leaned against a work bench and faced Faulkner. "I never would've guessed that. She acted like a woman possessed. You believed her?"

"She only said it once, right after Posey and her exchanged words about what the judge did for the family, she said 'someone told her that there would be a way' to save the farm. She said Posey understood how friendship worked, like old-time politics."

"When did that happen? She was putting up a good fight for someone who thought she might be rescued."

Faulkner perched on the driver's seat of the old car, one arm cocked on top of the steering wheel. He had a faraway look since he'd calmed down. "It was right after you and Posey came by the house. I wasn't there, but she told me after meeting Posey she didn't think she'd have to sell. She made a lot of phone calls after that, but I don't know who she talked to. If I walked in, she'd end the conversation. She also worked on the governor's campaign behind the scenes. Gave some money. She had every right to be pissed."

"What about the television interview?" Nightingale didn't bother to hide his skepticism.

"We both worked on finding media contacts. She acted single-minded, just like on everything she did."

Nightingale shook his head and gave a small breath of confusion and irritation. "Did you ask her if Posey said something to make things change?"

Faulkner had the look of a defeated Ulysses; all the pomp and anger had gone out of him, leaving a shell. He took a deep breath, drained his cola, and stood.

He shook his head. "I felt like a fool." He looked at the concrete floor. "I'd never been in love before. Her husband worshipped her, and he told me if he ever died that I should take care of her. She was kind to me. She didn't encourage me loving her, but I needed kindness more than anything, so I didn't question her." His voice wavered, almost broke.

"Your sister didn't like her. Anything specific?"

"They were friends in school—pretty tight. I remember

Constance coming home with Sue Nell when they were little. Then Constance got too good for Sue Nell. Sue Nell has always been pretty straightforward. I think Constance got in a phase that her daddy encouraged, when he knew all the right people. I thought Constance was over that. Anyway, it seemed like Sue Nell knew one woman, and I knew another. Sue Nell couldn't imagine that I cared for her."

"Was she happy about Constance's death?"

Faulkner grimaced. "That's an awful thing to say."

Too late, Nightingale realized he'd stepped in it.

Faulkner's words quickened. "She never thought anything would come of my 'infatuation.'" He knocked his knuckles against the metal car frame. "I'm saying the woman I cared for still thought her father's friends would save her. Never thought that I'd save her." A strange half-smile crept onto Faulkner's face. "I don't like any of you people. I don't like thinking about this. You need to leave."

Nightingale didn't want a meltdown like the one Faulkner had inflicted on the ELF guy. Faulkner acted just this side of crazy. Nightingale had learned to never look dogs in the eye if he wanted to avoid confrontation, so he didn't look at the former soldier. He put his hat on and walked out of the workshop and down the drive, the thud of his heart loud in his ears. He wondered if he'd hear a shot over the beating of his heart if Faulkner fired one.

35

O nce he made it to his truck, Nightingale backed out of the drive and headed toward town. Out of sight of the house, he took a deep breath. The sky looked brighter, bluer, if that was possible. Nothing like the thought of a bullet in your back to level your perspective.

No trembling in his hands. Surprising. He'd just had the crap scared out of him.

His mind went back to Hank Faulkner's trauma—a trauma he didn't want to test. The man seemed just enough on the edge of reality that Nightingale worried about what he might do. He'd had little experience with people whose anger and rage came as a disability. On the other hand, the criminals he knew were downright mean, or full of hate, or looking for revenge. You knew where you stood with robbers and killers.

At the same time, the anger that took over Faulkner's body and mind reminded Nightingale of the anger that stalked him. In the last few days, when he lost control, it seemed to come from nowhere, but now he knew better. At one point, Nightingale had thought that the anger that took over Faulkner's body might point to guilt; now he didn't know.

From what Nightingale had experienced, men took death and battle and blood in different ways. In Faulkner's case, the trauma of battle, seeing the blood and guts of his fellow soldiers and friends, meant that now he jumped at small, unexpected noises. His eyes wandered to scenes that only he could see, and he became silent. He seemed to have lost a piece of himself.

In the new brightness of the sky, Nightingale drove slower as his own anger came into focus. At this moment, he wasn't frightened, nor had he experienced a savage killing. Instead, he was mad that small-minded men decided to beat him up in hopes of driving him away. Because his skin was a little too dark? Or he worked for the governor? Didn't really matter. He and Faulkner shared one thing—no control over a situation. And they were both men accustomed to having control and giving orders.

As he drove into town, he thought he might understand this awful anger, this feeling that no man had the right to attack him. When he was young, only once had he regretted his dark skin. He had not thought of such a thing again until now.

He laid his weapon on the seat next to him, not knowing why. He felt embarrassed that it took a look into Hank Faulkner's private hell in order to realize that his own hell was not so bad. He might never be able to accept what had happened to him, but he needed to quit wallowing in it.

Before he took account of where he was going, he realized he was near McGowan's rented cottage. He didn't have a number. All he could do was look for McGowan's truck. Then, around the edge of a porch, at a small gingerbread-laden bungalow, he saw the familiar black bumper and vanity license plates. He pulled in behind the truck.

With no particular plan in mind, he walked to the porch and knocked.

A curtain moved inside. McGowan jerked open the door, his

eyes bloodshot, his face marked with creases from a pillow. "What the hell are you doing here at this time of morning?"

Nightingale stepped back. "My God, Roy, go brush your teeth. You smell like something died in your mouth."

McGowan growled and turned into the house, leaving the door open.

The living room opened into an airy kitchen where a laptop sat on the kitchen table. The smell of coffee and toast reminded Nightingale that he was hungry.

McGowan had stepped into the bathroom and now returned, brushing his teeth. He went to the laptop, closed it with a snap, and walked over and spit in the kitchen sink. "I hope you're here with good news. Help yourself to the coffee." He walked back to the bathroom.

Nightingale had a cup in hand when McGowan returned.

"So?" McGowan said.

"I made a deal with the governor, not you. I don't like it, but I'll carry through. *So*"—he emphasized the word in just the hard-assed tone McGowan had used—"why are you here? This state won't dry up in the span of a few weeks."

McGowan continued to towel-dry his hair. "Contrary to what you think, this state is not waiting with baited breath for you to go back to being a Ranger."

"That has nothing to do with what I said."

"It has everything to do with it. You're pissed because you think I'm here to check up on you, and I told you to not be a Ranger. Well, the world doesn't revolve round you. I'm here to be away from my wife for a few days. The little darling has asked for a divorce." He held up his coffee cup in a toast.

Despite the half-jest of the words, McGowan's face was lined with worry. His bloodshot eyes testified to a lack of sleep. Nightingale didn't know what to say. As boys, they had shared secrets. They had laughed about their wet dreams.

McGowan had once told Nightingale, "All I want is a million dollars and a home like the one you grew up in." They had laughed because the two ideas were so different.

Nightingale didn't really know the adult McGowan. They had never talked about marriage or love, or loss of love. But in the warm toasty morning, with the smell of coffee in the room, the sunshine through the window, Nightingale thought his friend might be hurting more from the divorce than he admitted. Nightingale heard the air conditioner kick on, and the noise jarred him into speech.

"Roy, I'm sorry."

"Me, too. But life goes on. What did you find out?"

"Hank Faulkner's sister owns land to the north of the Dearborn ranch. I talked to her. She's saying she'll see the state in hell before she sells. Papers from Posey's car says the veterinarian, Dr. Elliott, owns land to the south. I haven't talked to him yet."

For a minute McGowan had a faraway look. "Sorry, what did you say?"

"I'm heading over to talk to the vet," Nightingale said. He wanted to say more, offer to listen, but he didn't feel comfortable in being so direct. Now he knew why McGowan was in such a foul mood at the restaurant. "I may swing back by after I talk to him. I'm here if you need me." He sounded juvenile and immediately regretted what he'd said, but McGowan caught the words and held like a drowning man.

"Thanks, Oz. People have told me that divorce hurts—guess I'm finding out." He lifted one hand in goodbye and reached for his cigarettes, then stared toward the back window.

～

As Nightingale drove to the vet's office, he thought of the people he'd known who had divorced. He often heard it hurt worse than losing someone to death. Reminded him of Lucinda Williams's words, "You do not know /What wars are going on /Down there, where the spirit meets the bone."

He parked to the side of the driveway at the vet's office. Mrs. Elliott sat at the desk. He went to her and explained that he needed to see the doctor about a private matter. She raised her eyebrows and straightened her back. Her answer came icy cold. "I'll tell him, but you'll have to wait."

"Yes, ma'am. I'll walk around outside a little." He smiled at her and gave a hissing cat a wide berth as he walked out. He went to the fence surrounding the property and looked toward the trees. At one place, the trees folded to form an arch, and he could imagine Cayden walking through when he went to Constance Dearborn's house. He'd follow the path tomorrow.

Soon, the dogs, cats, and people were gone. Nightingale heard his name called. Mrs. Elliott waited at the door. Her tone still held glaciers. She didn't return Nightingale's smile. She showed him to the vet's office, then made a point of sitting in the chair beside Nightingale while the doctor occupied a large desk.

"My wife said you had personal business to speak to me about," Dr. Elliott said. "I must tell you that I have no secrets from her."

The words, the doctor's hands closed on top of his desk, made Nightingale feel like a fool because the woman had misinterpreted his request. "Of course not, Doctor. Your wife is your partner. I just didn't want the whole office to hear." He glanced to the side at Mrs. Elliott. Her face seemed a little pink. "The state is interested in buying your land that borders the south of the Dearborn property."

The veterinarian smiled. "I'm going to make your job easier. Yes, I'm interested, but I don't want verbal games. I need a decent offer on paper with authorized signatures. Above market value, mind you." He stood. "I know that Mr. McGowan was here when the governor campaigned. He'd be a good one to sign a contract, don't you think?"

Nightingale also stood. "Yes, sir."

"I'll need details of how they plan to change the flow of the water. What will it do to the town? And tell whomever you talk to that I want cash. Is that agreeable with you, my dear?"

His wife nodded and smiled.

The doctor circled the desk, kissed his wife, and opened the door. He followed Nightingale out to his truck. "Frankly, I don't think the land is suitable for what the state needs. The ground is porous caliche, but maybe an engineer knows better."

He continued to smile, too much to suit Nightingale.

Nightingale shook the man's hand and walked to his truck, amazed at the ease of the answers and wondering why this seemed like a disaster.

36

Nightingale didn't return to McGowan's house. He didn't forget his friend; he simply couldn't face him. He rethought his conversation with the doctor. He had discovered two things but didn't feel inspired by either. First, the doctor's wife had more influence than he had thought. Second, the doctor —and his wife—would sell the land, but that seemed anticlimactic. The vet had to be imagining a ridiculous sum of money.

Nightingale wanted a better look at the map he'd found in Posey's bag. He felt like he'd hidden it more than he'd studied it. Even though it was from the tourist office, he needed to see a rough outline of the proposed reservoir in print. Somehow a map always helped him realign his sense of direction, and in this case, because he was not familiar with the land, he needed a concrete reference. He also wanted to hear what Garrick had come up with about the ELF boys.

His thoughts returned to McGowan. He had no good advice for his friend about marriage or women. The divorce accounted for some of McGowan's mean spirit in the last few days, and that gave Nightingale consolation.

Aching from the bruises as he swung the truck toward the B and B, he noticed Emma Jackson's car, a vehicle that probably belonged to the cleaning crew, and Silas's car. Apparently, the cottage next door was still vacant.

As he locked the truck, he glanced around again. Telling himself that the likelihood of a beating two days in one week was unlikely, he pulled his jacket back to have better access to his weapon. He almost hoped someone was watching him to see that he had not left town and a second attack would not be so easy.

Before he went inside, he stood with his back to the door, giving the surroundings another slow assessment. Only then did he feel safer.

Inside the cottage, he pulled out the map. No answers jumped out at him. Interstate 30 divided the more northern counties away from the green, piney woods. Lakes and tributaries speckled the northeast part of the state. He put the map on the floor and stared down. Hell, it was no wonder there was a fight. Lakes and rivers, islands of blue water dotted East Texas. West Texas had rivers—the Colorado, Pecos, and Rio Grande were a few—but they were drying up. On the map, the western half of the state remained brown or yellow. The stark difference took a minute to sink in. There had to be a better way. He searched for Broken Rock as his phone rang.

"Nightingale, this is Patterson. I'm at Isabel Shepherd's house. Came to talk to her son, the one who you assured me would be here. Well, he ain't. He's gone, and his weapon is gone with him."

Nightingale hesitated. Maybe the kid found Garrick again. "Weapon?"

"He had a rifle. One that Constance Dearborn gave him."

"Who told you this?"

"We can talk about that later. You know where the kid is?"

"No." Nightingale bit back his sarcasm. "I'm sure he'll come back home," he said. "I wanted to talk to you about the environmental guys. My partner and I talked to them. You gonna be in your office later?"

"Sure, come on by. I've got to get a warrant out on this kid." He sounded smug.

Nightingale didn't try to change his mind. He pushed the red button to end the call.

"Mr. Nightingale." The voice of Emma Jackson accompanied a knock on the door.

For just a moment, Nightingale was glad he didn't have the puppy in the cottage. He hurriedly picked up the map, folded it, and pushed it under a pillow. He opened the door but not the screen door. "What can I do for you?"

"May I come in?" She stood with her hands clasped in front of her like she might break into prayer at any moment.

"Of course." Nightingale stepped back. "I just talked to the sheriff, and I was on my way to see him."

Her gaze moved around the room as if assessing any damage and finally came back to him. "I guess he told you that my father's rifle that had been promised to Silas is nowhere to be found."

"No, the sheriff didn't mention a rifle that had been promised to Silas." For two rifles to be missing seemed beyond coincidence.

The woman went to the window and swiped at some imaginary dust. As she reached, he noticed the bracelet she wore. "I think it was a twenty-two. It was a small rifle. I asked the sheriff to look for it at my sister's house. Silas doesn't ask much but the gun had sentimental value to him."

"I don't think I'll be involved in that investigation anymore, but I'll remember the gun. That's a lovely bracelet. Is it new or an heirloom?"

Emma Jackson blushed and smiled. "Well, thank you. My father gave matching bracelets to Constance and me. He had our initials put in them. Her bracelet is probably missing, too. There's no telling how much is gone with that boy hanging around. I'll mention it to the sheriff."

Nightingale inched toward the door and put his hand on it.

"So, you'll be here another week, you think?" Emma peered over at the unused kitchen space as she moved. "I had someone call today for a room or cottage when they come to town."

"I'll be here a few more days," Nightingale said. He walked outside with her and locked the door behind them.

In the truck, he phoned Garrick. "Has anyone called you about Cayden?"

"Audie Louise called right after I talked to you. She was mad and worried, told me he lit out again."

"Apparently, there's a rifle missing, too." Nightingale filled Garrick in on what the sheriff had told him. When Nightingale got to the hotel, Garrick was already outside, standing by his truck. He held up the blanket in his truck bed, showing Cayden's absence, and shook his head before climbing into the vehicle with Nightingale.

"What's the plan?" Garrick asked.

"We've still got some daylight. Might as well check out the path behind the doc's office. If I was a kid, I might think I could hide in the woods. But first I'm going by the cottage for some more meds for my aches."

"Maybe Cayden's momma could give us some ideas about where he might go," Garrick said.

"We need to see her, but not right after Patterson. He operates by intimidation. We probably need to give her time to recuperate."

"Yeah, give her some space," Garrick said. "Audie Louise reacts and talks before she thinks. Maybe the daughter would be better."

"The sheriff needs somebody who looks guilty. Even if he doesn't arrest Cayden, he'll have questions about the rifle, and I don't want a scared kid with a gun facing Patterson. We need to find him. What'd you find out about the ELF guys?"

"According to the man I know, somebody from Texas called the main ELF office in L.A. and said this would be good publicity for the cause. Called about six weeks ago."

"Any way to find out who called?"

"No. I checked as far up as I have sources. Feeling was that they'd let this slide. The higher-ups figured too much politics involved. They back off a murder quick."

"Do they leave Keel and Kirkland to twist in the wind?"

"They're amateurs. They'll probably leave. This is getting too dangerous for them," Garrick said.

"But you know how to find them if they disappear?"

Garrick nodded. "They didn't kill anybody, but I've got names and numbers."

"Any ideas where Cayden went to?"

"No idea."

Nightingale parked the truck in front of the cottage, and they both went inside. After downing pills and cold water, he said, "I try to remember that he came to you when he left the first time. If I was a kid where would I run?"

"Did it ever cross your mind to run when you were his age?" Garrick asked.

"No. Never wanted to leave."

"He told me his grandmother worried him with questions."

When they went back outside, Silas Jackson waved and yelled from the porch of the B and B.

Nightingale and Garrick walked over to him as he hurried down the steps.

"Mother said tell you to mention the bracelet if you see the sheriff. He's not returning her calls."

"Will do," Nightingale said.

After they were back in the truck and a block down the street,

Nightingale explained the bracelet that Emma said was probably missing. He had to tell about his time under the bed, too.

Garrick smiled but didn't tease. Instead he seemed thoughtful. "We do what we have to do."

At the vet's office, Nightingale parked the truck out toward the road, away from the traffic of the doctor's patients. He went in and told Mrs. Elliott that they were following the trail to see what it looked like.

Back at the truck, he said, "Mrs. Elliott told me to be careful and close the gates."

The late afternoon sun bore down as they crossed the brown stubble of pasture. At the far edge of the field, the other side of the white wooden fence stood between them and the woods. Garrick stopped, pushed his hat back a little, and cocked his head, looking at the trees bowed so the top branches made a rounded doorway. "Funny, ain't it?" he said.

"The arch, you mean?"

"Yeah," Garrick said. "Reminds me of one of those Grimm fairy tales my mother used to tell me."

"Fairy tales? This is the first I ever heard of it. I thought you were raised by wolves."

"I'll have to kill you if you say anything in public."

The thing about Garrick was that he was nosy, asking about a person's childhood. But ask the old man about his childhood, and he clammed up.

"I hate to bust your theory, but the trees on every back road I've been on have been like that. If the whole trail is like that, we'll call in the forestry department."

Garrick raised his hands in defeat, and they climbed over the fence.

Nightingale walked ahead. He'd never considered himself an expert tracker, but a path of beaten undergrowth and broken limbs wound easily into the woods. Cooler temperature came in the shade. After they had gone a hundred yards, Nightingale turned around. Garrick followed suit. The archway was nowhere to be seen.

"I told you it was weird. See"—Garrick waved a hand in the vicinity of where they had been—"it's disappeared."

Nightingale shook his head. "I was gonna point out how everything looks the same since we got further in. But this path is pretty obvious."

"Somebody has walked it a lot," Garrick said. "Is this one of those paths the tourists follow when they want to 'get back to nature'?"

"Good point. We'll have to ask the doctor. At least it's a little cooler."

"No sunshine. So we've got mold and moss. I've never been in this kind of landscape. This is like another planet."

Nightingale looked around again, trying to find a marker to remember.

"You see that old fence up ahead?" Garrick said. "Somebody must have had livestock up here at one time."

Nightingale held that thought and stared at the frayed barbed wire that he had missed. "Glad you saw that. And from this other side you can see the highway going into town. I wonder if the boy saw anything that morning."

"I asked him and he said no," Garrick said.

They turned back to the path and walked another hour up and down hills, away from the town, before the path split to the right and to the left.

"Damn," Nightingale said. "What do you think?"

"The trail to the left is the direction of the Dearborn place."

"I have no sense of direction, so let's go. We can double back if we don't see the house in half an hour. We'll have to go back, anyway. It's getting too dark to see much." Nightingale walked several feet up the path to the right and came back. "Further up is not worn like the other side. The grass and weeds haven't been tromped down too much."

He led the way again, moving slowly, holding limbs back so he wouldn't swat Garrick in the face.

Garrick hadn't said much.

"We'll never be like the Rodriquez boys back home. I wonder what they'd say to this terrain," Garrick said.

"Maybe we can ask when we get home, but I've decided that Cayden wouldn't hide in these hills and woods. He grew up in town, living in a house, and he didn't strike me as a kid who could rough it for very long. It's creepy out here, and as it gets darker—think about sleeping on the ground with the bugs and snakes."

"You're probably right. I sure wouldn't look forward to it."

They had topped a hill, and in spite of the trees, the roof of Constance Dearborn's house came into view.

Nightingale looked at his watch. "It took us close to two hours to get here." They could see the back yard. Nightingale whispered, "I don't want to scare any of the sheriff's men. They're liable to shoot us."

Garrick nodded and pointed toward the edge of the tree line. "Rosemary bush."

Nightingale said nothing, but there was the rosemary bush that Cayden said he broke a piece off of for Constance. Whoever shot Constance Dearborn had been in the woods and watched her through the big window as she walked to the kitchen. They had shot her. Then they left in a car that was hidden, just like the patrol car was hidden from their sight now.

A deputy came around the corner of the house and motioned to the men standing in the back yard. The deputy continued along the length of the back of the house, and the two men followed him when he turned the corner.

Nightingale and Garrick turned and silently went back the

way they came. It would be full dark soon, so Nightingale watched Garrick's white shirt lead them into the trees. Nightingale didn't want to talk about what he had just seen.

The shooter could have been Cayden Shepherd. The boy could have been in the woods when Nightingale pulled his truck around the driveway. When he saw Nightingale's truck, he waited, then rushed to the house, key in hand, to declare his innocence.

37

Nightingale's latest discovery made his heart heavy. Suddenly, his anger of the last few days seemed benign, even silly. At the crest of the hill, before leaving the woods, they stood side by side and looked across the field to the vet's clinic. "The kid could have done it," Nightingale said.

"If he did, he's a damned fine actor."

"Reckon we want him to be innocent?"

Garrick stopped, his hand pushing aside a low sumac bush. "What's this *we* business? You want him to be innocent. Do I need to remind you of the day we found Constance Dearborn? That boy was trembling all over and full of grief. The hell of it is he's still a child, but he could also be a con artist." Garrick smacked the bush, let out a disgusted puff of air, and walked a few more steps.

"He could have shot her, hid the gun, and made a great entrance after we got there," Nightingale said. He had a hard time saying it, but it had to be out there. They both slowed their pace. "The sheriff thinks he did it, and I see why."

"I can see the sheriff's argument. With Constance dead, the

kid stands to be rich if they find the will, or if the mother takes his DNA to court," Garrick said.

The urgency of the situation, in the form of aching bones, bore down on Nightingale. He wished for more help from Garrick and got arguments. Gut feelings didn't work here: be methodical, go step by step. He knew Garrick didn't want the boy to be the killer, but Garrick fought the only way he knew to fight—as an adversary, trying to be an asshole finding flaws in Nightingale's argument.

Once they left the path and were back crossing the pasture, Nightingale said, "I'm going to get Bandit for the night."

Several minutes passed with Garrick standing outside the truck when Nightingale came out with the puppy.

"Why'd you want me out here?" Garrick asked.

Nightingale put the puppy in the driver's seat and got back in. "The vet doesn't like you flirting with his wife."

A sly smile crept across Garrick's face. "How'd you come to that conclusion?"

"His land—or their land, to be correct—is southwest of Dearborn's. Mrs. Elliott let me know in no hidden terms that she has a say in everything. He fawns over her. Your conversation with her aggravated him when we were here the other day. You laughed, flirted, right?"

"Hmmm." Garrick kept smiling.

The ego—just amazing.

Nightingale shook his head, started the engine, and smiled as the puppy cuddled in Garrick's lap.

When Nightingale left Garrick at his hotel, he said, "In the morning, I'm going to talk to Cayden's mother and grandmother. Want to come?"

"Wouldn't miss it," Garrick said.

Nightingale drove to the cottage, looking forward to more pills and a stiff drink. He felt heartsick, what his mother used to refer to as "blue," but he'd decided to fight the mood. Probably meant a sleepless night.

THE NEXT MORNING AT 8:00, GARRICK KNOCKED ON the door.

Nightingale still had pain, so he moved slowly, although he could tell his muscles weren't as sore as they had been.

Garrick grinned as he stepped into the sunny, bright cottage. "I'd like a decent meal before we face these women," he said.

Nightingale envisioned a Whataburger. "Me too. I've got to have coffee."

As Garrick chowed down on a breakfast taco, Nightingale asked questions. "Did you talk to Cayden's mother at all?"

"No, but I think she has more say-so than we give her credit for. When I called about him being with me at the hotel, Audie Louise ordered me to bring him home. But"—Garrick drank some coffee and opened a salsa package—"I heard another voice in the background, muffled like a hand was over the receiver, and Audie Louise came back on the line and told me he could stay and to bring him home the next morning."

"Good. That had to be his mother. I met her, but she didn't tell me her name."

"Isabel."

"Okay. Finish your food. Let's go."

Garrick chunked the remainder of the taco shell in the trash, and they refilled their coffees and headed out.

Nightingale parked on the street, then they walked slowly, looking around at the aging houses, many of them in need of paint or a new roof. A white Honda sat almost out of sight at the side of the small brick house. Nightingale knocked.

Audie Louise answered. She looked past Nightingale to Garrick but then said to Nightingale, "What do you want?"

She didn't ask for an introduction, so Nightingale assumed she knew him from Garrick's presence. He explained where they'd been the day before. "I hoped to talk to Cayden's mother. I want to find the boy. Maybe she can give us some ideas of where to look."

"He's innocent," Audie Louise said.

From the darkness inside the house a lower, younger voice said. "Mother, let them come in."

The screen door made it hard to see inside; in addition, drawn blinds meant no light. The door opened slightly, and Nightingale stepped inside.

He squinted into the dark room, trying to get accustomed to the darkness. He searched for windows, then stumbled on a rug, resulting in Garrick bumping into his back.

"Sorry," Garrick said. "My eyes aren't accustomed to the dark."

Nightingale stood perfectly still, willing his eyes to adjust. He remembered his two cousins who still lived in Obsidian. During the summer, the inside of their house stayed as dark as a tomb. They battled the Texas heat by keeping the sun outside. Somehow, it made them feel cooler. He'd quit arguing with them about efficiency, just turned the air conditioner in his own house to cooler.

A lamp clicked on in a corner of the room.

"I am Isabel Shepherd. I am Cayden's mother."

Nightingale turned to the voice and saw the slender, dark-haired woman he'd met earlier at the cottage. She had a slight accent, just enough to make her words enunciated, clipped. She wore a starched white blouse tucked into blue jeans. In the shadows of the room, Nightingale wondered if she was trying for drama or was simply an overwhelmed parent.

"Mrs. Shepherd, I'm sorry we didn't call. We thought—"

"I don't mean to be rude, Mr. Nightingale, but for my son I am very worried." She clinched one fist at her waist. "He is scared. He trusts you and Mr. Garrick. He is a good judge of character, so I must trust you. What do you want?"

"Maybe we should offer them something to drink," Audie Louise Shepherd said.

In another room, Nightingale heard the whirr of a window air conditioner. His eyes had adjusted to the dim light, and he found himself staring at the younger woman, waiting for a response.

"They did not come here for tea. They know I need my son." The slightest quiver of emotion came on the last word. Tears glistened in her huge, dark eyes.

Her urgency was beyond that of a mother. She knew, as did Nightingale, the boy might get shot for many reasons, not the least of which was that he was part Mexican.

"We wondered if you had any idea where he might have gone when he ran away."

"I will tell you my thoughts." She didn't sit down. She brought both hands in front of her waist and stared at Nightingale.

She held up one finger, almost instructing and, Nightingale felt, listing her thoughts to herself as much as to him.

"Cayden wanted to know his father. He needed a father. Number two"—she held up two fingers and grasped them with her opposite hand—"he loved Miss Dearborn as much as a boy could who had only found a sister when he is nearly grown. Sometimes I was jealous he loved her so much." She drew in a long breath and stopped.

Audie Louise Shepherd had walked to a small chair and sat down. Nightingale looked at her as she stared at the floor.

"Was there anything else?" Nightingale asked. "Can you guess where he may have gone?"

Isabel blew out a deep breath and grasped three fingers with her left hand. "He used the rifle at the Dearborn house." At those words, she seemed to melt and lose her courage. She quit counting and folded her hands like she was praying. "Don't you see? She was his sister. He loved her. He told me his sister was teaching him how to shoot." Isabel put her face in her hands and drew another long breath before continuing. "The sheriff took Cayden's computer. It showed the sheriff what he needed to know —that Cayden was studying guns."

"How did the sheriff know he had a gun?"

"Silas Jackson told him," Isabel said.

"Damn." Nightingale glanced at Garrick.

Despite the woman's show of strength, she seemed filled with an electric fear, as if at any moment she might burst open.

Nightingale pulled out a business card. She flinched when he stepped toward her.

"Here's my cell phone number. If you get any ideas, any thought that might help us find him, call me."

Isabel took the card and looked at her mother.

Nightingale couldn't interpret their thoughts, but he knew something was imminent. He worried that if Cayden showed up at some point, she might take her son and run. She was desperate, and desperate people didn't think straight.

In the truck, Garrick said, "They know what can happen. That's why they're so scared."

"Let's drive by the sheriff's office."

Garrick snorted. "Fine, it's your wasted gas."

Nightingale made the loop around town. The sheriff was not at his office. He drove to McGowan's rented house.

A new, red truck had pulled in front of McGowan's vehicle in the driveway.

Nightingale nodded at the truck. "He said his son was coming to visit and go fishing."

McGowan answered the door, smiling like he was expecting them. "Come on in. I want you to meet my son, Darren." A blushing teenager came from the kitchen and shook hands with Nightingale and Garrick.

"You can unpack your things," McGowan said. "I'll just be a minute with these gentlemen, and then you and I can plan our day tomorrow."

The boy smiled, then walked to another room. The door closed softly, and McGowan rounded on Nightingale.

"I have two days with my son. We're going fishing. Tell me you've found the people who own this God-forsaken land so I can have a peaceful time with him."

Despite the whisper, the hiss of anger told Nightingale to be quick and leave.

"Sure, Roy. Sue Nell Faulkner owns the land to the north. I talked to her and her brother, Hank. She owns the land and says she won't sell—no matter what the price. Dr. Elliott, the vet, owns the land on the other side, and he's willing to sell, but he'll want a lot of money. And, he wants an offer on paper—no dickering back and forth 'cause of the neighbors, he says."

McGowan rubbed his forehead and walked into the kitchen. "Bad headache." He reached for a bottle of ibuprofen, poured several in his palm, and pulled a bottle of cold water out of the refrigerator. He kept his voice low. "Guess I came off too strong, but the timing on this really sucks." He gave a lopsided half-grin, and Nightingale remembered McGowan's wish for a "normal" family.

"Is there any hope on getting the Dearborn land?" Nightingale asked.

"The governor can declare eminent domain," McGowan said, "but she didn't want to bully this through. We may have to. I'll call and see what she's being advised for alternatives. What's happened with the kid?"

"He's missing."

"Missing—how? As in gone?" McGowan straightened his back and stared at Nightingale.

"Ran away. Scared, I guess, after Mrs. Dearborn was killed."

"Why should he be scared—unless he killed her?"

Sometimes McGowan astonished Nightingale in not relating to other people. Nightingale nodded toward Garrick. "We don't think he killed her. But since you told me to stay out of it, I don't have much info."

"That's the best thing. The sheriff can take care of that. I need your full attention." McGowan paced the kitchen. "Call me in the morning. I'll have work for you by then. Call early. Darren and I are leaving at six."

"Guess we're dismissed then," Nightingale said. He glanced toward a noise in the hall.

McGowan's son stood there.

McGowan gave a nervous smile, his all-business attitude changing so that his face softened, his personality altered. Suddenly, he was the doting father.

Garrick walked over to the teenager. "Hey, we've got a young man from here in town we'd like you to meet. Maybe we'll bring him over."

The boy grinned, looking momentarily cheered.

"God dog it, Garrick." McGowan stepped forward, pushing Garrick toward the door. "Darren, he's trying to make a joke and failing. Goodbye, guys." As he put his arm around his son's shoulder, he stepped back and slammed the door.

38

Neither of them spoke during the drive back from McGowan's house. Outside the hotel, Garrick opened the door and looked at Nightingale, his heavy eyebrows raised in question.

"I'll call tomorrow morning," Nightingale said.

Garrick nodded.

Nightingale watched the older man's back, straight but thin, as he walked in and appreciated that for now the questions had stopped. He guessed Garrick might be more heart-sick than he was.

Neither of them had the grit for an argument. Eventually, they would talk the day over, but not now. Now, he needed to think about McGowan and the confusion that came with him without the knife-sharp criticism from the old man.

McGowan had been in and out of his life, but he'd always been steady. He'd had a hard time growing up, but he'd always been honest, trustworthy, almost a Boy Scout in his everyday living. McGowan had a reputation among cops and the staff of several governors as a straight shooter.

People, he thought, remained pretty true to their young

character after they were grown. He thought back to McGowan's comment that he wanted a "good, solid family" more than anything. McGowan had said that before. His way to get that was hard work, which might or might not lead to money. Roy had worked his butt off for years in the trenches of politics, and money had never seemed to follow.

McGowan had been loyal from the moment they met. McGowan stood up for him, as well as his own beliefs. Nightingale now found himself trying to find clues in the years of their youth, looking for the past to help interpret the current time.

The only conclusion he could draw was that McGowan's current family was falling apart, just as his childhood family had. And the young McGowan seemed to want a good family life above all else. It had to be difficult dealing with the vagaries of politics while his family fell apart.

He had asked McGowan about another way to get the water project through but gotten a blanket "Not now, maybe later."

Legislators usually made laws to match the whims of their constituents. Very few politicians ever acted in the best interest of the state without being goaded into the action, and there was no telling how the polls would make them react given this avalanche of problems for the water project.

The confusion of thoughts and emotions mounted as he returned to the cottage, walked the puppy, poured himself a drink, and sat in his recliner to ponder. The fact was that Roy McGowan was in a unique position to finagle the governor and the water proposal in several different ways. Roy loved money and he was capable of manipulating a situation, but he would never murder someone. With that conclusion, Nightingale decided to call the governor the next day and ask some very direct questions.

In his estimation, he'd fulfilled his part of their agreement, but what if the governor continued to add requirements to his job? He knew himself well enough to realize that this series of problems was presenting more trouble than in his usual cases. Normally, people didn't tell him no as the governor had; people didn't watch his every move, as McGowan had. And, normally, he didn't have the well-being of his hometown hinging on his abilities to do the job he'd been ordered to do.

Nightingale still felt obliged to find Constance Dearborn's killer. The sheriff had not showed the concern needed because he thought Cayden was the shooter.

Nightingale let his head rest and leaned the recliner back as the puppy stilled in his lap. As Nightingale moved his hand along the dog's back to further calm it, he felt rather than heard a rumble coming from its innards, and the puppy raised his head. Nightingale put one hand on the furry body. "Easy, boy, did you hear something?"

A bedroom window rattled. The dog jumped off Nightingale's lap and lit out for the bedroom, woofing in full cry.

Nightingale picked up his weapon. If this happened to be the night visitors from his earlier encounter, he planned to shoot first.

He advanced slowly, staying close to the wall, his heart pounding in his ears. He stuck his hand into the room, flipped on the light, and weapon at the ready, looked into the bedroom.

Half of Cayden Shepherd hung through the raised window. Nightingale told the puppy to hush while he pulled the boy inside. Cayden stood, grinning at the puppy.

When the barking continued, Nightingale pulled a treat from his pocket and put the dog in his crate in the front room. He hit the bedroom light switch and hoped Emma or Silas Jackson wouldn't come barreling outside.

Cayden seemed mesmerized by the puppy, kneeling and poking his fingers into the kennel for the puppy to lick.

"Why aren't you at home?" Nightingale whispered while he

jerked together the blinds on the windows and front door. He imagined Silas had come out to eavesdrop at the door.

In the low light, the boy's eyes reflected fear, and Nightingale realized the boy had taken a risk and hadn't known what to expect.

Cayden looked sunken, like he'd lost weight but had grown an inch taller. He glanced at a box of cereal on the kitchen counter. "When did you get the puppy?"

"Cayden, do you realize how much troubled you're in?" Nightingale got milk out of the fridge and poured some over a bowl of cereal. He pitched some sugar packets on the table, continuing to keep his voice low.

The boy didn't wait for an invitation. He sat down and started eating like a starved person.

Nightingale waited while Cayden consumed cereal. After the bowl was finished, Nightingale picked up the milk and put it in the fridge. "Where have you been?"

Cayden glanced at the dog kennel and dropped to his knees beside it. He opened the door and the puppy bounded out, cuddled in Cayden's lap, and settled in to roll and flip and play.

Nightingale slapped his hand on the counter.

The boy flinched, and the puppy yelped and ran into his crate.

Nightingale fumed. "I asked you a question."

Cayden got up off the floor and sat in a chair, as far away from Nightingale as he could be.

"I went to the woods at first. I stayed a while in Mr. Garrick's truck. Then I got pretty hungry. We've had talk of someone who lives in the woods and steals food from campsites. People say he has a gun, so I was uneasy about that. I got hungry. I saw you when you parked your truck. I'm glad you moved to a cottage."

"Where's the rifle?"

"Grandma must have hid it." He didn't look up. Nightingale figured he was lying.

"She says you have it." Nightingale pushed the point. "If the sheriff or his deputies see you with a firearm, they'll shoot you." Cayden had stopped playing with the puppy, but his tired gaze remained fixed on the friendly pup. "Look at me," Nightingale said. "Do you understand that?"

The boy stared back. "Yes. I understand that. I can take care of myself."

So much for advice to a teenager.

Nightingale didn't like this role as savior, mentor, whatever. He felt inadequate as an authority figure. He didn't know what he expected, but he wanted Cayden to see the seriousness of the situation. Somewhere he had read that boys matured later than girls. Maybe that accounted for this running away and avoiding responsibility. To hear him tell it, Garrick didn't have difficulty with the boy. But he'd be fried in hot oil before he called the old man for advice.

Cayden really was still a child, a fourteen-year-old child. Nightingale watched him play with the puppy and knew that Cayden might survive without an adult, but he would evolve into an animal that Nightingale didn't want to imagine.

"So, what do you do now?" Nightingale asked. "I've been told you're a wanted man."

Cayden bent over, picked the puppy up and rubbed his face in the fur. Then he looked at Nightingale. "Can I stay here?"

"You can spend the night, but your mother has to be told in the morning. Understand?"

"Yes."

Nightingale hated himself. He didn't know how to read the boy. What was true and what was a ploy, or did a fourteen-year-old think like that? He wanted to say, "It will be all right." He thought of his own mother and father when he needed help, so he stepped forward and put one hand on Cayden's shoulder. "I'll be with you all the way. Just hold that thought."

Dog and child went to the bedroom. Cayden's muffled voice came through the air once.

Nightingale knew the dog was in the bed and didn't care.

He knew he wouldn't sleep, so he turned on the TV and sat in the chair, waiting for the boy and the puppy to be still. Then, thinking about avoiding hot oil, he called Garrick.

The Ranger insisted on coming over, and when he knocked on the door, they stood on the small porch for a minute. "You think he'll wake up if he hears us?" Garrick said.

Nightingale motioned him inside and started making coffee. He spoke in a whisper. "Bandit is in bed with him. We'll know it if he wakes up. I don't think an earthquake would wake him."

"What are you gonna do?" Garrick said.

"I don't think there's any choice." He went into his plan, giving good and bad. Then he asked Garrick, "What do you think?"

Garrick rubbed both hands on his temples. "I'll be back at six."

~

AT EIGHT O'CLOCK, NIGHTINGALE WOKE CAYDEN.

Garrick was already there, standing in the small living room.

When Cayden saw him, he said, "What's wrong? Have you called my mother? Why is Mr. Garrick here?" He threw the covers back and looked at the window as Nightingale stepped closer.

"We want to talk to you. We're worried about you."

"I can take care of myself."

"We're taking you to jail," Garrick said.

"No," he screamed, jumping off the bed and ramming his head into Nightingale's stomach.

After the encounter at the Dearborn house, Nightingale expected it and grabbed the boy's arms, twisting him around and to his knees at the bed.

"It's not just me," Nightingale said. "Garrick agrees. The sheriff thinks you're dangerous. He might shoot first and then try to talk. If you're there, you'll be safer."

No need to include that they were protecting the boy from himself, from his temper, his running away.

When Cayden dropped his head against the side of the bed, Nightingale loosened his grip, but Cayden continued to pull away and struggle.

Nightingale lowered his voice, trying to sound sensible. "We can have the sheriff come get you."

All struggling stopped.

Nightingale took half a step back, watching for any unpredictable movement.

The boy put his forehead against the mattress and sighed.

"We haven't changed," Nightingale said. He loosened his hold a little. Nightingale glanced at Garrick, who nodded.

"What does my mother say?" Cayden asked.

"We haven't told her, but she wants you safe. I'll call her before we leave," Garrick said.

After another long silence, Cayden, still kneeling, sat back on his heels, but didn't look at them. "I'll stay here. You can lock the door."

"Too many things can go wrong with that," Nightingale said. He didn't want to imagine the number of things that could happen.

Garrick stepped up. "Look, you want to be a man, so grow some balls and let us do our work. We'll have you out in two days."

Cayden pressed his forehead into the bed. His breathing had quieted, but Nightingale took long, deep inhales. An insistent clock ticked a different cadence against the breathing.

Cayden raised his head. "All right. I'll get dressed."

Garrick nodded. "Good decision."

Nightingale stepped back.

"I want a shower."

The lawmen looked at each other, but Cayden shook his head as he started toward the bathroom.

"That window has bars," he said.

39

S howered and dressed, Cayden stood in the doorway from the bedroom like a soldier waiting for orders.

Nightingale nodded to Garrick, who motioned to the boy, and without a word, they all marched to the truck and drove to the jail. Like going to a funeral, Nightingale thought.

He hoped he was doing the right thing. He had mentally played out every scenario and thought the sheriff would protect the boy. Now it was too late to back down. At the jail, Nightingale went in while Cayden and Garrick waited.

Nightingale went straight to the sheriff's office. "I have the boy outside," he said.

Patterson sat back in his chair and eyed Nightingale through cigar smoke. "And?"

"You said you were getting a warrant for him."

"He's a juvenile. Did he have the rifle?"

Nightingale hated this game of one-upmanship. "He doesn't have the rifle, but I figured you'd want him in your jail so he wouldn't get hurt by some gun-happy citizen. I'd hate for a kid to be shot because of a rumor. Besides, if anything happens to him, I'll kill you."

The sheriff chomped the cigar, frowning, looking irritated. He crossed his arms over his chest and leaned back.

"He'll be safe here for a little bit. You know I can't keep him. I hope this ain't some half-assed trick. Goddamn, he's fourteen. I'll call his momma. Besides, look at the construction. I've only got this one cell that's usable."

Nightingale cursed inside. This was not going as planned.

The sheriff carefully placed the cigar on an ashtray and misted it with a small bottle of water. "Where'd you find him?"

"He turned himself in to me. Said he didn't do anything wrong. I gave him my word that you'd see that he was protected. Somehow he got the impression your deputy might hurt him."

The sheriff grimaced and squinted again. "I'll say something to Ed Howard. He called in sick today."

"I told the boy that you'd have this solved in two days. Reckon that'll be a problem?"

"You sure are making a lot of promises for me. Two days, my ass." The sheriff's voice rose in frustration. He stood and walked out into the hall. "I'm calling his momma, and if he takes it on hisself to grab a gun and have a shootout it's not my problem."

Nightingale moved in so close he felt Patterson's breath. "There you're wrong. Everything about that kid is your problem."

Patterson's eyes shifted. He shoved his stomach around Nightingale and led the way down the hall. The cells were in a state of disrepair: most doors swung loose on their hinges.

"If you come up with his rifle and we get the ballistics report, we might have part of it done." The sheriff crossed his arms—the monarch in his kingdom. "I'm leaving in ten minutes. Got an appointment."

Nightingale had pushed as far as he dared. He stood at the door and waved Garrick and the boy inside.

The sheriff opened the cell and didn't bother to lock it. "It ain't fine, but it's clean. Michelle"—he nodded toward the female deputy—"will bring his meals. He'll stay warm and dry."

Nightingale glanced at the window air conditioner, blowing out tepid air. The place was already hot. Construction workers were nowhere to be seen.

"Cayden, you want me to bring anything?" Nightingale asked.

The boy dropped onto a cot. He squinted at them. "I haven't done anything wrong."

Nightingale already regretted this. His father's words came to him: "No good deed goes unpunished."

They said nothing else until they returned to the hotel. Garrick paused before he opened the door. "I hadn't asked directly, but what is McGowan using to make you stay on this thing?"

Nightingale glanced at Garrick and then back in front of the truck. "I promised the governor to protect Posey."

"That's not what I meant. You can't be responsible for the man dying from diabetes."

"I know, but then Mrs. Dearborn was killed. The sheriff is out of his league, but I think the kid will be safe for a day or two. Especially with the deputy out sick. McGowan is a good friend. He has to do what the governor says."

Garrick nodded. "Right." His tone conveyed enough cynicism for an hour-long argument, which would accomplish nothing.

"This whole plan is threatened by the legislature coming back. They can't convene for several months, but they can make noises in the news."

Garrick stared at the landscape. "McGowan knows you'd rather solve a murder than sell land."

"Seems to me that's the right thing to do. There's no sale now unless the vet comes through, but this boy is weighing on me,"

Nightingale said. "We need to find the rifle. See if you can find out if his grandma is telling the truth. Then call your friends in Austin. Find out if they've heard anything new on Posey's death. I'm going to the Dearborn house and those woods up behind the house. Maybe we missed something."

And, maybe, just maybe, he'd find something to prove the boy's innocence. But right now, that prospect looked grim.

40

A fter Nightingale left Garrick at the hotel, he drove to the Dearborn ranch. Hank Faulkner's silver truck sat parked on the drive to the barn. Nightingale guessed that Faulkner was taking care of food and water for the horses and few cattle that lived there. He didn't care to talk to the man again, but he figured they needed to be aware of each other's presence since the place looked deserted.

Just outside the fence surrounding the feedlot, he yelled, "Faulkner, I'm looking around the place."

A door at the barn creaked, and Faulkner poked his head out. "Okay. I'm feeding the horses. Just milked the old heifer. I'll be leaving soon." He waved one hand, and the door shut.

Nightingale turned, not worried as he had been two days before about his back. Faulkner sounded calm. He probably realized he'd overreacted the day before.

He walked to the corner the house, surveying the encroaching woods that stood less than a football field away. As he stood at the house and looked up the slight incline, the forest seemed dense, unfriendly. He noted his word choice, wondering if his take on the stand of trees was because this territory was so foreign to him.

He thought of the police photographer from Tennessee who had been in Broken Rock the last year. She said people who lived in the Appalachians were more guarded in their emotions, reflecting closed lives in the trees and mountains that surrounded them. People out west, like him, usually said what they thought, didn't hold back, like in the flatlands.

He wondered why he'd remembered those observations. Armchair psychology, he'd called it then, but now he rethought his accuracy. These Piney Woods, with the shrouding trees, could hide tiny things or large murderers.

The shooter had probably braced against a tree. One good shot was all it took.

But he and Garrick had found no evidence. But why? If he knew why, then he would know who. Or, could it have been an accident?

He walked the length of the house, looked at the bullet holes in the big kitchen window. Then he meandered back.

Posey came to mind. The only thing that Posey and Constance had in common was the water plan. One wanted it and one didn't, but they both were dead.

Then, too, there were the political ties. Nightingale tried to remember the conversation between Posey and Mrs. Dearborn. Faulkner had said the woman thought Posey would not make her sell because he understood politics like it used to be in her daddy's day.

The person who talked politics around here was McGowan.

"Hey, Nightingale," Faulkner said. He stood several feet away, a looped rope in one hand. "You look deep into it, but you need to come see what I found in the hayloft."

"Sorry, guess I was thinking about how far away the shooter was."

Faulkner glanced toward the woods. "I try not to think about it." He shook his head as if to shake away the thoughts. He might never look anything other than heartbroken. "This way." He motioned with one hand, and Nightingale fell into step with him.

"Constance fed the horses and cows. She bought hay one year for the winter, but it was in the big rolls so most of it stayed in the pasture. The loft still had hay in it from when her daddy owned the place. I got up there yesterday and decided to knock some of the hay out, get rid of some rats at the same time. You'll have to follow me up the ladder."

Nightingale mulled over two days before when he'd felt like Faulkner might shoot him. Nothing seemed amiss. "Hope this is important."

"You can't trust anyone, can you?" Faulkner put one hand on a rung of a crude ladder made of pieces of lumber that were nailed up between studs and spaced for climbing to the loft. The barn was probably sixty years old, but the ladder seemed sturdy enough.

Nightingale followed slowly, not as nimble as he once was, using that as an excuse for caution. He heard Faulkner's steps after he disappeared through the opening above. He put one hand on the gun at his back, only to realize he would look stupid trying to shimmy through the hole with a gun in his hand. Worse, he could climb and hide the weapon. To hell with it—he stuck his head up and peered around.

He was at the second story, his head sticking out with the rest of him down below. Rough-cut lumber had been nailed across beams to make a storage area for hay. Two gaping fourteen-foot-tall openings at each end of the barn allowed an area for pitching hay down to animals.

To one side, under the eaves, Hank Faulkner squatted. "You coming up here, or you scared I'll do something crazy?"

"You forget I was beat to a pulp a few days ago," Nightingale said. He finished the last few steps, then stood, brushing hay from his torso.

"What I wanted to show you was this." Faulkner used a pitchfork and pointed to a rifle, still covered in flecks of hay dust and straw. "I was scooting old hay bales, and the pitchfork hit the metal. It sounded odd. I pushed more hay back and here it is. I think it's the one Constance gave to the kid. She gave him a few lessons in firing it, but I can't figure out why it's up here."

Nightingale looked at the area next to Faulkner. Even under the hay and in the shadow, the dark wood of the forestock and gray metal of the barrel spoke for an older weapon. Nightingale stepped closer. "It was just like this?"

"Yep. Weird, right?"

"Did you touch it?"

Faulkner managed a caustic huff of air. "I'm not an idiot."

Nightingale glanced at him and zeroed in on the small rifle. "Wonder when it was last fired?"

"They didn't practice that last time he was here. Probably the week before that, which would be about three weeks ago."

"Was he any good?"

"Does a bear shit in the woods? Yeah, the kid was born to it. I said it was young eyes, but he was good."

"I'll get some gloves and take it to the sheriff. Thanks for telling me. Do you come up here every day?" Nightingale tried to think how and when Cayden might have left the weapon in the hayloft.

"You're wondering if I put it there, and the answer is no." Faulkner made no attempt to hide his aggravation. He stood, brushed his hands together, and walked toward the opening in the floor. "I've done my chores. The animals don't make half-assed accusations, so I'll see them again tomorrow. You'll not find my prints on that weapon. I'm guessing you can find your way out."

He disappeared down the ladder, and Nightingale heard him cursing as he kicked and stomped out of the barn.

Nightingale stared at the weapon, then leaned closer. He smelled the oil from cleaning—or did he imagine it? After he heard Faulkner's vehicle move down the drive, he climbed out of the loft, got gloves and a ragged towel from his truck, and went back to retrieve the rifle. Out in the sunshine, he handled the weapon gingerly, trying to walk nonchalantly to his truck, all the time aware the sheriff or anyone else could drive up at any minute.

Once he made it to his vehicle, he laid the weapon in the back floorboard and looked it over again. The rifle, which looked to be a contemporary Model 1860 Henry, incorporated a firing-pin block safety that prevented the hammer from hitting the firing pin unless the trigger was fully depressed. He used a pocketknife to move the rifle, but he didn't want to cause any reason to question the evidence, so he covered the weapon and wished he had more things to put on top of his cargo.

He wondered if the boy had lied, or if Constance Dearborn or Faulkner had put the gun in the barn. Nightingale's spirits sank as he thought of reasons for hiding the rifle. Every idea pointed to Cayden's guilt. The boy didn't have to know about a will to see the farm as his way to save his mother from a life as a maid, money for an education for himself, and the list went on.

The other possibility was Hank Faulkner. He could have left the gun in the loft at any time, but today was the best opportunity because Nightingale was there to witness finding it. Could he have killed Constance? He said he loved her, but he'd also been in a war and suffered trauma. He knew that Constance didn't return his love.

Nightingale sat in the truck, staring at the fields across from the Dearborn house. He tried to simply observe, let speculation leave his mind. But the minute the engine turned over, he thought about Cayden in jail. "I didn't do anything wrong." Could the kid be pathological and not realize what he had done?

Half-way distracted, he turned left out of the drive, still picturing the boy.

A horn blared a second before he saw the oncoming vehicle.

He hit the accelerator and aimed the truck for the ditch just beyond him.

They almost missed. The vehicle clipped his rear fender, screeching metal on metal.

The impact left him shaking.

Brakes shrieked as the truck that clipped him slid sideways for a hundred feet before finally coming to a stop.

Nightingale shoved open his door, looked at the gouge down the side of the truck, and decided he was off of the pavement enough that no one else would hit him. Then he eyed both directions of the road to make sure no one else was headed that way.

Darren McGowan came running out of the driver's side of the red truck. The lanky young man headed for Nightingale. "Are you okay, mister?"

Roy McGowan's familiar figure slid out of the passenger side and held to the door. "Hell, Nightingale, when did you start driving like you were a hundred years old? My God, man, my mother gets out of the way better than that. And what're you doing out here anyway?"

McGowan's slurred words meant he had been drinking, and the boy was driving too fast. But Nightingale was supposed to be working on a contract, not a murder. "I met Faulkner out here to see if he'd talked his sister into selling her land. She's still a no-go."

McGowan glanced at Nightingale's truck and then back at his

son's. "Let's just have our own insurance take care of this. If you're okay with that, we're headed back to talk to the governor." He looked away, like a guilty schoolboy, and grinned. "She called while we were fishing, and I didn't answer."

Nightingale returned the token grin and looked up the incline at the house. McGowan had had too many beers, and now they were all in shared guilt of several types.

"Sorry about your truck," Nightingale said.

The boy had a rueful smile. "It's okay. Just adds to the one Dad gave it last week. Glad you're okay."

Nightingale stuck out his hand to shake, and Darren awkwardly offered a limp hand in return.

"Hate to hit and run, but we've got to get back." McGowan put an arm around his son's shoulder and leaned on him to sway back to their vehicle. The boy got in the driver's side, and the truck pulled slowly onto the road.

Had a trooper been there, they would all have done the same thing—the accident was minor. He had some fault in it, but he'd been caught at the Dearborn house, and he'd lied about it. What's more, McGowan was drinking too much, and his son was covering for him. Both adults had been terrible examples for the younger man. Nightingale stood a minute, watching them leave. The agreement to use their own insurance was fine, but Nightingale was, yet again, being less than honest. Somehow, deep inside, something more bothered him.

He stared and squinted at the truck as it faded into the distance. There was more to this than a water deal. He hated that word—deal—it sounded dirty. He hated that he'd gotten drawn into a political skirmish.

He glanced at the towel-covered weapon in the back floorboard. Murder could not be ignored. He'd sold his soul, and somehow or other he had to retrieve what was left of his own inner compass.

41

Sitting at her desk, balancing her checkbook, Emma Jackson's mind wandered. She touched the bracelet on her arm and realized she missed her sister. She couldn't account for the feeling of emptiness. At least twice, Emma caught herself reaching for the phone, only to remember that Constance was dead.

She needed people around her who cared. That's why she enjoyed the people from church so much. They gave her strength —like Mr. Wilson, who owned the funeral home, a friend of the family for years. A friend who had stuck with her when Father died and Constance wanted to cremate him.

"That's not in the Bible," Emma said.

Constance reddened, and Emma thought her sister might hit her.

Constance had a fit, telling the undertaker that Emma was deranged, but Emma held firm. Mr. Wilson was there every day. Constance had made so many people mad, no one wanted to hear her bitter words, let alone put up with her temper. When the days became a week, Constance said, "All right, bury him. He's gonna stink to high hell if you don't." Finally, Conrad

Alexander was buried with all the pomp that Emma could muster from her church-going friends. Then the will was read.

Neither one of them had expected what their father had done. Just as Emma never expected to see her sister's corpse, even though there had been times she wished her dead.

She'd had to identify her sister's body. Patterson knew who Constance was, but he made Emma go to the morgue and look at her dead sister's face. She stood back, unwilling to be close. She thought she would faint from the smell, antiseptic mixed with a sweet, awful death smell. Her knees buckled. Silas put one arm around her on one side, and Patterson was on the other. They held her. Her feet didn't touch the ground. And it truly was Constance. Darkness clouded Emma's head. Silas and the sheriff helped her to a bench in the waiting room. At that moment, she forgave her sister for the past wrongs. It hadn't been easy.

The last few years had been toxic. They didn't speak to each other. But now that Constance was dead, Emma thought of things she wanted to tell Constance, or questions she wanted to ask.

Emma rubbed her throbbing temples when she remembered the last horrible conversation with her sister. Constance had kept bringing up the boy, like he meant something to the family. "He's our half-brother," Constance said.

"No, Papa would not lower himself to that."

"Emma, he was a man. Yes, he would, and he did."

Well, as a Christian, Emma forgave Constance. It had been hard, harder than she'd imagined. After all, Constance was the one to first throw out names, calling Emma overly righteous, and full of Christian *carte blanche*.

Emma glanced at the numbers in the checkbook and then eyed a smudge on the front windows. She put down the checkbook and went for the vinegar water that she had in a spray bottle. Stuff was great on glass. There was something else she could tell Constance, but the woman didn't seem to care about saving money, so there was no need to call.

She grabbed a roll of paper towels and headed toward the soiled glass. She was enjoying squeaks of cleanliness when Silas came down the stairs, heading for his car. Emma turned from the window, going into the conversation with her son that she was having in her head.

"Silas, what do you think we should do about the property that the state wants for the water plan? It will be ours now. Even if we're grieving Constance, we have to be practical."

Silas stopped and looked at her like he didn't know her. "Mother I hadn't thought about such a thing. If someone is going to shoot me over it, I don't want to have anything to do with it."

The answer took Emma off guard. "Surely, no one shot her because of . . ." The image gave Emma too much to consider. Her hands dropped to her side. "The sheriff said it could have been a hunter's accident."

"I'm going to the library," Silas said. "May go by the grocery. You need anything?"

"I don't think so. The library?"

"Getting a head start on a class in public speaking," he said. "See you later."

Emma waved the vinegar cloth, glad to hear he was thinking of school. She went back to her checkbook.

SILAS TURNED THE SENTRA TOWARD THE LIBRARY, AND when he'd driven four blocks, he turned the car toward the jail. He didn't really lie to his mother. After all, he intended to go to the library. It just seemed like a good idea to go see Cayden first.

They'd met several years earlier when Silas went out to one of the cottages because he was bored. The summer heat had him irritated from the sweat when his thighs rubbed together. If his mother would only keep the air conditioning a little cooler, he could be comfortable.

For years, Silas had heard the story of his wayward grandfather and how he'd been seduced by the hussy, Isabel. His mother didn't tell him the tale. He didn't know how he first heard it. Like many myths, it was just there, but this myth involved people he knew. The bastard offspring was Cayden. As he grew older, Silas kind of admired the old man's spunk.

The kid had been about ten when Silas met him. Silas smiled, remembering that first meeting. For the first time in his life, he had felt superior to someone. The kid was smart-mouthed and loved to read. They hated each other.

Silas enjoyed the antipathy so much that he'd look for the kid when his mother came to clean. He'd hang around the car or go to a cottage just to find Cayden and aggravate him. Then the kid began to secretly pick at Silas. A shirt went missing, his bed was short-sheeted, his billfold moved to a place where he would never leave it.

It became a game of one-upmanship. Who could be the cleverest in aggravating the other? They began smiling when they saw each other. Sometimes Silas left paperback books off his bookshelf for Cayden to find. The books disappeared and reappeared a few days later, no matter the subject matter. When Silas left for summer camp, he gave Cayden a copy of *Tales from Shakespeare* and the first two Harry Potter books.

Silas always chose a day when Emma was gone to talk to Cayden. "I guess you know you're probably kin to me," he said on one of their meetings.

"Yep," Cayden said.

They never acknowledged specifics. They continued to trade harassments, but the flavor of their relationship changed. They had become comfortable with each other.

Silas liked thinking of Cayden as a younger brother, even though to be correct he was a half-uncle. No matter. Silas cared about him. It seemed natural to try to find out how the kid was faring in jail for a crime that Silas was sure Cayden did not commit.

At the jail, Silas went inside. The girl deputy said the sheriff was not there. Cayden had skipped out when she was in the bathroom. She didn't seem too concerned, though she did say the sheriff would not be happy. And Silas was definitely concerned.

So now, driving around town, he chewed over what his mother had told him and what he had heard from people around town. Gossip abounded in Beulah. He had to sift through the real and imaginary, and that was particularly difficult because people quit talking when Silas came around.

And, too, he had to sift through what his mother told him. Like the rifle. She told him to ask the sheriff about it because Aunt Connie had said she was saving it for him. Then, come to find out she had told the sheriff that the rifle belonged to Silas when she knew Cayden already had the gun.

As much as he hated to admit it, his mother was a convenient Christian, doing anything to promote her own cause or twisting her views to make things go her way. It had never been convenient for her to admit that Cayden's father was her father, so she said mean things and created bad situations for the child. Silas couldn't say that to anyone. He just kept it in his heart—his mother had a vicious streak and he was the only person who knew.

Silas cared for Cayden. He didn't know if he loved him like kin, but he thought he probably did. He wanted nothing to harm the kid whom he'd come to know in the last few years. So he drove through the streets, parking every so often to get out and walk and talk loud to old people while looking for Cayden, thinking maybe the boy would hear him. He'd had no luck with the cell phone but still hit recall every so often in hopes of reaching him. What he planned after that, he didn't know. Something would come to him.

After his last walk down Maple Street, he climbed in the car and muttered, "Damn."

From the back seat, a voice said, "Are you here to help or to turn me in?"

42

Nightingale drove slower than usual, expecting someone to honk and give him the driving finger at any minute. Then again, he was in a rural community—they were used to people moseying through their day and on their highways. Every once in a while, he'd glance back, look at the towel covering the rifle, and start a new line of thought.

He pulled the truck into the parking lot at the jail, surveying the two vehicles and several empty parking slots. The sheriff's car was not there.

His phone rang. It was McGowan.

"Meet me at the bar." He gave no time for a reply, but sounded sober.

Now Nightingale was glad the sheriff was gone. He leaned around and covered the small rifle better by tucking in the corners of the towel, then put the truck in gear.

~

IN THE WANING AFTERNOON LIGHT, THE BAR SEEMED dirtier than Nightingale remembered. Not that he expected change, but some of the situation had rubbed off on him. He felt dirtier by the day. Maybe a cold beer would help. Roy McGowan was already seated and had two beers on the table.

Nightingale decided to be a better friend. He pulled out a chair and sat down. "Is your boy okay after the accident?"

"Yeah, that was bad luck for both of us. He's gone back home."

"What else? How's he taking the divorce?"

"He'll be okay." McGowan shrugged. "He won't have to listen to our arguments. And once this is over, I'm going to spend more time with him. But I wanted to tell you the medics found more drugs in Posey."

Nightingale sat back. He felt like McGowan was looking to blame Posey for much of what was wrong.

McGowan glanced over his shoulder to his right and left, then lowered his voice. "You ever hear of Special K?"

"Yeah. A date rape drug. Called the Black Hole where I'm from."

"He was full of it. Liquor and the drug killed him."

"The governor knows this?"

"She does, but we're sitting on it."

"You're what?" A surge of disbelief flooded Nightingale's body. "Pardon me, but you need to tell our governor that is the dumbest thing I've ever heard. Hell, I'll tell her if you're too scared." Nightingale leaned in toward McGowan. "Okay, we'll let Posey's death go. But the governor owes it to Constance Dearborn to find her killer. A murder is best investigated as soon as possible after it happens."

McGowan squirmed in his seat and shushed Nightingale with his hands. "Calm down. That's why she's the governor and you and me ain't. This water deal is the primary thing to her right now. This state will be lost as far as investment and growth if this fails. She can't have the diversion of Mrs. Dearborn's death take over the press coverage."

Nightingale took a deep breath to put back the air that Roy's words had knocked out of him. Surely, he'd misunderstood. "That's not right, Roy. You have to make her understand that when people see how she put this woman's death above her ambitions, it will be political suicide."

With his eyes half open, his jaw clenched, McGowan's voice took on a smooth delivery that Nightingale had heard before. "Glad to hear your take on this." The fingers of his left hand tapped an even one-two one-two-three beat on the table.

Nightingale realized he'd get no further information because of Roy's anger. He changed tactics. "You insinuated that Posey had used drugs. Maybe . . ."

"That will be considered."

McGowan stared at Nightingale like the Ranger was a different person than the one he had known for twenty years. Nightingale returned the stare, figuring it meant nothing good.

"I planned to come up here and talk to the Dearborn woman, but someone shot her. I'm thinking this thing has been jinxed for years. A hunter probably shot her accidently. Anyway, you've been a help with Faulkner and the Dearborn place. Just leave investigating to the sheriff. Frankly, I told the governor that you're too invested. She wasn't having it, wants you to stay a few days."

Nightingale didn't breathe, didn't move, didn't let his eyes leave McGowan's. "No."

McGowan acted like Nightingale had said nothing. "The governor likes you."

"I signed on to watch out for Posey, and he died. If you think he was killed, I'll find the man who did it, and I can find out about the explosion."

McGowan's face hardened. His eyes became dark voids of anger. "We don't have time for you to be Superman."

This was beyond politics. Nightingale cursed his naiveté for not seeing the depths of the struggle. Why had he not seen it? This was more than power, it was money, big money and corruption and murder. And those people in Broken Rock, his friends and family, might be doomed. Like a puzzle, things were falling in place, but nothing was totally in focus.

"Oz, after all your reading, don't you see how this will break the state if we don't get it finalized? Once things get going it'll be like the roads, it will get done and people will watch, maybe they'll be pissed, maybe they'll wonder and wail, but eventually they'll be glad. We have to have a water plan. This is about the future, our children."

After McGowan's passionate words, Nightingale paused and forced himself to cool down. After all, McGowan was having personal problems. Obviously, he didn't see the depth of the damage that he, Nightingale, saw.

McGowan scooted back in his chair, recoiling from his emotions for a moment, reflecting Nightingale's cooler voice. "What have you got against Patterson? He's solved murders before. What about these environment nuts? And what about that boy? Seems to me there's no shortage of possible suspects."

"The sheriff won't tell me if he thinks the environmental guys were responsible for the explosion. You need to pull some rank here. He may have information that would help."

McGowan looked at him sideways and took a swallow. "You don't have a clue about politics, do you?"

Nightingale leaned closer. "I know enough to say you should lower your voice in here or the whole county will think we're conspiring to overthrow the government."

McGowan frowned. "Let's get out to the parking lot." He

threw a twenty on the table and ambled to the door like he had all the time in the world.

Outside, McGowan went to the Suburban and leaned against it. "This is over my head. People closer to the governor are talking to her. If we lose momentum on this, it'll take us twenty years to get papers signed. As it is it'll take twenty to get all the dirt moved and infrastructure built. Hell, if we have one more delay, then you might as well pack your fiancée and move 'cause there won't be any water anywhere. We'll have a war."

"I won't do it Roy. I'm beat. I quit."

McGowan looked up at the starry sky and snorted his exasperation. He opened the door, turned, and pitched his sunglasses into the seat. "Oz, I'm gonna pretend I didn't hear you. One way or another this will happen." McGowan came close, almost whispering. "Don't forget our deal."

Nightingale didn't move when the vehicle sped away. His throat burned. Dust filled his nostrils, and when he unclenched his jaw, grit scraped on his teeth.

He should feel vindicated, but he didn't. This was not over.

43

Nightingale glanced back at the sound of "Whiskey River Take My Mind" coming from the bar. He pulled off his hat, smacked it against his leg, and started toward his vehicle. For God's sake, there had been a murder, maybe two; he'd had to put a fourteen-year-old in jail for protection; and he doubted that anyone would carry through on the pledge of water for Broken Rock. This whole deal stunk.

He had a choice, and he'd made it. He didn't want to ask people to sell land that they loved and cherished. He wanted justice for Constance Dearborn.

He drove and considered what he would do next. He had resigned, but law enforcement was in his blood, and he felt good for the first time in several days. He headed back to the B and B to consider his options.

As he pulled the truck into his space in front of the cottage, his phone rang.

"What the hell is going on?" Garrick's voice cut the evening air. "Josephine Holly just called me and said someone at the Canadian River Municipal Water called her. They're cutting off our water tomorrow. Supply has petered out. The whole town,

Nightingale. All 657 of us. Why do I think you know something about this?"

Cold sweat broke out on Nightingale's back. The band of his hat got hot. He didn't answer immediately. He knew what had happened.

"I'll call you back," he said. He pushed the End button, giving Garrick no chance for reply.

Damn McGowan and damn the governor.

Anger washed over him, reminding him again of the fists and kicks pummeling his body days ago. He was glad no one was around. He stopped the truck, got out, and walked around the vehicle once, cursing under his breath.

He didn't like it, was surprised by it, and he hadn't given the governor credit for playing so rough. He had not thought a woman could be tough. He'd dealt with other governors, sometimes senators or mayors, always men or their second in command. And he had worked for them in a variety of jobs—from seeking murderers to ferreting out bribery to cheating at bookkeeping. He kept things strictly business, as did the officials. He made a point of keeping the badge visible. He expected hard decisions from everyone—except a woman.

He had made his politics mute—no one knew if he was a D or an R, and he kept it that way to make sure he was fair. In this case, he'd thought he'd known what the governor wanted from the outset, but now he felt like the goal was changing and he was not in the game.

He had studied the water problem in West Texas and kept an eye on what the legislature did or didn't do periodically about the statewide shortage. The Canadian River Municipal River Authority controlled all of the water that went to western towns like Broken Rock, Obsidian, and Sand Dune. Aquifer water had been assigned to the larger cities like Abilene and Lubbock, who then doled out portions when the drought became unbearable.

But now the governor had called someone who called someone else, and the effect was the water cut-off for Broken Rock.

As much as he wanted to blame McGowan, he knew the governor was behind this. Somewhere in the back of his mind he had thought McGowan might intervene, might see that things worked out for his hometown, but he knew this was chicken shit on his part. Might as well deal with the devil face to face.

When his temper had cooled, he picked up the phone and took a deep breath. After McGowan's terse hello, Nightingale said, "I've thought about it."

"And?"

Nightingale waited for more and nothing came. "The dead can wait."

"Glad to hear it."

"Exactly what do you want out of me, Roy?"

"Stay here. Stay out of murder investigations, and make sure no one shoots me if we get a contract from the vet."

Neither of them said anything else. Inside his gut, inside his heart, Nightingale promised Constance Dearborn that he would find her killer. Anybody who dished out this kind of poison didn't deserve public office. He'd campaign against the governor, go door to door if he had to, but for now he'd let it go.

Bitter thoughts would not let him be. Back in his bedroom, he pulled the bottle of Jack Daniels out of his luggage and poured two fingers in the glass that was on the bedside table. His neck and shoulders felt like lead had been poured over him. The governor was a spectacular politician. She said she was interested in Posey's death, and he believed her. She said she cared who killed Mrs. Dearborn, and he believed her. But actions were the true gauge of a person. Her actions were those of a cold-blooded politician.

He couldn't stay still. He paced, looked out the window, and when he saw a light in the kitchen of the Sycamore, he decided to visit, get his mind on something else.

He walked up the front steps, not trying to be quiet, but when he opened the kitchen door, Silas stopped talking to his mother, and Nightingale knew he'd walked in where he didn't belong.

Nightingale held out a carafe. "Sorry to interrupt, but I need some ice. The fridge is not keeping up yet."

Silas took the carafe to fill it. "Mr. Nightingale, we've heard that Posey may have been murdered. Is that true?"

Here was the opportunity to campaign against the governor. "I've been told to stay out of any investigation." He tried to not sound bitter like a rejected lover.

Several thoughts congealed at one time. Small-town rumors had a lot going for them. And sources for him with access to the sheriff's office were standing in front of him. Resentment swelled at the thought that he was not investigating Posey's death. But he wasn't responsible for this mess. He had heard that revenge was best served cold; he would add regret to that.

NIGHTINGALE STOPPED BY HIS TRUCK BEFORE HE WENT back to the cottage. After the walloping he'd gotten, he hesitated about taking the rifle inside, but that seemed safer than leaving it in the truck. With the weapon wrapped in the towel, he hugged it close, went into the cottage, and called Garrick.

"The water won't be cut off for Broken Rock. That was a mistake." He didn't give Garrick a chance for questions. "More important, Faulkner found Cayden's rifle this afternoon and gave it to me. I'm calling the sheriff, and I want you to be a witness when I hand this rifle over to him."

In the brief silence, Nightingale figured Garrick was beating back his curiosity.

"No problem. I can take pictures with my phone. You going to the jail or is he coming to you?"

"I'll let him make the choice. It's his investigation."

The call to the sheriff was not as pleasant. "What the hell were you doing at the farm again? You're supposed to be out of this."

Nightingale imagined Patterson turning red as he blustered, unable to do anything at this point except cuss and yell. "Bring it to the jail," he said. "I'll meet you there in twenty minutes."

Nightingale waited for Garrick at the cottage. He pulled the curtains shut after putting the rifle on the kitchen table, feeling slightly melodramatic.

But as he and Garrick donned gloves and then took pictures, turning the weapon one way and then the other, he felt more at home in this job than he had in a long time.

"Can't tell a damned thing about this rifle without a lab examination," Garrick said when they headed to the jail.

Nightingale had to agree, but he felt better now that he knew where the weapon was.

Patterson led them back to his office. He pulled out a pair of gloves himself and bent over the rifle as it lay on his desk. "Smells like oil. You said Faulkner claimed that he'd just found it. You believe him?"

"Don't know what I believe anymore. When do you check to see if this is the murder weapon?"

"I'll drive it into the lab in Dallas tomorrow. They have the bullet that killed Constance. I'll have to leave the rifle." Patterson moved the gun in small increments as he talked, bending close like he was observing a rare diamond.

Nightingale raised his respect a notch.

Patterson took a deep breath and straightened his spine. "Does that suit you?"

Nightingale ignored the sarcasm. "You want me to take it for you?"

"No," Patterson scoffed. "You boys heard from the kid?"

Neither Nightingale nor Garrick answered. Nightingale walked slowly, churning over the fact that, once again, the boy was missing. Why did it seem he was the only one who gave a damn? Even Garrick didn't mention it, and Nightingale wondered why. Side by side they walked to the door, then directly out to the truck.

When they were in the truck, Garrick turned toward Nightingale. "So when are you gonna tell me who shut off our water supply and why?

44

A heat wave of hope swept over Silas when he heard Cayden's voice. He flipped the fan on the car's A/C up another notch and looked to the right and then to the left, finally glancing in the rearview mirror. Thank God, the kid was okay. Silas tamped down his excitement.

"There's a towel on the seat. Cover up. Did anybody see you get in here?" He started the engine, purposefully clamping his lips together. If anyone saw him talking in an empty car they'd be suspicious, or worse yet, think he was as disturbed as his mother.

"I don't think so." Cayden's voice sounded muffled.

"Good. Stay down. I'm gonna drive and think."

"Is the sheriff still looking for me?"

Silas made sure he turned on the blinker at the stop sign, waved at Mr. Stevens, then headed for the highway out of town. "I guess he is. I went by the jail, but I didn't see his car."

"Do they really think I killed Constance?"

Cayden had uncovered his head.

Silas swerved, trying to bat him back down with one hand. "For God's sake, stay covered. These windows aren't tinted. I know you didn't kill her. We just have to keep you hid for a few days. Any ideas where you can stay?"

"Maybe the barn at the farm."

"We can try that. I've gotta stop and get gas. You stay down."

Silas got out and went inside to pay for the gas and get something to eat for both of them. For once, being overweight was no issue. He picked up two of everything. Back in the car, he pitched a bag of chips to Cayden, swigged some cola, and continued up the road. He slowed at the farm. "We can't go in there now. Cop cars are still hanging around."

He pulled the car off a small side road and bumped back into the trees. When he stopped the engine, he opened the other cola. "Here, drink this, but keep your head down. We may have to shave those curls to keep you out of sight."

Cayden crossed his legs as he sat on the floorboard, talking to the back of Silas's head. "Why can't I just go back and tell them I didn't do it. Why don't they believe me?"

Silas didn't like being the giver of advice. Just because he was older didn't mean he was wiser, but he couldn't let the kid down. "Let's think about this. You came in right after Constance was killed. The rifle is missing. You'll probably inherit the farm. Any ideas where the rifle is?"

"No. I thought Grandma had it. That's what I told the Ranger, but I was just talking, and besides, I was mad at her. The last time I saw it was when Connie and I shot at some targets at the farm. She kept it."

"The sheriff says he's searched for it." Silas mused to himself, trying to think where the rifle could be. In the back of his thoughts, he worried about his cousin. The boy had a quick temper, not a trait conducive to working with the sheriff. And he seemed to maintain a far-fetched trust in people that they would do the right thing. Silas felt too wise to trust much of anybody. "Reckon that hired hand knows anything?"

"Maybe." Cayden handed a candy wrapper to Silas. "You don't want to leave this in here for your mother to find."

"Right." He stuffed the wrapper in his shorts' pocket. He had an idea. "I think I know where to put you." He grinned and started the car. "Get under the towel, and I'll explain while I drive." This had to work. He would make it work, no matter what.

45

Nightingale had the truck on the street before he answered Garrick. "The only person with the power to turn off the water is the governor."

"What are you not telling me?"

Nightingale whipped the truck around a corner, angry with himself. He'd never been a good liar. Then he told Garrick about the job, how it had morphed into a semi-sales position and ended with the governor's promise of water for Broken Rock, if Nightingale helped get the Dearborn sale done. "I'm guessing she wants me to kowtow and she had to prove she could get to me."

"This is not just a case of a woman proving she's got balls," Garrick said.

They were back at the B and B, and Nightingale wanted Garrick gone. He'd had enough advice, and he didn't like admitting he'd screwed up. "I'll call McGowan tonight, see if I can get details. Go on back to your room. We'll start again early in the morning."

"Start what?"

Nightingale blew out a frustrated breath. "I'm finding Cayden. The governor's wishes can wait."

Garrick shook his head as he walked back to his truck. "I'll be on the lookout, but I doubt that he'll come to me again."

Nightingale got out and surveyed the parking lot as best he could under just street lights. He had left the porch light on at the cottage, as well as the lights inside the house. This particular spot of real estate had plenty of light. He wished he'd noticed the lack of light sooner the night he was waylaid. With hindsight that he hoped he didn't need, he pulled the snub-nosed .38 from the small of his back to complete his walk to the cottage.

Once inside, he locked the door and went through each room before turning off the lights and settling in the recliner with a tumbler of Jack Daniels.

About finding the boy, he had little hope, so there seemed to be no purpose in talking again to Cayden's mother. Who knew? Maybe the kid would show up. He didn't seem like the type to hoof it off to a city and lose total contact with his mother and grandmother.

Nightingale swirled the liquor in the glass the same way he was swirling ideas. He'd go tomorrow to McGowan. He had thought he would call but nixed the idea, recalling their latest arguments. The man knew the governor, and despite his own personal problems, he had insight that Nightingale needed.

Nightingale turned off the floor lamp and dozed, hoping for inspiration for the coming day. When he awoke, he didn't know how long he'd been asleep, but he needed to walk and take some ibuprofen for the stiffness that had settled in his muscles. From the window in the kitchenette, he noticed that the light on the porch of the B and B was out.

He glanced at the clock. Five minutes beyond midnight. The porch light bothered him. It usually stayed on all night. Every other light twinkled happily.

He went to the front door, pistol in hand, and pushed the barest space open at the curtain. Nothing moved. Not a sound.

He stood in the darkness, hoping for a chance at the cowards who had attacked him. This time, he was prepared.

Barely breathing, he listened to the hand of the kitchen clock as it made its way around, marking each second. Had to be the loudest clock he'd ever heard. After fifteen minutes, still no light and no sound.

At 12:35, a light came on upstairs in the B and B.

He blinked and rubbed his eyes. The light was on in the room Posey had occupied. Nightingale puzzled over it for a minute.

Then the light was gone.

He could only guess that Silas was making good on his wish to stay in the room. Nightingale walked back over to the recliner. He laid back in it and glanced at the window.

The porch light was back on.

He heard nothing and finally drifted back to sleep.

True to his word, Garrick knocked on the door at 8:00 a.m.

Nightingale had made coffee before anything else. Movement still pained his ribs, so he'd downed pills and had a hot shower in hopes of loosening his muscles.

Words were not wasted between them. Everything would be revealed as necessary.

Garrick pitched a paper bag on the counter. "Sausage sandwich," he said and pulled out his own sandwich, then sat at the table with his coffee.

"How do you plan on finding the boy?" Garrick said.

"Don't know yet. We're going to see McGowan at his house first. I want this water business to be off my plate, and I'm not leaving town with this murder open. I think I can be low-key enough that I can get both done. McGowan will stick to the water deal, and between the two of us, we'll get some land bought. If all else fails, the governor can work through an eminent domain declaration on the Dearborn land. She's in charge, so she has to make a tough decision. McGowan will leave, and I can work on finding the murderer, if the sheriff still hasn't nailed someone."

Garrick grunted and finished his sandwich. "You know she's right about water wars?"

"Yeah, and right now I know this needs to go forward."

"Just thinking out loud. This is about the future."

"Garrick, the vet will sell for the right price. Even if they have to redraw the plans, they'll have the land. Come on, we'll go to McGowan's and see if we're still a go." A burning anger remained with Nightingale, but he knew he was right.

McGowan opened the door for them, smiling, his head wet from the shower. "Come on in. Governor called already. She personally talked to the vet, so the contract gets signed this morning. Coffee is done. Help yourself. You going with me to Doc Elliott's?"

McGowan sipped his coffee and looked out the back window. To Nightingale, he seemed almost mellow.

"You're better off without me on this errand," Nightingale said. "After that, you won't need me."

"Can't let it go, can you?" McGowan's glance slid sideways, and one corner of his mouth tightened cynically.

"Guess not. Let me know when you get back."

Nightingale and Garrick walked to the front porch, pulling the screen door shut. A familiar-looking figure came around from the side of the house. It took a second before Nightingale registered that a bewildered-looking Cayden stood in front of them.

"That truck." Cayden whispered and pointed to the candy apple red truck McGowan's son had driven the day before.

Nightingale didn't take in the words. "What are you doing here?"

"I was in your truck."

Nightingale stepped toward him. "Where have you been?"

The boy stepped back, skittish, like he might run. "I saw that truck the day Connie was killed." His voice cut the muggy air, then silence crystalized as he looked at the house.

"Looks like you found your stray," McGowan said. He smiled, walking down the steps as he stuck out his hand to shake. "Aren't you going to introduce me?"

"Sure." Nightingale had several things running through his mind. He tried to process Cayden's words as he said the names, adding, "Mr. McGowan has a son a little older than you."

"You like my son's truck?" McGowan walked closer to Cayden. "Why don't you go over there and look at it?" McGowan stared at Cayden, getting close and putting one arm on the boy's shoulder.

Cayden flinched.

"I won't bite," McGowan said.

Cayden stood firm and didn't step with him to the shiny truck.

"We're headed back to the B and B," Nightingale said. "We've got to get Cayden home."

"Come with me," Garrick said. The boy stepped closer to the old Ranger. They started toward Nightingale's vehicle.

"I'll let you know how the meeting with the doctor goes," McGowan said. He exuded confidence.

"I don't know why I'm here, Roy."

"You're indulging a politician," McGowan said.

The early morning air got quiet.

Nightingale didn't like McGowan's smart-assed attitude, but his unease couldn't be totally blamed on McGowan. Cayden appearing like some magician had conjured him irritated Nightingale's sensibilities. Where had the boy been in the truck? And how did he get there?

Nightingale watched Garrick walk with the boy. Garrick

looked up and around at the clouds that had suddenly darkened the sky. Then his arm tightened slightly as he gave the boy a squeeze. Something had changed. Garrick hadn't said a word, but when he glanced back, his eye contact had a warning.

McGowan started up the porch steps, then turned and came down instead, lowering his voice. "That boy killed his sister, Oz. It's plain as this scar on my chin. You don't want to see it, but it's there. I've always been good with judging people. You know that. You need to be careful."

More pieces to the puzzle fell into place. No matter how much he cared for McGowan's friendship, suddenly, his friend looked dirty.

46

Nightingale backed the truck out, taking the opportunity to turn and look at the boy as he drove.

Cayden had scrunched himself into a corner of the back seat. The smell of day old teenage sweat rose from his clothes. He stared at his fists. His complexion had paled under the tan, and Nightingale guessed his few days of independence had caused the unhealthy pallor.

Nightingale wanted to put the boy at ease, but McGowan's words stayed in his head, words that he and Garrick had said before.

Garrick stared straight ahead.

"Where have you been?" Nightingale asked. He glanced in the rearview mirror.

The boy looked out the window and then back at his fists, doubled in his lap.

As he drove, Nightingale studied the boy's face. He didn't know how to proceed except as he always had. Honesty had been the best thing. It still would be.

At the B and B, Nightingale took a long breath. "We need to talk, and I'll bet you need to eat. Let's go inside a minute."

Cayden stood by the truck, his eyes shifting from one man to the other like he might bolt at any minute. "You don't believe me, do you?" His voice shook, sounding even younger than his years.

"We haven't heard your story yet," Garrick said. "All you've done is run away every time we've tried to help. Come on inside, and tell us where you think you saw that truck."

Once inside, Nightingale pulled out the cereal box, milk, and bowl. "You can talk and eat."

Garrick dug packets of sugar from his pocket and scattered them next to the cereal.

"I saw *that* truck the day Connie was killed." Cayden ripped open a sugar packet, dumping the contents onto the cereal, then pouring milk.

"Where?" Nightingale asked. His mind went back to the walk through the woods.

Garrick pulled out a chair and sat at the table, nursing his coffee.

"From the top of the ridge you can see traffic coming into town. I was walking out. He was driving in."

"You told us you didn't see any different traffic," Nightingale said.

"I thought it was a tourist—somebody I'd never see again."

"How do you know it was that truck?"

Cayden took a mouthful of cereal and barely chewed before going on. "It's one of a kind, like Mr. Garrick's. If you knew your trucks, you'd know." His voice gained confidence. "It has fender flares; it's got fuel-forged wheels. Nobody in this town can afford that stuff."

The implication was deadly.

Nightingale glanced at Garrick.

Cayden saw it. He pushed away from the table. A spoonful of cereal clattered in the bowl. "You don't believe me."

"Yes, we do. You've given us a clue, but we can't have you running around with us because the sheriff is looking for you. We want you to be safe. We're taking you home."

Nightingale called Isabel Shepherd. He spoke so that Cayden could hear him; no need to reinforce the boy's charges.

Cayden didn't finish the cereal. He stood, looking like he had the day they took him to jail.

Nightingale talked as he drove them to Cayden's home. "Garrick and I want to help you, but you've got to help us by staying at home."

Cayden said nothing.

When Nightingale glanced back, he could read no emotion on the boy's face.

At Cayden's home, both men walked him to his house.

Nightingale said, "Promise me if you get a wild hair to leave, you'll call me."

"Yes, sir. I will."

Nightingale didn't believe him.

Isabel came out and hugged her son. She sent him inside and turned to the two men. "What do I do? I love him and want him home."

"Don't try to tell him what's best right now," Garrick said.

"My mother's lectures, you mean?"

Garrick nodded.

"I will take him with me to clean tomorrow. He is a good helper."

"I asked him to call me if he wants to leave or talk," Nightingale said. "I don't know what he's thinking, except he feels like we don't believe him. We're concerned for him. Keep a close eye and call me if you think he's about to run." Nightingale looked at the house, where he guessed Cayden stood watching them. "He doesn't trust me, and I guess for good reason."

They were back on the road before Garrick said what was on

their minds. "Was Roy McGowan, or his kid, here? Or do we check all of East Texas for a spiffed up red truck?"

"You call Austin and see if your friends can find new licenses for trucks in these counties. If they can, check every town in a hundred-mile radius. You can do that while I talk to Silas."

At the B and B, Garrick went to the bedroom and closed the door to make his calls.

Nightingale called Silas and asked for help with the television.

In a few minutes, Silas knocked on the door. He said hello and took the remote from Nightingale.

As Silas fiddled with the remote control, Nightingale said, "Did Cayden stay with you last night?"

Silas looked up from the batteries and the remote. "Why would I have the kid in the house?"

"I think someone has been helping him, and you're the obvious person."

"Why?"

"You're both misfits, and you're related. We're trying to help him."

"You don't need help with this?" Silas pointed to the television, and when Nightingale shook his head, Silas blew out a long breath. His face turned red with anger. He laid the remote on the television. "What made you think he was in the house?"

"Lights in Posey's bedroom," Nightingale said. "'Course, it could have been a ghost."

"Yeah, and jackasses fly." Silas gave another frustrated huff and walked to the door. "I don't know much about what's going on, but the kid did not kill Aunt Connie. He worshipped her." He walked out, slamming the door so the glass rattled.

After he left, Garrick said, "That wasn't much help."

"You're wrong. He never said he didn't have the kid in the house."

"Okay, so what does that prove?"

"I don't know specifically, but I'm working on it. How did your call go?"

"You mean after they stopped laughing? This state is not real sophisticated. You seem to forget that we're keeping taxes down and cutting services."

"Don't start—what did they say?"

"They'll check, but it will take a day or so. Too bad the sheriff hates you. We could use some local help."

"Let's talk with McGowan. I need to check on the contract anyway."

"When're you calling the governor? She needs to level with you. 'Course, that may never happen."

"Due time. Due time," Nightingale said.

THE RED TRUCK THAT WAS ELICITING SO MUCH DISCUSSION was parked in the drive by the house that McGowan had rented. He had backed the truck in, moving it since their earlier visit. It still reminded Nightingale of a toy, not a working vehicle like the ones the farmers he knew owned.

Nightingale swung his legs out of his ride to go to the house and sensed the appeal of the truck.

Garrick, likewise, started toward it, as if drawn by a magnet.

From the left, a door opened.

"You want to see the truck?" McGowan asked.

"Yeah, I wondered about damage after the scrape we had. I thought the other side was damaged," Nightingale said. "Obviously, you can still drive."

"Visit with the kid was great. The truck runs great. The vet's still talking 'bout more money, but that shouldn't be a problem."

Nightingale faced McGowan. "Cayden says he saw a red

truck, like this one, going into town on the day Mrs. Dearborn was shot."

McGowan squinted. He didn't seem surprised or happy. "I thought as much. You want to see inside, or what?"

"Have you seen another truck like this in these parts since you've been up here?"

McGowan crossed his arms, didn't smile. "No, and I was in Austin on the day she died. Call the governor if you want."

"Just wondered."

"The vet says it's well known that the kid would inherit the farm from the Dearborn woman. She told some people. You need to think about that before you start concocting stuff or asking embarrassing questions."

"I guess that old gossip telegraph is reliable."

"Damn, man." McGowan threw both hands up in frustration. "You've been one of the best Rangers in the state. You're like Wyatt Earp, but it's never been because you stuck your neck out for a needy cause."

The words hit close, and Nightingale turned to hide his anger. "We have to do what we think is right." He had no evidence except the boy's word and this sour feeling in his gut.

"Sure you do." McGowan came close. "But you've pushed it far enough. I'll say it straight. Don't implicate my son or me in this mess because you feel sorry for a Mexican kid." He walked up the steps into the house without another word.

It came to Nightingale to wonder why he had enjoyed friendship with this man for so many years. He was smarmy, aggressive, full of himself, and unpredictable. He made those around him feel like they'd failed. But it wasn't failure, it was humiliation.

Garrick didn't share his embarrassment. They walked away, side by side, and in the truck Garrick said, "That guy will find out about karma. He's way too proud of himself."

47

Back at Nightingale's cottage, Garrick made coffee and poured them each a cup. Nightingale got out the lined tablet he had scribbled on. They sat at the kitchen table.

"I'm calling the governor."

"I'll go out for a walk so you can have privacy. Open the front door when you're done."

Nightingale nodded and picked up his phone. He wasn't sure he could get through to the lady and he didn't know what he planned to say, but he could follow her lead.

After the third, "Let me check," he heard her voice. She was cordial, congratulating him on securing a good water future for the state and for Broken Rock. At first, her words sounded like a political speech. He heard a door slam on her end, and the tone changed: she became a real person. Her voice grew more serious as the politics drained out of her words. Then she stopped.

Nightingale said, "Ma'am, I need to know if McGowan was in Austin on Thursday."

"I'll check my calendar." Again, he heard papers move. "I talked to Roy that afternoon in my office."

"Thank you." Relief rushed over him. He had suspected his friend, even though he hadn't admitted it to himself.

"Mr. Nightingale," the governor said, "I know you have certain career callings. But I need you in that town for a few more days. No matter what happens. Mr. McGowan has had a lot of personal issues. There are some problems. I don't know how honest he has been with me lately." She spoke slowly, emphasizing each word. "I trust you, even though you may not like me right now. Is that clear?"

A commitment to service that Nightingale hadn't heard in years came to him. Did this have an evangelical flavor? No. The governor was firm, not wanting miracles, just his presence.

He said "Yes" and put the phone down. He pushed the front door open, pulled out the bourbon, poured a good splash in his coffee, and sat down with his thoughts.

When Garrick came back inside, Nightingale said, "McGowan couldn't have shot her. He was in the governor's office that afternoon."

"You think his son did it?"

"Do you remember the kid? He'd faint if you put a gun in his hand. That puts us back to a stranger or Cayden. Or maybe—"

The phone rang. It was Isabel Shepherd. "Mr. Nightingale, my son is gone. I heard his phone, and when I checked, he was gone."

"Any idea where he went?" Nightingale wasn't surprised but he did feel anger with himself and the boy. He almost prayed. *One more chance and I'll keep him with me, no matter the consequences.*

Her voice broke. "No."

Nightingale mumbled, "We'll look for him."

Garrick said nothing, just picked up his hat and headed for the door.

Night was just falling. The darkness would not be good for a search.

"The light is on in the B and B, but the car they share is gone," Nightingale said. He hesitated, almost went in and asked for Silas, but thought better.

"Where're we going?" Garrick asked.

"First, I'm gonna drive 'round his neighborhood and then we're going to the Dearborn ranch. I think he's with Silas. No telling what they think they're doing."

Nightingale made a quick tour of Cayden's neighborhood, flaring the lights on full into bushes when either he or Garrick thought they saw movement or shadows. It didn't take long.

From there, they went to the ranch. He parked far down the drive, despite the gate being open. Emma Jackson's car was parked behind the house.

Nightingale breathed a sigh of relief, hoping the two would be near the car.

Darkness swallowed most of the light. Clouds slithered across the moon. Nothing showed in the house. The one spook light outside, several feet from the house and surrounded in a strange, humid mist, gave off little light.

He imagined Cayden and Silas were inside the house, but they could be in the barn. What could they think they were doing? Then he saw the flicker of a flashlight through a window in the house. It was weak, waving up and down and then gone.

He didn't want to surprise them. He hesitated about shouting out his presence. Some sense told him to wait.

"See that light?" Garrick asked.

"You stay here," he said to Garrick. "I'm going to the other side of the house. They must be inside." He stuck close to the front of the house. His eyes adjusted to the darkness by the time he had secured a place at the bedroom window.

Then a figure ran across the back lawn from the woods and toward the back door.

Who? There was no logic for the appearance of anyone, unless it was someone sneaking up on the people they already knew were in the house.

Nightingale waited, his hand opening and closing around his service weapon.

Inside the house, he heard Cayden. "Why are we here?"

"The will." Silas's reply was short, out of patience.

"I don't understand," Cayden said. "The sheriff has the will."

Nightingale felt himself grin, vindicated that the boy would argue with anyone.

"I heard something." Again, Cayden's voice came through the window, then silence filled the space.

A drawer slammed shut. "Mr. McGowan is meeting us here," Silas said. "He knows more about this. He told me he could get you cleared and—"

A light in the inside hall came on.

Nightingale ducked.

Cayden whispered, "You don't need a gun."

"Sorry." McGowan's confident voice hit the salesman mode. "I came through the woods. Didn't know what kind of critter I might see. Didn't mean to scare you."

"Silas said you can clear me," Cayden said.

"We'll talk. You all go ahead and search that desk and the boxes in the closet. Hard to see with only a flashlight."

"You didn't answer my question," Cayden said.

"I know, kid, but I've got this covered. I figure you can admit that you saw somebody in the woods that you forgot about. There's all sorts of hunters, and there's even a guy who's been hiding out up here for years. Could have been him that shot her, by accident, mind you. Once you say that, I'll back you up and you'll be clear."

"How will you back me up?"

"I'll say I was driving into town and saw you hiking toward her place after the time she was killed."

"Why?"

Nightingale worried that he knew the answer. McGowan had been there in his son's red truck.

"The alternative is that you called me up here and I found you both rifling through papers." McGowan's voice lowered, adding an unfunny sarcasm. "Or, maybe you like this better, you were both already dead. You'd killed each other."

"You told me you would make everything right," Silas said.

Nightingale peered around a corner and saw Silas step in front of Cayden.

"Get behind me, Cayden. I got you into this—"

McGowan fired.

Nightingale shot through the window and heard McGowan's second shot almost immediately.

Silas screamed and fell to the floor.

Nightingale ran for the front door. He didn't know if he had wounded McGowan or not. The door gave on his first try.

Garrick ran in from the kitchen. He had a flashlight.

"Bedroom," Nightingale said.

The door was shut. Silas sobbed behind the door.

"He's got the boys," Nightingale said.

"What next?" Garrick asked.

Nightingale took a deep breath and slowly let it out. No more shots. "McGowan, come on out. These kids can't help."

A long pause prefaced McGowan's words. "This has to work. The whole state will be dry or in a war over water." He sounded like he was talking to himself, trying to be an evangelist, but too weak to carry it off.

"Roy, you've succeeded. You said the vet will sell, and you can get him the extra money," Nightingale said. With those words, more of the puzzle cleared. The extra money would be for McGowan. A straw buyer. McGowan was buying land cheap that he knew was in the state water plan and selling it high.

McGowan didn't answer right away. And the wait confirmed Nightingale's thoughts. McGowan had shot Constance Dearborn and then drove like hell to get back to Austin that same afternoon. Cayden had seen the red truck.

"This half-breed needs to be out of the way."

He sounded tired, probably blood loss, but that could make him not care, too.

"Roy, you have a son. You don't want him to know you killed a boy his age."

"You always were an uppity bastard—don't think you're giving orders here or playing psychiatrist to get to me. And you're not getting points. That boy is my wife's son. He doesn't give a rat's ass about me."

Damn, the self-pity was a whole new battle.

"He does care. I saw that boy after he plowed into my truck. He's worried about you. You raised him."

Silence—nothing good came of that.

"This hurts." That was Silas. "I think I'm dying." He sobbed again.

"Roy, let him out. Him dying won't help you at all. Garrick can get him to a doctor. You can stay, or you can take my truck and leave."

"Too much talk," McGowan said. "Go kid, get your fat ass out."

The door swung wide and Silas Jackson scooted across the floor, leaving a bloody streak in his wake. "I can't make it," he said.

Garrick knelt and pulled the younger man out into the hall and to the next room.

Through the crack when the door opened, Nightingale glimpsed Cayden. McGowan's arm was wrapped around the boy's neck, and blood ran down Cayden's face, darkening McGowan's sleeve. A bullet had hit McGowan's shoulder, and on that side, the damaged arm held a pistol, which dangled against Cayden's chest. The boy's head rolled forward. His eyes closed. He needed help.

"You owe me, Nightingale."

"I know that, Roy. I always will. You'll get out of this fine, if you'll just quit. You didn't kill Posey, did you?"

"Nope, the bastard just died on me. That was the beginning of the bad luck. This kid has been shot. You've lost your touch. Me and him." McGowan started humming. "Me and you, you and me . . . perfect family."

Tamp down the panic. McGowan was lying, but Cayden lay limp against McGowan's chest.

"You both need a doctor. Why, Roy, why?" Nightingale risked another peek around the corner and into the room.

A little boy's voice called out, "Is that you, Daddy?" McGowan's face, sliced with the partial light from the hallway, glistened with sweat.

Could he be hallucinating? The bloody arm draped over Cayden had not moved.

"It's not your father, Roy."

"Please don't lie, Daddy. I knew when you left that you'd come back. Have you seen Mama yet?"

"Let the boy go, Roy."

"Nope, can't do that. I told Daddy I'd keep him here and skin him."

What now? Sweat ran into Nightingale's eyes, and he tried to flick it away, all the while staying just outside the door frame so McGowan couldn't see him. Leave the hall light on or not? That thud had to be his heartbeat. What next?

Silas no longer moaned. In the distance, an ambulance siren screamed.

"Roy, you need help. I'm here. Just push the boy away and we'll get you to a doctor."

"He's been shot. I'll have to skin him."

"I'm coming in to help you. The ambulance is here. See the lights?"

Outside, the yellow and blue lights pulsed around and 'round.

He pushed the door wider and heard a zing as a bullet whistled by.

React. Point. Pull.

McGowan grunted and slumped.

Something ran into Nightingale's eyes, blurring his vision as he scrambled to the boy. He reached for him and felt warm, thick ooze on his shirt. Garrick stood in the hall waving to people coming in. More lights—good thing, electricity. He held the boy close, rocked him. Medics pulled him away, putting the child on a stretcher.

Next to him McGowan moaned, "Daddy, are you there?"

He kicked McGowan's handgun away. Regret filled his heart. "Yeah, Roy. I'm here."

48

Nightingale and Garrick left the hospital together.

"Go home and get some sleep," a doctor had told Nightingale.

Nightingale's shoulder had cuts from the broken window, so Garrick said he'd keep an eye on him, and he drove Nightingale's truck back to the cottage.

The hospital had called Emma about her son. While he waited, Nightingale watched her huff into the emergency room, ignoring Cayden's mother and everyone else while she demanded to see her son.

At the cottage, Garrick opened the door and walked directly to Bandit's crate. The puppy whimpered and almost flew outside.

"That puppy has the right idea," Garrick said. "I'd like to piss on this town, too. A night like this makes me kinda wild."

Nightingale grinned at the enjoyment the dog got out of racing around the yard, sniffing and marking territory. "That's why I need a dog—to keep perspective." He laughed for the first time in days.

"Nobody's supposed to be as tense as you've been. We need coffee."

Nightingale rubbed his eyes, trying to get the fuzz off his thoughts. "What'd you find out about everybody while I was being taped up?"

"Cayden is okay. One of your bullets grazed his head and that accounted for a lot of blood. Silas may need some surgery. Both of them have mothers with them. McGowan lost a lot of blood, but the doc thought he'd be okay. You got him with the first shot and the second, but he'll survive. Doc said he was talking odd." Garrick shook his head while he poured water into the coffee maker.

Nightingale settled back in the chair and blew out a deep breath. McGowan's last words didn't coordinate with what he thought he knew about the man, and it bothered him.

"Did McGowan kill Constance and Posey?" Garrick asked.

"He killed Constance. But Constance helped Posey along. She came to the B and B, and if she didn't outright kill him, at least she helped him die. We'll find her bracelet under Posey's bed. I don't know details, but McGowan was the front man for the campaign and met Constance then. He probably made her promises about not having to sell the land, and then he found out he couldn't carry through.

"He also found out that if he knew what land was to be bought he could make money through some fake buyers, which he was doing in other parts of the state."

"Was Posey in on that?"

"No, Posey came on strong in the other direction. Neither one knew what the other had said. Constance thought Posey was going to force her to sell, so she helped him die."

"She was the woman who Cayden saw go into Posey's room?"

"Right. Probably disconnected his insulin or something and slipped some drugs into his drink."

"Why did McGowan shoot Mrs. Dearborn?" Garrick squinted, a sign he was thinking.

"Constance was dug in, and he saw her as a serious threat. Who knows? He may have offered to have one of his corporate buddies buy her land. If he offered that and she knew about the straw buyers, she was a problem. He decided to kill her."

"But how?" Garrick asked. "You said the governor said he was in her office that afternoon."

"Shot her then drove like hell back to Austin. Used the stepson's truck thinking anybody who saw it would think it was a tourist. That should have solved everything, but then he had Cayden and a will to deal with." Nightingale tried to not think how close Cayden had come to death.

"He started a cycle he couldn't stop," Garrick said.

"Right. He was afraid the water plan would fall apart. His home life was going to shit, and this project was his ticket to save the day. Legislators were uprising. They can't do much when they aren't in session, but they make everyone uncomfortable and promise anything. McGowan was worried on all fronts.

"His wife was threatening to leave. He had his house mortgaged to the hilt, and I'm betting he was using the money from the house to be a silent partner in buying property out west. When it came time for the state to buy the property, McGowan stood to make a nice profit."

Nightingale twirled his coffee cup around in the puddle in the saucer, talking to himself as much as to Garrick. "I feel bad for Roy. I knew his father left them, but it was after high school. I guess you never grow up enough for parents to leave."

"It affects anybody at any age," Garrick said. "Used to, people stayed together come hell or high water. But I don't know that I believe that stuff McGowan was saying. That was too handy. He never struck me as the type who wanted his daddy around enough to go off the deep end. That odd acting will be convenient for his defense."

"I hadn't thought about that. Maybe I'm more naïve than Bandit."

"You believe people are good. Nothing wrong with that. So how well did Mrs. Dearborn and Roy know each other?"

"I'm speculating, but they met in the campaign. Remember Faulkner talked about her thinking somebody would save her? That's why she went to see Posey. She thought he was treating her like a commoner, and she had been told something different."

Garrick's eyes slid sideways. "Sarah told me she'd seen McGowan in the restaurant once with a lady. That had to be Constance. I figured she had him mixed up with somebody else."

"You shoulda told me," Nightingale said. "That might have helped."

"Sharing information goes both ways. You didn't tell me any of the political dickering that was going on. So don't get on a high horse about me leaving things out. And speaking of dickering, will the governor be including Broken Rock in that water plan?"

Nightingale let the criticism roll off. "I think so. But I want to talk face to face."

"One last question. Who gave you that beating?"

"I'm guessing McGowan was behind that, although Ed Howard, the sheriff's deputy, has been absent during the last few days. I'm betting he has some bruises he doesn't want me seeing. He's hated me since that run-in we had in Amarillo. He's a bigot and a hoodlum. I'll talk to Patterson about that. We'll have it cleared before I leave."

"Good. Sun's coming up. What're you gonna do about Josephine?"

"You said one question, but Josephine doesn't want what I want."

"That sounds like one of those philosophical quizzes I do in my head."

"I know I still enjoy Rangering."

Garrick nodded agreement. "I think there's more to it."

"Ah, hell, Garrick, I don't know. Can't I have some private thoughts?"

Garrick grinned. "Sure, I didn't mean to be a burr. I know I'd like to have a good woman to finish out life with. Everybody thinks I chase women 'cause I'm a horny old cuss, but that ain't it. I told you about the hole in my heart from Nancy dying. I need somebody who gives a shit about me. You might need the same." He reached down and pulled the puppy up onto his lap.

Nightingale didn't know what to say to the old man. He stood and refilled his coffee. Maybe it was the lack of sleep, but he felt a sentiment creep in that he'd been trying to place and couldn't.

"I guess that's it. I thought I wanted marriage, to settle down. I wanted somebody to sit by me on the porch as we grew old. Looks like I won't have that."

He felt uncomfortable; he'd said too much. He put his palms flat on the table and stood. "Enough of this. If the governor lets me go back to being a Ranger, I'll have my lesson learned. I'll be happy."

DISCUSSION QUESTIONS FOR

A PROMISE of WATER

1. Have you read anything, other than this novel, about a world-wide shortage of potable water?
2. Do you think people in the West (where droughts are more common) are more aware of the possibility of a water shortage than people who live in the East?
3. Do you think government officials often make bargains with civilians to gain what they need politically?
4. Did you like the story better after Jack Posey was dead? Do you think Posey understood Nightingale and if not, did he try to understand the lawman?
5. Do you know anyone who is committed to justice for victims of crime?
6. Do you know anyone like Sutton Garrick? Do you think Garrick loves or admires Nightingale?
7. Do you understand the bitter relationship between Emma Jackson and Constance Dearborn? What accounts for their bitterness?
8. Do you think Constance sees Cayden as a younger brother? As a son?
9. Do you think Cayden really loved Constance as a sister?

10. Have you ever considered the possibility of a water shortage where you live?
11. Caring for your fellowman is one of the subtle questions in the book. Would you be willing to share potable water with someone you didn't know?
12. Do Hank and Sue Nell Faulkner have a typical brother and sister relationship? Is Sue Nell a problem for Hank caring for Constance Dearborn?
13. Did you like Bandit and his role in the book?
14. Did you feel sorry for Roy McGowan at the end of the book? Were you surprised at the climax?
15. What do you think happened to Cayden Shepherd?
16. Nightingale doesn't understand women; do you think he needs a woman to love in his life, as Garrick keeps insinuating?
17. Does Nightingale change by the end of the book? Does he learn anything or grow in character?

ACKNOWLEDGMENTS

Writing is a joy and hard work. It seems I have been writing forever. And when I look through old manuscripts I see that it's true: I have been writing forever.

Thankfully, people along the way have encouraged me. Some of the best help came from the Novel In Progress group in Austin, Texas. Everyone in that group is smart, helpful, and kind. They are the best.

I especially want to thank my editor, Patsy Shepherd. The cover designer (and man of a thousand talents), Tosh McIntosh, has been patient and amazing. My publisher and marketing expert, Laura Resnick-Chavez, is indispensable. And to Lolly, thanks for proofing and keeping me mentally together.

Leanna Englert is a friend, fellow writer, and supporter without whom I would never have finished.

To my daughters, thank you for encouraging me. You all are the best blessings I have ever had.

ABOUT THE AUTHOR

Sharon Scarborough has been a mother, a teacher, a rural mail carrier, and a realtor. Her work has appeared in *18 Almanac, The Washington Star, Paris-Post Intelligencer,* and *Country Song Round-Up.* She lived and worked in Austin, Texas, for twenty-three years before returning to her native Kentucky, where she now lives.

CONNECT WITH THE AUTHOR ONLINE

Blog: sharonmscarborough.com
Facebook: facebook.com/smscarborough